Roundup
on the
Picketwire

**Center Point
Large Print**

Also by Allan Vaughan Elston and available from Center Point Large Print:

Guns on the Cimarron

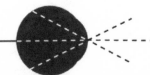

**This Large Print Book carries the
Seal of Approval of N.A.V.H.**

Roundup
on the
Picketwire

ALLAN VAUGHAN ELSTON

CENTER POINT LARGE PRINT
THORNDIKE, MAINE

This Center Point Large Print edition is published
in the year 2012 by arrangement with
Golden West Literary Agency.

The text of this Large Print edition is unabridged.
In other aspects, this book may
vary from the original edition.
Printed in the United States of America.
Set in 16-point Times New Roman type.

ISBN: 978-1-61173-392-1

Library of Congress Cataloging-in-Publication Data

Elston, Allan Vaughan, 1887–1976.
Roundup on the picketwire / Allan Vaughan Elston.
pages ; cm
ISBN 978-1-61173-392-1 (library binding : alk. paper)
1. Large type books. I. Title.
PS3509.L77R68 2012
813′.52—dc23
                                        2011050270

To every neighbor, stranger and *compañero* who ever unsaddled for the night at a certain ancient adobe ranch, scene of the author's boyhood, on the San Ysidro road.

Roundup
on the
Picketwire

CHAPTER I

The seven hundred miles had taken nearly four months of Johnny Diamond's young life. But his big dun gelding was still fresh as he left the headwaters of the Dry Cimarron and reined uptrail toward Capulin Gap.

Not that Johnny Diamond had ridden those seven hundred miles from Lampasas, deep in Texas, in one continuous grind. He'd stopped briefly at ranches along the way, working day pay for money to live on. At no time had he traveled fast. The lazy bay pack mare he led limited him, generally, to a running walk.

"We're most there, Hackamore."

Hackamore twitched his tall ears and snorted. He was an ugly brute, ungainly in build and unfriendly by disposition. It was his habit to kick or bite at anyone other than Johnny who came near. He had a long conical head and pale green eyes set wide apart. With a bit in his mouth this big, smoke-colored horse wouldn't move an inch. Which was why Johnny always rode him with a hackamore. Kipling, in this year of 1884, hadn't yet told his tale about the raw rough dun of a certain colonel's son:

With the mouth of a bell and the heart of hell
and the head of the gallows-tree.

Just such a brute was Hackamore and Johnny
put up with his ill temper for the sake of his
endurance. The horse was too short coupled for
his height, but he had long sure legs and a deep
chest. He could climb like a bobcat and seldom
got winded.

Far in the distance uptrail, hoofbeats clashed on
the gravel. Presently a band of horses came in
sight and Johnny saw that they were being driven.
Remounts, he supposed, on the way to some
roundup.

He reined a little way off the trail, pulling the
bay pack mare after him, to give the remuda room
to pass. But when the horses galloped by, heading
for the Dry Cimarron below, he concluded they
weren't roundup remounts at all. They looked like
half-wild range mares. Two cowboys were
hazing them along. They went by too fast for
Johnny to read brands. He waved to one of the
men but got no response. Then they were gone,
down-trail, in a cloud of dust.

Some rancher, Johnny guessed, was moving his
breeding herd from one range to another. "But
he oughtn't to run 'em like that, Hack. A mare
could easy lose her colt, bein' jostled along that
way."

Johnny resumed his own progress toward the

gap, at a walk, the saddle creaking under his buckskinned legs. The last mile to the gap steepened, scrub oak brush closing in from both sides.

In the gap itself, a V between two rimrocked mesas, the scrub oak gave way to wild cherry. That, naturally, would be why they called it Capulin Gap. Johnny stopped on the summit to rest his animals and to twist a cigaret. Behind him lay New Mexico, brown and butte-studded. Ahead he could see Colorado, a shade less brown and with here and there the greenish ribbon of a cottonwood creek.

Las Perdidas County, Colorado! Johnny Diamond now saw it for the first time and the sight brought a grimness to his lips. He took from his pocket what seemed to be, but wasn't, a tarnished copper coin. Johnny thumped it into the air, caught it in his open palm as it came down. He sat staring at it, his eyes suddenly cold and hard and his mouth bitter. He remembered back six years ago when, as a boy of fourteen, he'd first seen this tiny disc of copper. It had sickened him, then, and he'd cried like a child. At the same time it had given purpose and direction to his life.

Now, a man of twenty, he was here to fulfill that purpose. Whenever he thought of it, which was often, it changed him from a pleasant, gentle-mannered boy to a flint-hard, ruthless

11

hunter of men. It made him mean and tough and stubborn, just like the rough, raw brute of a horse he rode.

Those he hunted were three in number. Beyond that, Johnny Diamond knew nothing about them except that they'd once lived, and might still live, in Las Perdidas County, Colorado.

Alive somewhere in that vast sea of grama, streaked by cottonwood creeks, walled on the south by high, box mesas, on the west by a saw of snowy cones. A county as big as an eastern state, spotted with plazas and ranches. How on all that vast range could he find three men whose names he didn't know, whose faces he'd never seen? He couldn't even be sure, after the passage of six years, that they were here at all!

He spurred Hackamore down the Colorado side of the gap. The pack mare followed lazily, dragging at her lead rope.

Again the dun snorted, slanting his ears forward as he always did when he heard oncoming horsemen. Those who came into view, heading at a fast pace uptrail, were five in number. Cow-hands. Like Johnny himself, each was belted with a six-gun and had a carbine in his saddle scabbard.

"Looks like they're on the prod about somethin'," Johnny muttered, and reined to a halt.

The five riders thundered up on lather-flecked mounts. One of them, a shaggy man with a cold, slab-like face, sang out: "Howdy, mister. Didja pass a bunch o' range mares lately?"

"Sure did," Johnny admitted. "Forty-fifty of 'em, maybe. They went by too fast for me to read brands."

"How far ahead of us are they?"

"About ten mile by now, I'd say."

"How many men was drivin' 'em?"

"Just two," Johnny said.

The shaggy man turned to his companions. "Fog along after 'em," he directed. "When you ketch up with 'em, start throwin' lead."

Four of the riders raced on south toward the gap.

It made the situation clear to Johnny. The two he'd passed were horse thieves and these men were hot after them.

"Sorry I didn't try to stop 'em myself," Johnny said. "But I thought it was just some outfit pushin' its stuff from one range to another. Smoke?"

He offered makings and the shaggy man rolled himself a cigaret. "Sansone's my name," the man announced. "Top rod at the Circle D. Haven't run across you anywhere before, have I?"

"Not likely," Johnny said. "I'm new to this range. How far is it to the county seat?"

" 'Bout forty-five mile. You hit the main east-and-west road at San Ysidro. Turn west there."

"Thanks. Don't need any help, do you, handlin' those bronc rustlers?"

Sansone gave a laugh and shook his head. The harshness of the laugh foreboded ill to the horse thieves, once they were caught. Johnny was glad he wasn't being recruited to help. He had a mental picture of a summary court held under the nearest tree, and of that he wanted no part.

And, although this man's manner seemed friendly enough, something about Sansone repelled Johnny. His lips made a thin cruel line and his eyes were like pale chips of ice. The man tossed back the makings and glanced at Johnny's laden pack mare. "You can't make Las Perdidas tonight. But you can stop at Ronaldo Rivera's place on Grosella Crik. They'll be glad to put you up."

The dun horse, Hackamore, took a vicious bite at Sansone's mount. Johnny jerked him out of reach. "None of that, Hack. Folk'll think us Texans haven't got any manners." To Sansone he said: "Thanks. A bunk'll feel good for a change. I been campin' at water holes, lately."

"If you're stoppin' at Rivera's," Sansone advised, "you better slick back yer hair. Don Ronaldo's got the best-lookin' gal on this range. I'll be foggin' along now." He dug in with his spurs and loped south after his men.

Johnny proceeded on in the opposite direction, toward San Ysidro.

Again he was in a scrub oak canyon, descending along a streamlet. In a little while the oak gave way to cottonwoods. He came out of the foothills at the edge of a wide, level prairie. The trail, presently, joined an east-and-west road and here lay an old and jaded adobe plaza. San Ysidro.

There was only one street, ankle deep in dust. A saloon, a general store, a barbershop and pool hall. A row of mud shacks. Johnny heard the distant pounding of a hammer on anvil and knew the place had a blacksmith shop somewhere.

He dismounted at the store and went in for tobacco. A Mexican woman waited on him. Outside again he saw half a dozen cow ponies tied at the saloon. Two were branded Circle D and four had a Lazy M. Clicks of pool balls, a hum of talk inside the saloon and a clang of hammer on anvil were the only sounds.

An odd thought struck Johnny. Since five Circle D punchers were chasing horse thieves, why would two other Circle D men be loafing here at a saloon? Why weren't they also in the chase? Something about that chase vaguely disturbed Johnny. Something he couldn't quite pin down. He sensed a contradiction somewhere. Sansone with his friendly voice, and yet with his cold, slab-like face and killer's eyes!

It was no particular concern of Johnny's. Shadows were long and he'd better push on to the next creek. He remembered the tip from Sansone. That he could stop overnight at the ranch of a man named Ronaldo Rivera. Presumably it was right on his way to the county seat.

Sansone had referred to him as "Don Ronaldo," which suggested a *hacendado* of some importance. Johnny wanted to know people of importance and especially people who'd been settled on this range for a long time. Gringos were likely to be either newcomers or drifters, but a Mexican hidalgo would, almost certainly, be an old-timer here. And since Johnny was chasing a six-year-old clue, only citizens who'd lived on this range at least that long could by any remote chance be of help to him.

Boots came clumping up the walk. Johnny turned and saw a man with a round amiable face. His denims were muddy. He looked like a ranchman who'd spent the day irrigating his meadow.

"Hi," Johnny said. "Can you tell me how far it is to the Rivera layout?"

"Sure can, young fella." The man pointed west along the road. "Two hours at a slow jog'll put you there. Right where the road crosses Grosella Crik. You aim to stop overnight there?"

"If they'll put me up," Johnny said.

The stockman smiled. He took off his gloves. His big red hands cupped over his stubbled chin to light a cigaret. "They'll put you up, all right. He's an okay hombre, the senator is."

"Senator, did you say?"

"Sure. I supposed you knew that. Don Ronaldo's

16

been state senator from this district since 'seventy-six. And will be as long as he lives, I'm bettin'. Gets all the Mex vote, and there's two Mexicans in this county for every gringo. Fact is, Don Ronaldo pulls most of the gringo vote too. I always vote for him myself."

"Is he home now?"

"Yep. And his casa'll be yours the minute you knock on the door. He's that kind of a guy."

"Thanks. I'm Johnny Diamond from Texas, case I ever see you again."

"I'm Buck Perry of the Lazy M, down this crik a piece." A thought struck Perry and he added, "Since you're headin' fer Don Ronaldo's, you might as well take him a message from José Pacheco."

"Who's José Pacheco and what's his message?"

"José's the blacksmith here." Perry thumbed toward the far end of the street. A little while ago Johnny had heard a hammering on an anvil in that direction, but the sound had stopped.

"I left my bronc there to be shod," Perry explained, "and José asked me if I aimed to ride by Don Ronaldo's place tonight. He wanted to send a message there. I said I wasn't goin' that way. So José said he'd send it by someone else."

"I'll take it," Johnny offered promptly. As the bearer of a message he should be all the more welcome.

Buck Perry went along to show him the way to

17

Pacheco's shop. It was the last adobe on the street, directly on the bank of Ysidro Creek and overhung by a giant cottonwood. "Don't reckon he's got my bronc shod yet. But I can't go nowhere till he does. Here's the place."

They turned in at the smithy, which had a hard cinder floor with a forge and bellows at the deep end. Perry's horse stood there, three shoes on and one off.

"Criminy!" Perry froze at the entrance, and so did Johnny Diamond.

José Pacheco lay prone beside his forge. A horseshoe, still pink from heat, lay on the anvil. One of Pacheco's outstretched hands held a hammer, the other a pair of tongs. Blood stained the man's leather apron. His face had the waxen cast of death.

Buck Perry and Johnny Diamond ran to him. The body, with a bullet hole through the heart, was still warm.

"I was talkin' to him not mor'n twenty minutes ago." Perry turned his shocked face to Johnny. "How come we didn't hear the shot?"

The answer, Johnny thought, was clear enough. Clarion sound as Pacheco pounded his hammer on the anvil! A shot, coinciding with one of those resounding hammer beats, would have been absorbed and smothered. No one down the street would have heard it. The place had an open back door, through which the killer had retreated unseen.

CHAPTER II

There being no peace officer at this small plaza of San Ysidro, Buck Perry himself took charge until the sheriff could be brought from Las Perdidas. Johnny gave up all thought of riding on this evening. As a co-finder of the body, he would need to be questioned by the sheriff.

Four of Perry's own riders were at the saloon and he dispatched one of them on a fast ride to the county seat. The others he deputized to make a list of all men known to be in San Ysidro at the hour of the shot. "It happened a few minutes before five, Slim. Count noses. And guns. Chances are the guy slipped right up the crik bed to the back door of the cantina. Or mebbe to the pool hall. Then again he might've forked a bronc and lit out fer the mesas."

Johnny helped investigate the last possibility. Cottonwoods and wild plum along the creek would have given ample screen to the killer's retreat. If so he was safe from pursuit. Because many head of stock, both bovine and equine, had watered at the creek, scarring its mud banks with innumerable hoofprints.

Perry, taking a late supper with Johnny at the

cantina, had a discouraged look. "We've counted noses and we've counted guns. Present in the plaza at time of shot, one hundred and twenty-six human beings. Which includes women and *niños.* Total number of gun-wearing males, seventeen. Of these, nine are ranch hands loafing around the saloon, pool hall, cantina or barbershop. A minute's all it would take for anyone to let fly with a slug and then slip back to where he was a little while before. No one can swear just who walked out and in and just when. Could have been anybody in the plaza. Or some mesa outlaw that nobody saw at all. I'll sure be glad to dump this in Ad's lap."

"Ad's the sheriff?" Johnny inquired.

"Yeh, Adam Sawyer. And Ad's nobody's fool, either. Used to practice law down at Capulin, on the Dry Cimarron. When he moved over to the Colorado side, folks right away elected him sheriff. Not much to look at, Ad ain't. But smart as a whip."

There was a rentable bed up over the cantina but Johnny didn't like the looks of it. He took his animals down below the road and made camp under a creek cottonwood. Rolled in his blankets there he looked up at the stars and wondered. About a message which Pacheco had wanted sent to Don Ronaldo Rivera. Was that why he'd been killed? A simple plaza blacksmith, José Pacheco, with no known enemies. A peaceful man who'd never harmed anyone. Yet all of a sudden, a bullet through his heart!

Had someone wanted to silence José before he could send certain information to an influential citizen of his own race? Johnny could think of no other motive. A blacksmith, serving customers from all over the range, might learn many things. He could come upon a fact which needed to be passed along to a high authority like Ronaldo Rivera.

Johnny slept soundly and awakened with the sun in his eyes. Hackamore, hobbled, was grazing along the creek bank. Johnny caught up the bay pack mare first, grained her, then brought the gelding in on a lead rope.

He'd just finished breakfast when he saw a band of loose horses being driven down the plaza street. They came loping across the road with five cowboys driving them. One of these, Sansone of the Circle D, pulled up at Johnny's camp.

"I see you caught up with those rustlers," Johnny said.

Sansone made a sour grimace. "No such luck. They seen us comin' and took to the hills. Chased 'em till dark, then lost 'em in the brush. So we came back and picked up the mares. We're hazin' 'em home, now, to the Circle D."

"Circle D's down this creek, is it?"

Sansone nodded. "Yeh, right where it hits the Picketwire River."

He loped on down the San Ysidro to overtake his men. Johnny gazed after him, wondering if he'd passed through the plaza too hurriedly to learn about José Pacheco's murder.

Johnny walked up to the general store and found Buck Perry there. The storekeeper and his family had blank looks. "We know nothing, señor. José was a man of peace and our good friend."

"Did he have any relatives?" Perry prodded.

"A married daughter who lives at Thacker, señor. Only last Sunday José went there to visit her."

Johnny asked, "Do you know what message José wanted sent to Ronaldo Rivera?"

Again they looked blank. "He does not speak to us about a message, señor. But if it was for Don Ronaldo it was of great importance. A *pobre* like José would not disturb Don Ronaldo with small matters."

Johnny went outside with Buck Perry. "Nothin' we can do now," Perry muttered, " 'cept wait fer the sheriff."

"They said José had a daughter at Thacker. Where's that?"

"Thirty-odd mile due north on the main line of the railroad. Just a whistle stop."

"Anything between here and there?"

"Nothin' but a million acres of grama sod and about fifteen thousand head o' cattle."

"What brands?"

"Mostly Rick Sherwood's Circle D, Ronaldo Rivera's Bar L, and my Lazy M. A few shoe-stringers run in there too."

It was noontime before Sheriff Adam Sawyer arrived. He came loping up on a blaze-faced sorrel and looked, Johnny thought, a good deal more like a courtroom lawyer than a sheriff. Ad Sawyer was tall and paper-thin, black-visaged, with a bony, angular face of almost Lincolnian homeliness. An alert shrewdness gleamed from his deep-set, piercing eyes. His coat too was black, long and somber, buttoned tightly over his chest. His black, center-creased hat would have suited a Congressman. Nothing but his spurred boots marked him as a rangeman. If he carried a gun it was somewhere under the coat.

He swung to the walk and confronted Perry. "Let's have it, Buck."

Perry presented Johnny Diamond and explained how the two of them had found José Pacheco. "He wanted a message sent to Senator Rivera," Buck finished. "About what, we don't know."

Adam Sawyer stroked the sharp angles of his chin for a moment, then whirled and crossed to the saloon. In a moment they heard him barking questions at customers there.

"He'll shake everybody down," Perry said. "And lyin' to Ad Sawyer ain't easy."

For more than two hours they watched Sawyer stride from house to house in the plaza, checking alibis, sifting for every possible scrap of information. Negative responses floated to Johnny through the open doors. "Dunno nothin' about it, sheriff. I was right here shootin' pool with Ferd Smith." "Heck no, sheriff. I didn't hear no shot. I was . . ."

Late in the afternoon Johnny grew impatient. He sought Sawyer out to ask, "If you don't need me for anything, Mr. Sheriff, what about me ridin' on?"

Sawyer gave him an oddly calculating look. "You're from Lampasas, Texas, and you're on your way to Las Perdidas."

The abrupt statement, with a touch of severity in it, puzzled Johnny. How did the man know?

"That's right, Mr. Sheriff."

"I haven't time to talk to you now," Sawyer said. "But look me up tomorrow at my court-house office. I want to give you some advice."

He turned sharply to his duties, leaving Johnny confused. What advice? And why had the sheriff used that scolding tone? A flush of resentment climbed from Johnny's neck to his suntanned face.

But no use making an issue of it now. He crossed the road to his camp to pack and be on his way. He could get as far as the Rivera ranch by sundown and stop overnight there.

Then he recalled a remark of Sansone's. Don

Ronaldo had a good-looking daughter. Chances were he had one of those fancy haciendas where even the *mayordomo* wore braid on his pants. *And me lookin' like a tramp!* The thought inspired Johnny to change his shirt and shave.

Once he was shaven, with a black silk shirt and bandana to match, and with his wavy, sun-bleached hair carefully brushed back with a deep part on the left, Johnny Diamond didn't cut a bad figure himself. He wasn't tall by Texas standards, but tall enough. His back was straight and his muscles had springs in them. Hardship and poverty had printed more years on his face than he'd really lived. In repose it was strong, purposeful, at times gallant.

He took off his gunbelt and wrapped it in the pack. It wouldn't be polite, he thought, to ride up to a peaceful hacienda wearing a gun.

But a carbine was in his saddle scabbard as he swung aboard Hackamore. The road led almost due west, paralleling a line of box mesas along the Colorado-New Mexico border. And here on the flats the grass looked good to Johnny. No sage or greasewood to speak of. Mostly it was bunch grass and grama, with here and there a spot of bluestem in the swales.

As Johnny progressed the mesas on his left loomed higher and higher. A sheer palisade of rimrocks fringed their tops. Below these the aspen parks made olive-green blotches, and

25

below the aspens a dense mass of conifers. On the lower slopes conifers gave way to scrub oak until at the very foot these petered out entirely, the land leveling off into a sea of grama sod.

From successive rincons of the mesas came creeks, all flowing northeasterly to join the Picketwire River. Johnny passed grazing cattle, three brands predominating. Circle D; Bar L; Lazy M. Once he saw the dust of antelope on the run.

He crossed McBride Creek and some six miles further on sighted another creekline ahead. It reached from a crack in the mountain, crossing this road at right angles. Alfalfa meadows flanked it for miles. Grosella Creek, from what Buck Perry had told him. On a slight eminence just this side of it stood what at first seemed to be an adobe town. At least there was a street with houses lining it on either side.

Johnny turned into it and saw that it was just a big Mexican rancho. These adobes were the peon quarters. The master's house stood at the far end, against a cottonwood grove, circled by a plastered adobe wall painted robin's-egg blue. There were barns, corrals, a steepled church, a two-story bodega with a pulley well in front of it. All made a quadrangle alive with chickens, burros and fat little brown *niños* at play.

The adult population in sight was clustered at a roundpen corral below the main barn, where a shouting applause in Spanish indicated a bronco was being ridden.

Johnny Diamond, leading his pack mare, rode to it and dismounted. The roundpen had smooth spruce poles. Standing outside of it, and observing with approval the show within, was one who could only be Don Ronaldo Rivera himself. A smallish thin gentleman of poise and dignity, with a goatee at his chin, and with a cigarito between his aristocratic lips. Every inch a caballero from his wide velour hat to his polished boots. He was in his middle fifties, Johnny thought, and the entire history of the Spanish conquest seemed stamped on his face.

All his attention, at the moment, was on a pitching horse in the roundpen. Seated on the top rail on all sides were vaqueros, cheering the horse on, predicting a quick spill for the rider. But the rider stuck. The rider wasn't Spanish, like the others, but a gringo redhead not much older than Johnny himself.

"*Caramba! Qué diablo!*" yelled the gallery as the horse continued to circle the pen, making the stirrups pop with every pitch.

It was a nice exhibition. The redhead held the reins high, fanning with a sombrero in his free hand.

When it was over, Don Ronaldo Rivera turned and saw a young stranger.

"Señor?" he greeted politely.

Johnny had a winning smile and used it. "My name's Diamond. On my way to Perdidas. I'm wonderin' if you got an extra bunk at the bunkshack where I could . . ."

"*Por supuesto.*" The *hacendado* didn't let him finish. "You will make yourself at home, señor."

"Thanks," Johnny said. "I've ridden all the way from south Texas and a sod bed gets kinda hard, sometimes. You're Senator Rivera, I take it?"

"That is true, señor. At your service."

"Then maybe there's somethin' I oughta tell you. It happened yesterday as I came through San Ysidro." Johnny proceeded to tell about the killing of a blacksmith named Pacheco. "He had a message for you, senator. First he asked Buck Perry to bring it but Perry wasn't coming this way. So I offered to bring it myself but I was too late. Nobody knows what the message was."

Don Ronaldo was shocked. "José Pacheco!" he exclaimed in genuine grief. "He was my friend. Always he came to me when he had a problem. Or when he was in trouble. *El pobrecito!*" He clapped his hands and called out: "Miguel. *Apurese!*"

His *mayordomo* came on the run. "*Mira,* Miguel. *Qué triste!* Our friend José Pacheco, *el herrero de* San Ysidro, has been murdered. You will go there at once, Miguel, and arrange for his funeral. It must have many candles and the expense will be mine." These and other instructions erupted from Don Ronaldo in rapid Spanish.

He then called a boy, directing him to stall and feed Johnny's horses. "You yourself, señor, will be my guest at *comida*."

He linked an arm in Johnny's and led him to the main house. An elderly servant admitted them. The outer wall was four adobe bricks thick and going in was like passing through a short tunnel. The walls had been built that way, Johnny supposed, in the old days to withstand attacks by Indians.

They entered a sala with tinted walls and a puncheon floor. An organ stood at one end. At the other end a fireplace had two formal, high-backed chairs in front of it. Candlelight showed carved wooden saints recessed into the walls. "Wine for our guest," murmured Don Ronaldo.

The *mozo* brought wine. The host pushed an open box of cigaritos toward Johnny. They were wrapped not in paper but in covering taken from an ear of Indian corn. Not to offend, Johnny took one. "Now you will tell me more," the senator entreated, "about poor José Pacheco."

"Nothin' more to tell," Johnny said, "except we sent for the sheriff and he's there right now shaking everybody down. Some think the killer never left the plaza. Others claim he's some outlaw who high-tailed to the mesas. Me, all I got's a hunch I can't prove."

"A hunch, señor?"

"It's that somebody didn't want Pacheco to send you that message."

Rivera stared. Yet a credulous look formed on his face. He puffed daintily at his cigarito. "In the mesas," he said, "there are many *ladrones*. Often they drive away my cattle. Perhaps José learned of a guilt and wished to send me word."

"Speakin' of *ladrones*, I passed a couple of 'em drivin' a bunch of Circle D mares. Some Circle D men caught up with 'em and brought the stock back. The rustlers got away, though."

Rivera sighed. "Always they get away."

In a moment he glanced at the mantel clock and some slight worry furrowed his brow. He rang for a *mozo* and inquired, "Have the young ladies returned yet?"

"*Todavía no, patrón.*"

"We will hold supper for them," the master directed. To Johnny he explained: "My daughter has a guest, her cousin from Las Perdidas. Today they rode up into the canyon to pick berries."

He moved to a window which looked southward toward the mesa. Johnny took a stand beside him. Directly under the window lay a little lake, a perfect oval a furlong in length and half as wide, giant cottonwoods spaced evenly around its perimeter. At the far end of the lake stood the ranch church. The quiet beauty of it charmed Johnny Diamond.

"There they come!" his host exclaimed. Two young ladies could be seen loping toward them. "They are fine *muchachas*, señor, full of life and laughter. They will be glad to have your company." A thought struck him and he chuckled. "But we should balance the party. *Two* señoritas should have *two* cavaliers." Again he summoned a *mozo*. "Pablo, you will request Señor Wiggins to dine with us at the house."

The *mozo* went out and scampered toward the bunkshack.

"Señor Wiggins," the senator explained, "is *el colorado* who breaks horses for me."

Johnny grinned. The redhead! Hard-riding buckaroo of the roundpen. How thoughtful of Don Ronaldo! Two ladies. Two cowboys. A gracious host and dinner for five.

The two girls galloped into the ranchyard. Back of them rode a *mozo* with a basket of wild raspberries. The young ladies themselves, although both dark, didn't look at all alike. Johnny could hardly believe they were cousins. One was vividly Spanish, the other definitely gringo. One looked like she'd been schooled in an Old Mexico convent; the other might have been a campus belle at some Yankee college. The Spanish girl rode a side saddle and wore a long, sweeping skirt. The gringo girl rode astride, in corded pants and doeskin jacket. She swung to the ground with the grace of a rodeo rider.

The Spanish girl let the *mozo* help her dismount.

They came into the house and Johnny saw at once that the Spanish girl was easily the more beautiful. She might have stepped out of a portrait in a Madrid gallery. Yet it was her tall, free-limbed cousin who drew, and held, the quick interest of Johnny Diamond. The one was all curves and softness and shy smiles; the other, as hipless as a boy, had glow and vigor and an exciting personality.

Don Ronaldo presented them. "My niece, Florence; and my daughter, Felicia. My guest, Señor Johnny Diamond."

The niece gave him a frank, quizzical appraisal. "From Texas?" she inquired.

Johnny nodded. But how did she know? Did all Texans look alike?

Felicia murmured a welcome and then the girls disappeared to change for dinner. A moment later Chuck Wiggins, his red hair sleeked back and his face shining, arrived from the bunk-house.

When the girls reappeared, each in evening dress, the promptness with which Chuck Wiggins attached himself to Felicia left Johnny no choice. He offered an arm to Florence. She gave him a strangely puzzled look, and he wondered why. Also she vaguely reminded him of someone he'd seen before; and again he wondered why.

The dining sala was in a separate house. To reach it they had to cross a wide open patio where paper lanterns hung from neatly trimmed box elders. An ancient sheep dog came up as they passed, and Florence gave it a pat on the head. Stars were out by now, the light shimmering on the little lake beyond. From the bank of it came the strumming of a guitar.

Don Ronaldo led them into a building of two rooms, one a kitchen, the other a dining sala. Supper was of *cazuela* and roast grouse and during it the senator, in courtesy to his guest, directed the talk in English. Both he and Felicia spoke it with a marked Spanish accent; but Florence had no accent at all. More and more Johnny couldn't understand how the two girls could be cousins.

"You must tell them about poor José Pacheco, señor. *Qué triste!*"

So Johnny retold the tragedy of San Ysidro. Felicia's sensitive face showed shock. "Have they sent," she asked, "for Uncle Adam?"

The senator nodded and Johnny sensed the truth. Adam Sawyer, the sheriff! If he was Felicia's uncle, he must be Florence's father. So that was why she'd reminded him of someone! Although the girl's features didn't have Adam's angular Lincolnic homeliness, a certain family resemblance was nevertheless there.

Felicia turned troubled eyes to Don Ronaldo.

33

"This message José wanted to send you! Could it concern Ernesto?"

The *hacendado's* brow clouded. His response to Felicia was brusque, almost a rebuke. "Let us not speak of Ernesto."

A silence fell over the table. Who, Johnny wondered, was Ernesto?

CHAPTER III

Later, in the patio, Chuck Wiggins made his own personal objective quite clear. The absorbing interest of his life, Johnny could see, was Felicia Rivera. It explained why this gringo redhead had taken a job here, as horse tamer, on a ranch where all the other hands were Mexican vaqueros.

Don Ronaldo, leaving youth to amuse youth, retired to his study. And presently Chuck Wiggins enveigled Felicia inside to play and sing at the organ for him. Under the mellow light of lanterns, Johnny lingered in the patio with Flo Sawyer.

All evening she'd been looking at him with an odd and puzzled speculation. Quite suddenly she said, "You're not at all like I thought you'd be, Johnny Diamond."

It confused him. How could she have known

of his existence? And why should she think of him at all?

"I expected," she explained with a cryptic smile, "that you'd be hard-eyed and glowering and sullen."

"What made you think that?"

"You saw my father at San Ysidro. Didn't he tell you?"

"Only that he wanted me to report at his office in town. He said he had some free advice."

"He received a letter from the sheriff at Lampasas, Texas. It said you were on your way here. On some mission of revenge. My father disapproves of revenge. He thinks it's an ugly motive." A coolness came to Flo's voice as she added, "And so do I."

Resentment flushed Johnny "It's a free country," he said stiffly.

"That is true," she agreed. "But I still agree with my father. He will advise you to drop this revenge mission of yours and go back to where you came from."

"What else," Johnny demanded, "did the letter say?"

"It said a Texas ranch was raided six years ago. An entire family was wiped out with the exception of a fourteen-year-old boy. The boy grew up and when he was twenty he found a clue to the background of the raiders. It made him think they'd come originally from this Colorado county.

So he loaded his guns and set out on a seven hundred mile ride to find them."

"What's wrong with that?" Johnny challenged.

"It's taking the law into your own hands, isn't it? Appointing yourself judge, jury and executioner. If we all did that, there'd be chaos on every street corner."

Johnny's mouth drooped stubbornly. "Chaos! That's exactly what I found when I got home from school one night, six years ago, and saw hot ashes where the ranchhouse had been. The stock all driven off. My father and my brothers shot dead! How would you like it yourself?"

The sternness went out of her face and her voice softened. "I wouldn't like it. And I feel awfully sorry for you, Johnny Diamond. But unlicensed, personal vengeance isn't the answer. We have peace officers to handle things like that."

"I waited six years," Johnny retorted, "for peace officers to handle it. They handled it by concluding it was a raid by Commanche Indians. Indians, they said, always raided like that. They'd ride up to a ranch and kill everybody, burn the buildings and run off the stock. But in the raid on our place, I don't figure it was Indians."

"Why?"

"Tracks showed there were just three of them. Indians don't raid in three-man gangs. And I got other reasons for thinkin' it was three white men, and that one of 'em came from Las Perdidas."

"Very well," Flo Sawyer agreed. "Suppose you're right. Then why don't you just show your evidence to my father, the sheriff here? Let him take over. You can depend on him to . . ."

An interruption came in the courteous voice of Don Ronaldo Rivera. They hadn't seen him enter the patio. "With your permission, señor. Flo, guests have arrived to see you and Felicia. The Señores Sherwood and Cranston. They await in the sala."

Flo stood up, and seemed thankful for the interruption. "Yes, Uncle Ronald. Felicia and I were expecting them."

Her uncle said to Johnny "They are friends and neighbors. You must come in and meet them."

Johnny followed them into the sala where he found Chuck Wiggins looking glum. "Looks like they're all dated up," the redhead whispered.

The two arrivals were presented as Rick Sherwood, owner of the Circle D, and Val Cranston. Sherwood looked thirty, Cranston a trifle older. Of the two, Sherwood was the more personable. He had height and dignity. His chin was deeply cleft, his eyes slate-gray and penetrating. He wore tailor-made corduroys, the double-breasted coat fitting snugly over his broad sloping shoulders, its creamy color contrasting sharply with his raw, windburned skin. His mouth had a self-willed set, Johnny thought.

The slate-gray eyes brushed over Johnny and dismissed him, almost with an amused contempt. The other man, Cranston, lacked Sherwood's assurance. He was softer, less virile, less aggressive, not born to the saddle as was Sherwood. He might be a clerk or a politician.

Sherwood's date was clearly with Flo, and Cranston's with Felicia.

Chuck Wiggins drew Johnny aside. "Look, pal," he whispered. "Four's company and six is a crowd. Those guys got our time beat, for tonight anyway. Reckon we better shag our carcasses down to the bunkhouse."

Johnny nodded. He thanked Senator Rivera and said his goodbyes. "I've been a long time in the saddle, so I'll be turnin' in."

"Our house is yours," Rivera said warmly. "You must visit us again."

Johnny's last word was with Flo. "I'll look you up in town some time, if it's all right."

"Of course," she agreed. But her tone wasn't encouraging. And Johnny himself wondered why he'd even want to see her again. If he did, she'd probably give him another lecture. And as for looks, she couldn't hold a candle to Felicia.

Outside, Wiggins guided him to the bunkhouse. It was a long, adobe affair, with a recreation room where a half dozen Mexican vaqueros were playing cards. In a room beyond, Chuck pointed out a bunk for Johnny.

Then the two went out on the steps and lighted cigarets.

Organ music from the main house depressed the redhead. "And just when I thought I was gettin' somewhere!" he mourned. "Them guys sure moved in on us. Why couldn't they fall in a crik, on the way over here?"

Johnny smiled. "Do they come often?"

"Cranston does. Sherwood don't because Flo's generally in town. He keeps hangin' around her old man's office. Flo keeps books for her old man at the courthouse."

"How big is the Circle D?"

"Biggest spread in the county. And they say Rick Sherwood started out with nothin' but a dugout in a sand bank. A smart cookie, Rick is."

"And Cranston?"

"He's state brand inspector for this district. He has to be on hand at the loadin' pens every time anyone ships out cattle. Senator Rivera got the appointment for him. If he likes you, the senator can get you anything you want. A pass on the railroad. Or a job at the courthouse. Or a pardon if you get tossed in the clink. But don't get me wrong. Don Ronaldo's as honest as daylight. Offer him a bribe and he'll challenge you to a duel."

"How long you been around this range, Chuck?"

"Four-five years, I reckon. Why?"

"Did you ever see a man wearing a pair of boots with a gilt design around the tops like this?" Johnny took an envelope from his pocket and made a sketch. It showed a row of diamonds with the corners slightly overlapping.

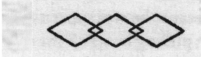

Wiggins looked at the sketch. "Linked Diamonds? Is that a cow brand?"

"Used to be," Johnny told him. "My dad used it a long time ago in Texas. Just before he died, he had a pair of fancy riding boots made to order. They were just like any other cowboy boots except they had these linked diamonds etched in gilt around the tops. Halfboots, they were, comin' only part way to the knee."

"Never noticed any like that," Wiggins said. "How come you wanta know?"

This young redhead seemed friendly, observing, and completely without guile. And Johnny needed a confidant.

So he told Chuck about the raid six years ago down in deep Texas. "I was just a kid. My dad and my two older brothers made me go to school in town five days a week. Saturdays I'd ride to the ranch to do chores over the weekend. I got home one Saturday morning and found 'em dead. The buildings had been burned to the ground and the stock driven away."

Chuck swore softly. "That was sure rough, pal."

"My dad had sold some cattle and hadn't banked the cash yet. The raiders took it. Dad lay on his back in the ranchyard with a bullet through his heart. He was in his sock feet."

Wiggins blinked "You mean one of the raiders swiped his boots?"

"Must have. The boots were gone. Then the raider did something else to dad. No Indian would have done it. Only a white man with a ghoulish sense of humor, mixed, maybe, with spite and superstition."

"What did the guy do?"

"Just before riding off, he took two copper pennies from his pocket and laid 'em on dad's eyes. Maybe for a laugh. Maybe for spite. Or maybe because he was superstitious and didn't want a dead man to see him pulling boots off the dead man's feet. Anyway that's how I found my father. I was only fourteen. It made me so crazy mad I snatched those pennies away and threw 'em as far as I could. Then I rode to Lampasas and told the sheriff."

Wiggins twisted another cigaret. "So ever since then, you been lookin' for a man wearin' those boots. But they'd be wore out by now, wouldn't they, after six years?"

"The heels and soles would. But they could be renewed. The tops'd be scuffed some, that's all. If you keep renewin' the heels and soles, you can make a good pair of boots last a long time."

"But why would they be up here in Colorado?"

"My home was gone," Johnny said. "So I took a job on the next ranch and worked there six years. Sundays I'd go over to the old place and poke around. And just this spring I found somethin'. Looked like two copper coins. They were buried in the dust, and tarnished, about fifty yards from where I found my father that time. I'd thrown them as far as I could, remember? It took six years to find 'em again. And when I did, I saw one of 'em was a penny and the other was just a penny-size disc of copper. Not a coin at all. That raid was at nighttime. I figure the man thought he was fishing two pennies from his pocket, in the dark there. But one of 'em was this."

Johnny produced from his own pocket a coin-like disc which he'd polished until it was now quite bright. He showed it to Chuck Wiggins. On one side of it was printed: "The Picketwire Bar, Las Perdidas, Colo." The other side said: "Good for one beer."

"A beer check!" exclaimed Wiggins. "Many a time I've been in that Picketwire Bar. It's the oldest saloon in town. On lower Commercial, right by the river."

"It must've been operating in 1878," Johnny said, "six years ago. A customer picked up a beer check there. He went to Texas with two other

42

men and made a raid or two. Maybe he came back here to his old stamping grounds, and maybe he didn't. But it's the only lead I've got. So I'm running it down."

"Chances are he *did* aim to come back," Wiggins guessed, "or he wouldn't've hung on to that Las Perdidas bar check so long. But he could be dead by now. Or he could be runnin' with some gang of outlaws up in the mesas. Any way you look at it, he's a needle in a haystack."

Johnny admitted it. "If he came back, he brought those boots along with him. He could be wearin' 'em right now." Seated there on the bunkhouse steps, Johnny's eyes sparked like diamonds in the dark. "All I want is an even break with him."

"You need any help," Chuck assured him with a warm sympathy, "just call on me."

CHAPTER IV

An afternoon later Johnny got quite a different reaction when he faced Sheriff Adam Sawyer in an office at the Las Perdidas courthouse. Sawyer was particularly dour at the moment, having just returned from a futile effort to run down the killer of José Pacheco at San Ysidro.

He listened to Johnny's story and looked at the bar check. His eyes were stern. His response was: "I can't blame you for feeling bitter about this, young man. It was a raw deal for a fourteen-year-old kid. But you're a man now. And a man ought to have better sense than you're showing."

Johnny flushed. "You've no call to talk that way, sheriff."

"I've a call to stop unauthorized man hunts," Sawyer snapped. "In the first place, you haven't got a chance to find your man or men. One of them, let's admit, passed through this town more than six years ago and accumulated a bar check. Maybe he was on his way from Montana to Mexico. We don't know that he ever really lived here. Even if he did, we don't know that he ever came back. And even if he did come back, what have you got? Nothing but a pair of boots the man probably wore out and threw away three or four years ago."

Johnny's jaw squared. "There's no law against lookin' for him."

"Right. But there's a law against shooting him down when you find him. That's your plan, I take it?"

"He'll get an even break," Johnny said.

Sawyer glowered. "Bosh! That even-break business gives me a pain. It may legalize killings on some ranges, but not on mine. You're out on a crusade of personal vengeance. Forget it and go home. 'Vengeance is mine, saith the Lord.' Which means it isn't yours, Johnny Diamond."

Johnny had a rebellious look when he went out. He didn't like being preached to. First the sheriff's daughter. And now the sheriff himself. Talking to him like he was a renegade schoolboy! Your father and your brothers get massacred and they expect you to take it lying down! Johnny Diamond was in no such mood. Maybe he couldn't find those raiders. But nobody could talk him out of trying.

He walked to the corner of Main and Commercial and stood there, watching the life of the town. It wasn't a gun-toting town. An ordinance, promoted by Adam Sawyer, stipulated various hotels, saloons and corrals where side-arms must be checked by men coming in from the range. Johnny's gun was still rolled in his pack, which he'd left with his two horses at a livery barn.

Traffic streamed by in the Main Street dust. Ranch wagons, cow ponies and loaded burros. This thoroughfare was, or had been until a few years ago, the old Santa Fe Trail itself. Any highway traveler from Missouri to Santa Fe would still have to pass this corner. Adobe and pine-board stores flanked it now. Spurred boots thumped along the plank walks. Tinpanny music issued from the saloons. The intersecting streets, running north and south, were steep, climbing from the Picketwire River to the upslope of a towering knob, shaped like a saddle horn, at the west end of Fisher's Mesa.

Johnny paid small attention to faces. He looked at boots. Cowboys, merchants, miners, gamblers, busy men and idle men, were tramping or riding by. A needle in a haystack, Johnny thought morosely. Hardly a chance in a million he'd see the boots stripped from a dead man six years ago in Texas.

Five blocks down Commercial, in the trough of the town, he heard a train come in. The depot of the Santa Fe railroad was there, right where Commercial Street crossed the river. The rails had arrived here in 1878, they'd told him, the very year of the raid in Texas. Which made Johnny's quest seem all the more hopeless. For during rail construction a legion of drifters and grafters would have been here. Any one of them could have picked up a beer check at the Picketwire Bar and gone outlawing down Texas way. Such a drifter would have no reason to return here.

A buckboard, drawn by matched trotters, came whirling down Main. A *mozo* from the Rivera ranch was driving it and on the seat by him was Flo Sawyer. Evidently she'd terminated her visit to her country cousin and the host had supplied her with a conveyance home.

46

As she went by, Johnny took off his hat and waved. She didn't see him. The buckboard turned uphill toward the better residential section of town.

Later a dusty horseman pulled up and dismounted. Johnny recognized his round amiable face and stubbled chin. "Hi, Mr. Perry. Anything new out your way?"

Buck Perry popped dust from his gloves and shook his head. "Ad Sawyer turned the plaza inside out," he reported, "and couldn't find a thing. Looks like Pacheco's killer got clean away with it."

"You said Sawyer used to be a lawyer. How come he turned sheriff?"

"He was practicin' law down in New Mex, twenty-odd years ago, when he married Elena Rivera. She was a sister of Ronaldo Rivera. We had a crime wave up this way a few years back, when the railroad came in, and we needed a smart sheriff. So Rivera persuaded his brother-in-law to come up and take over. Bein' ace-high in politics here, Rivera can pull any string he wants. He can make a sheriff or a county clerk or a brand inspector with a nod of his head."

"Is his wife still living?"

"Nope. Both the sheriff and the senator are widowers now. Havin' daughters the same age, they get along fine together. Except that the senator's an easygoin' sort and the sheriff's got a streak of Puritan in him. Ad takes his sheriffin' plenty serious. Which reminds me, I better check this gun before I get pinched."

They crossed to the Toltec Hotel where Johnny already had a room. Buck Perry drew a forty-five from his belt and checked it at the desk. He hurried out, then, and Johnny went on up to his room.

The room had a bare floor and raw pine walls. There was a cot and a bench seat. The washstand had a cracked china bowl and pitcher. Johnny's slicker roll lay on the cot. He unwrapped it and took out a pair of boots.

They were handsome, shiny boots which had never been worn. Just before leaving Lampasas Johnny had had them made to order by the same bootmaker who, long ago, had supplied his father with a similar pair. Linked diamonds, in gilt lines, circled the boot tops.

Johnny removed his old footwear and put on the new. He tucked his trousers in, leaving the boot tops exposed. He washed, brushed his sun-burned hair and made three neat dents in his tall Texas hat.

Spurless, he went out and walked north down Commercial. The Picketwire Bar, they'd told him, was near the bridge where this street crossed the river.

He found it there, a shabby old place with cracked mud walls. Ranch ponies were tethered in front and next door was a barbershop with a bootblack stand on the walk. A railroad clerk was getting his shoes shined.

Johnny went into the bar and bought a cigar. The place had a sawdust floor and a beery smell. There was a cheap free lunch laid out on a plank against the wall. Flies buzzed. The bartender had drooping mustaches and looked Irish. The place didn't look tough. Just cheap and old and dirty.

Three stock hands were drinking there. Johnny waited till they went out. Then he clinked an old copper beer check on the bar. "Do you still pass these out?" he inquired.

The Irishman leaned elbows on the bar and squinted curiously. "Nope, not in my time. But I only took the place over coupla years back. Where'd yuh get holt of that thing, anyway?"

"Down in Texas," Johnny said. He put the copper check back in his pocket. "By the way, does a customer ever come in here wearin' boots like mine?"

The man leaned further over the bar and peered down at Johnny's boots. He could easily see the design of linked diamonds.

"Nope, don't recollect ever seein' any boots like that. But I'm back of the bar most of the time. Don't generally see a customer below the waist. Whatsamatter? You had a pair of boots stole?"

"Yeh," Johnny said. "It was a long time ago. The boots'd be old and scuffed by now."

He went out to the walk and found the

bootblack's chair empty. Johnny mounted it and bought a shine. The man who served him was an elderly Mexican. "They are new, señor. They need no polish so I shall just brush them a little."

"Ever have a customer with boots like 'em? I mean old boots with the same design around the tops."

"I do not remember any, señor."

"Any other shine stands in town?"

"There is one in the depot. And one in a pool hall on Elm Street."

"What about cobblers? I mean places where you could get a half sole or new heels."

The man named three such places. "But why do you ask, señor? You do not need new heels."

Johnny tipped him and went on. He spent the rest of the afternoon covering the places named. It was fruitless. No bootblack or cobbler could remember boots like Johnny's.

He checked with the clerk at the hotel to make certain there were no other shine stands around town.

"That's all of them," the clerk said. "But you'll find one down at Chico. Chico has a shoemaker too."

"Where's Chico?"

"Four miles down the river. The narrow gauge from Denver comes in there. A wide-open town,

Chico is. Tough, I mean. A good place to stay away from."

In the morning Johnny took Hackamore out of the livery barn and rode four miles down the Picketwire. Sunflowers stood high along the banks, with here and there a cottonwood grove. Ahead lay an expanse of open grass reaching to the Kansas horizon.

On the north, to his left, two snow-capped domes reared to the clouds. Twin peaks, as uniform as beehives. On the south, to his right, ran the chain of box mesas which marked the New Mexico line. The main line of the Santa Fe railroad followed the north bank of the river.

When he came opposite the Chico plaza, Johnny forded the river and rode into a shabby street. The place seemed to be about one third the size of Las Perdidas but with about three times as much vice in sight. Johnny saw a half dozen honkytonks featuring games and women. A drunk was pushed out of one of them. Men lounging on the walks looked like the off-scourings of the range. Some of them wore guns. Evidently the ordinance of the county seat didn't apply here.

Everything on this street was false-fronted frame. However, Johnny found a more sober part of town when he turned a corner. An older section built of adobe bricks, with shops and cantinas and a pepper tree or two.

Here Johnny found the one cobbler of Chico. He was a stolid little man of Germanic features, sitting cross-legged at his last. But Johnny drew a blank when he asked about the boots.

"Who does the shoe shining around here?"

"He is Frankie Valdez," the man said. "At the barber's you will find him."

The barbershop was a one-chair establishment. A customer there lay back with his face lathered. An Italian barber was shaving him. A shine stand was on the walk outside. The shine man was dozing and Johnny had to shake him awake.

"Rub the dust off these boots."

"It is a pleasure, señor." Frankie Valdez was a thin little Mexican with the eyes of a ferret. Prying, greedy eyes, Johnny thought.

"Ever see any boots like these? Old ones, I mean. Linked Diamonds around the tops."

The small eyes narrowed a bit. "Why is it you ask, señor?"

"I'm chasing a *ladrón*. All I know about him is he once had boots like mine."

"Are you a sheriff, señor? Is there a reward?"

"I'm not a sheriff," Johnny said. "And there's no reward. But I'd pay ten pesos out of my own poke."

"Ten pesos if I remember boots like your own, señor?" The sum clearly impressed Frankie the bootblack. Ten dollars didn't come often into his life.

"My name's Diamond and I'm at the Toltec in Las Perdidas. Think hard, Frankie. If you can remember, bring the tip to me and I'll pay you the ten pesos."

Frankie licked his lips and looked both ways along the street. "At the moment I can think of no one, señor. If I do, I will come to your hotel for the ten pesos."

"Do that," Johnny said dryly. He concluded that this sly little scamp was on the make. He might show up with a false tip merely to collect the ten dollars. It would be easy enough, and without risk. He could name a man no longer living and claim that such a customer had once come to him for a shine.

That seemed to exhaust the possibilities of Chico and Johnny rode back upriver to Las Perdidas. He left Hackamore at the livery barn and walked down Commercial to his hotel.

A saddle horse tied in front of it stopped him. The horse was young, looked like he might have Morgan blood, and had four white stockings reaching to the knees. There was a white star in the forehead. Otherwise the horse was mouse-colored.

Johnny's pulse quickened. He circled the animal, looking closely at the markings. The brand was Circle D. There was no vented brand. Johnny opened the beast's mouth for a look at the teeth. Four years old.

In the lobby Johnny spoke to the desk clerk. "Does a guest here own that mousey horse out there?" The mount could be seen through the front window.

"There he sits," the clerk said. He pointed to a guest who was seated on the lobby divan reading a newspaper.

Johnny went to him. The man lowered his paper and looked up with a smile. He had a soft plump face with sideburns hanging low on either cheek. "Hello," he said. "Met you out at the Rivera ranch, didn't I?"

Val Cranston, the brand inspector! An appointee of Senator Rivera himself. And a leading candidate, according to Chuck Wiggins, for the favor of Felicia.

"I was admirin' that bronc of yours out there," Johnny said. "A Morgan, isn't he? Raise him yourself?"

Cranston gave him a blank look. "No. I bought him a year ago from the Circle D. Why? Want to trade me out of him?"

Johnny shook his head. "I just got an eye for a good horse, that's all. It's not often you see markings like that."

It was then he noticed something which alerted him. Cranston was evading his eyes. The man looked to the left, then to the right, then down.

Looking down his gaze fell on Johnny's boots. Boots with a design of linked diamonds.

Sight of them seemed to spellbind Val Cranston. And to startle him. When he looked up again, his plump face was a shade less rubicund. "What's the matter?" Johnny prodded.

"Nothing," Cranston said. His tone had strain in it. He brought out a handkerchief and mopped his forehead.

I've hit something, Johnny thought. *Something I wasn't looking for.*

CHAPTER V

Johnny went out and hurried to the courthouse. The sheriff's office door was open and Johnny found Adam Sawyer at his desk. The girl at a smaller desk, making entries in a ledger, was Flo.

"Howdy," Johnny said. "You folks busy?"

Adam Sawyer laid down a quill pen. His smile had no welcome in it. "Not at all," he said with heavy irony. "What with an unsolved murder on our hands, and a dozen reports about missing cattle all over the county, we've nothing to worry us at all. What's on your mind, young man?"

"Boots. Like these, only old ones." Johnny looked down at his own.

The sheriff's eyes fixed on the linked diamonds

design. So did Flo's. "I had 'em made," Johnny explained, "to match the ones swiped by those raiders six years ago."

"For what purpose?"

"I showed 'em to every shoemaker in town here. Did the same at the shine stands. Both here and at Chico."

"Any results?"

"None," Johnny admitted.

"Naturally," Sawyer echoed dryly. "That trail's too cold."

"But I ran on to somethin' else, sheriff. A mouse-colored horse."

"What mouse-colored horse?" Sawyer's tone was impatient.

But Flo was attending with interest. Her interest, though, seemed entirely judicial and impersonal. She was dressed in sober gray today. She looked alert and capable, Johnny thought.

"Those Lampasas raiders ran off our stock," he said, "includin' an eight-year-old brood mare. She was a good breeder and had been bringing us a colt every year. The colts were always marked exactly like she was. Mouse-colored all over, except for four white stockings, knee high, and a white star in the forehead."

"Did the raiders run off her colts too?" This inquiry came briskly from Flo.

"No," Johnny told her. "The colts, with our Linked Diamonds brand on 'em, had been sold before the raid. But the mare herself, if she's still living, could have had five more colts since then."

Sawyer's expression changed. A shade of tolerance came into his voice. "You mean you've found such a colt on this range?"

"That's it," Johnny said. "Tied right in front of my hotel. A four-year-old with those same markings. It's branded Circle D."

"If it's a Circle D," Sawyer concluded with decision, "it's an honest horse. Rick Sherwood runs the Circle D. And take my word for it, young man, he's completely trustworthy."

"He doesn't own the horse now. It belongs to Val Cranston."

The sheriff gave him a piercing stare. "See here, young man, you're barking up a wrong tree. Cranston's our local brand inspector. What are you trying to start, anyway? A witch hunt? Color doesn't prove anything. There must be thousands of mouse-colored mares in the world."

"Ours," Johnny said stubbornly, "had Morgan blood. So does this bronc of Cranston's."

Sawyer's annoyance mounted. "I own a Morgan horse myself," he said sharply. "So do lots of people."

"All I want, sheriff, is a check on it."

"And just how, young man, would you do that? You say this colt is only four years old. And the raid was six years ago."

"I want you to take a look at the Circle D range

herd and see if there's a fourteen-year-old mouse-colored Morgan mare in it. With four white stockings. If there is, see if there's a blotted brand alongside the Circle D. If you can't read through the blot, you could shoot the mare and skin her. The blotted brand would show on the underside of the skin."

Flo Sawyer had a shocked look. "Are you suggesting," she challenged, "that Rick Sherwood could have been one of those raiders? That's positively ridiculous!"

Adam Sawyer echoed her tone. "The looniest thing I ever heard of, Johnny Diamond. Sherwood's highly respected all over this county. Often he's been a guest at our house. And at Senator Rivera's. Flo and I have known Rick for—" he turned to his daughter—"how long have we known him, Flo?"

She thought a minute, then said, "For five years, dad."

"But not for six?" Johnny questioned. "What was he doing *six* years ago?"

They didn't answer that one. And Johnny said: "If you won't look for that old mare, sheriff, I'll look for her myself. Just thought I'd let you know. So long."

He could feel cold stares aimed at him as he left the office. And he could hardly blame them. Sherwood stood high with them. He might some day be Adam Sawyer's son-in-law. Naturally the suggestion of a criminal past outraged them.

And chances were, Johnny admitted, that they were right. Certainly the color of a horse wasn't proof. At best it was only a thin pointer. But even a thin lead had to be chased down. He'd ride the Circle D range and look for an old mouse-colored mare. A range mare might or might not live to be fourteen years old.

Another idea hit Johnny. Suppose the mare had died a year ago. Even so, her last two or three colts should still be on the range. Her progeny of four years ago now bore the saddle of Val Cranston. What about a three-year-old? A two-year-old? A yearling? If a stepladder of such increase were found in the Circle D herd, Rick Sherwood must explain where he'd acquired the producing mare.

It was suppertime and Johnny turned into a restaurant on Main. When he came out it was dark. Cranston's horse was no longer hitched in front of the hotel. And then Johnny remembered he hadn't told the Sawyers what had alerted him more than anything else. Cranston's startled reaction at sight of Johnny's boots.

As though that design meant something to the man. A ghost from his past?

It didn't seem possible. Cranston looked too soft and clerkish ever to have been a hard-riding raider. He might, though, have guilty knowledge of a raid in which he hadn't participated himself. But no use springing it on Sawyer. Sawyer would call it stupid, hair-brained, a distorted figment of Johnny's overwrought imagination.

Johnny entered the hotel and went up to his second floor room. The room was dark. He fumbled for a match to light the kerosene lamp there.

The slight creak of a floor board made him take a quick sidestep and whirl about. Something whizzed past his neck, skimming his shoulder blade. Johnny snatched at it, gripped it . . . a hand with a knife in it. An assailant grappled with him in the dark. A clubby fist smashed into his face.

Johnny's knee came up, catching the man's groin. His right hand held doggedly to the knife wrist, twisting. "Drop it," he said, and kicked again with his knee. He heard a bone in the wrist crack. A thud came as the knife hit the floor.

Guessing where the man's chin was, Johnny swung hard at it. His knuckles smacked into hair and he knew the man was bearded. The man jerked free and Johnny dived for a clinch.

He missed entirely, in the inky darkness, and his head hit a wall. The impact brought a spitting pain, leaving him groggy for a moment. He got up, groping for something to strike with. His hand touched the china wash pitcher.

Johnny gripped it and stood ready to crack down. The man could have a gun and might shoot at any sound. So Johnny made none.

Neither did the other man. Johnny imagined him on all fours groping for the knife.

His knees buckled and he went down. He didn't know what hit him. For half a minute he knew nothing at all.

He came dizzily to his senses and saw a faint light from the hallway. The door was open now. Which meant that the man had retreated. Johnny got to his feet and lighted the lamp. A knife with a six-inch skinning blade lay on the floor. He didn't touch it.

He stepped out into the hall and looked both ways. At the front end, steps went down to the lobby. At the rear end other steps led to an alley. The knifeman, Johnny concluded, had arrived and departed via the alley.

He went down to see the desk clerk. The clerk had heard nothing, seen nothing. "Send word to the sheriff," Johnny said. "Tell him somebody tried to knife me in my room. The guy has a cracked wrist bone and a beard."

Johnny went back upstairs. He sat on the cot and looked around. An overturned bench-seat told what the man had struck him with. A man with a beard! Both Cranston and Sherwood were smooth-shaven. Whoever he was, he'd sneaked in here by the alley entrance to wait in the dark for Johnny Diamond.

The window shade was drawn. The man must have pulled it down to keep street light from

61

coming in. Johnny raised the shade and looked down on Commercial Street. It was peopled with the usual night traffic. Saloon customers; loafers; a sober citizen or two. A heavy cart loaded with hides rumbled by.

Then Johnny saw Adam Sawyer. The sheriff was on the run, a tall black-coated figure heading straight for this hotel. His lean, bony face was grim as he turned in just below Johnny's window.

As fast as his long legs could carry him, Adam Sawyer came dashing up to the room. His tone had a faint apology in it. "I seem to have underestimated you, Johnny Diamond." He loomed tall and thin there, staring down at the knife on the floor.

"You mean about the mouse-colored horse?"

"No." Sawyer's white teeth clicked on the negative. "Forget the horse. It means nothing. Sherwood and Cranston are above suspicion. But your boot clue was hot. It's already drawn blood."

"Not mine." Johnny grinned wryly. "The guy missed me."

"He hangs out at Chico," the sheriff said broodingly.

"Who?"

"The knifeman. You interviewed a bootblack there. A sly little man named Frankie Valdez."

"That's right. I asked him if he'd ever shined

any boots like mine. Offered him ten pesos if he'd hand me a steer on 'em.'"

"Which was a mistake," Sawyer said dourly. "Frankie Valdez always did like to make a dollar on a shakedown. Petty blackmail would be right in his line. He remembered shining a pair of boots like yours. So he said to himself, 'If this gringo offers ten pesos, maybe the other man will give fifty to keep my mouth shut.' So as soon as you were out of sight he went to the other man to see what he could get."

"What makes you think so, sheriff?"

"I don't have to think," Sawyer snapped. "I *know*. Because word just came from Chico that Frankie Valdez lies dead in an alley there. Knifed."

He stooped to pick up a knife from the floor. "With this same blade, I'll wager. After sealing Frankie's lips, the man hurried straight here to seal yours."

Johnny couldn't doubt it. The sequence was pat and logical. But it went deeper than that, Johnny thought. "By killing me," he said, "the man could stop me from looking for the boots. That's not a good enough reason. It would be easier for him to toss the boots in the river."

Adam Sawyer ignored this. "The hotel clerk says you didn't see him. All you know is he has a broken wrist and a beard."

"Maybe the wrist is only sprained. I gave it a

twist, that's all. I poked him in the chin and it felt hairy."

Sawyer heaved a sigh of exasperation. "I wish to Jupiter you'd stayed in Texas. You spawn trouble everywhere you go. First you ride into San Ysidro and there's a killing. You ride into Chico and there's another killing."

Johnny gave him a pale grin. "Now that I'm in your lap, sheriff, anything I can do to help?"

"I'm riding to Chico," Sawyer announced, "to turn that den of perdition inside out. You may come along if you like."

Johnny headed for the door. "I'll go saddle my horse, sheriff."

CHAPTER VI

Starlight made dim shadows along the river as they rode down its right bank. A coyote skulked across the trail and an owl hooted from a cottonwood snag. Sawyer had lapsed moodily taciturn. He made no response when Johnny questioned him about the citizenry of Chico. Nor would he comment when Johnny puzzled about why the man hadn't simply thrown an old pair of incriminating boots in the river.

Something else puzzled Johnny too. At dinner

with the Riveras two evenings ago, Felicia had mentioned the name Ernesto. To which her father had replied sharply, almost in a tone of rebuke, "Let us not speak of Ernesto."

"Who," Johnny queried now, "is Ernesto?"

This time he drew a response. "If I don't tell you," Sawyer whipped at him, "someone else will. Ernesto is the black sheep of the Riveras."

"Some no good son or nephew?"

The sheriff shook his head morosely. "Eighteen years ago, in the sixties, vaqueros of the hacienda had their last fight with Indians. Most of the Indians were killed. The rest took flight, leaving a dead squaw and her papoose on the battlefield. The vaqueros took the baby home to the ranch. Don Ronaldo felt pity for it, adopted it, and named it Ernesto. Ernesto grew up as his foster-son. But he was wild and undisciplined. He wouldn't go to school. He hung around dives at Las Perdidas and Chico. He broke Don Ronaldo's heart. A year ago Ernesto killed a man in a quarrel over a saloon woman. He escaped to the mesas and has been seen running with a gang of outlaws there. There's a murder warrant out for him. If you want to grieve Don Ronaldo, who's salt of the earth himself, just mention Ernesto. Which I hope you won't."

They rode silently on. Ernesto, Johnny reasoned, couldn't be tonight's knifeman. A nineteen-year-old Indian doesn't have a beard. Nor would he have been old enough to take part in a raid six years ago. So Ernesto didn't concern him. Ernesto Rivera, born a savage and reared amidst a gracious Spanish culture, had reverted to savagery again. It made just one more off-color streak in the strange pattern of life here.

They came opposite Chico and forded the river. Against the night light, the town looked more squalid than ever. "A den of perdition," Sawyer had called it. They rode into its false-fronted street and stopped at a place whose sign said: *EL PESO DE ORO*. Sounds of revelry came from inside.

"A man named Syd Orme runs this joint," Sawyer said. "They call him Shotgun Orme. I prosecuted him for a killing one time but he alibied himself out of it. Stay here and watch the horses while I go in."

Johnny didn't like it. The sheriff was treating him like a boy. But the man's stubborn look meant he couldn't be talked out of it. Johnny had to stand there and watch him push in, alone, through the swinging, latticed doors.

A piano was rattling inside. Boot thumps on the floor meant dancing. For a better look, Johnny climbed back into the saddle and rode Hackamore onto the walk. From this height he could see over the latticed doors and into the barroom.

Men were dancing with tawdry women. They paid no attention to the sheriff as he elbowed through them. Other men lined the bar, and beyond it loomed an enormously fat man in a double-breasted white jacket. His voice boomed out. "Look who's here, gents. My old pal and college chump. The sheriff hisself. Have one on the house, sheriff." His eyes and his tone were derisive. The man's hog-jowled face glistened with sweat and Johnny could see bulging red muscles at his neck.

"Let's have no comedy," Sawyer said harshly. "A man has been killed within ten yards of your alley door, Orme."

Orme leaned his huge elbows on the bar. He had long thick arms and the shoulders of a wrestler. "So they tell me, sheriff. Frankie Valdez, wasn't it? I always knew he'd come to a bad end."

"Where," Sawyer demanded, "is Constable Martínez?"

Orme shrugged. "Search me, sheriff." He looked, Johnny thought, like a huge bloated spider, hairy-handed, the sweat standing like drops of oil on his nearly bald head.

A glassy-eyed cowboy spoke from an end of the bar. "He's at Frankie's shack, if you want him."

Sawyer stepped to the latticed doors and talked over them to Johnny. "Valdez lived in a one-room shack down by the D and RG depot. See if you can find the town constable there. Get what information you can from him. Wait for me

67

there. Soon as I shake this joint down, I'll join you."

Riding his own horse and leading the sheriff's, Johnny proceded to the narrow gauge line depot. An elderly Mexicana with a shawl over her head pointed out the Valdez jacal.

In it Johnny found Constable Pedro Martínez. He was a wiry little man, all nerves, with a sallow, harassed face. His badge of office was on his suspenders and a gun was stuck loosely in his belt. He was fussily sifting through the effects of the late Frankie Valdez.

Frankie himself lay on a cot, covered with a sheet. The room had a dirt floor and a musty smell. Johnny introduced himself and gave his message.

Martínez heaved a sigh of relief. "I am glad he is here, the good sheriff. Myself, I have no talent for these matters."

"It was you who found the body?"

"*Sí*, señor. I am patrolling the alley at sundown and there he is. Near a trash can with a knife wound through his heart. The body is still warm. What does the good sheriff say for me to do?"

"We're to wait for him here. He's checking alibis at Orme's bar."

"Orme! *Qué diablo*!" Fear mottled the constable's eyes and he lowered his voice. "He is *sinvergüenza*, señor. But I am sure it is not Orme who kills him. I have already ask and he has not leave his bar between four 'clock and sundown."

"Did anybody leave about sundown for Perdidas, on a fast bronc?"

"I do not notice, señor."

"Did Frankie have a family?"

"Once he has a wife," Martinez said. "But she runs away with a wool buyer to Santa Fe. When the wool buyer deserts her, she goes to Las Vegas where now she lives in sin on the Calle de la Amargura."

"You'd think," Johnny remarked dryly, "she could have found enough sin right here in Chico. Did you ever see or hear about a pair of boots like mine?"

The constable, after a look at Johnny's Linked Diamonds boots, shook his head.

"The guy who knifed Frankie," Johnny said, "rode straight to Perdidas and tried the same play on me. Who's mean and tough enough around here to do that?"

"There are many, señor. Evil men come here to drink and to play cards. *Ladrones* from the mesas. Some of them will kill for a few pesos. Often they shoot up the plaza. I think I shall resign my job, señor. Do you have a cigaret?"

Johnny gave him the makings and rolled one himself. An oil lamp lighted the room. It was smoking a little. Johnny turned the wick down.

"Is there a medico in town?"

"A doctor? He lives at the white cottage on the corner."

"I'll check with him, constable. You keep an eye on the sheriff's horse."

Johnny led his own horse to the corner cottage. A man with a brown owlish face answered his knock. "You're the only doctor in town?"

When the man murmured an affirmative Johnny asked if a patient had stopped in this evening to have a sprained wrist treated. "A bearded man, I think."

"No one has been here, señor."

"Is there a drugstore in town?"

"Across from the post-office."

Johnny rode there and found the place open. The druggist was a gringo with a cheroot hanging from his lip and a green eye-shade over his eyes. "Anybody stop in this evening," Johnny asked him, "to buy linament for a sprained wrist? Maybe a man with a beard."

"No one like that, mister. Mamie Griggs was here, though. She came in for a box of gauze bandages."

The information alerted Johnny. "Mamie Griggs? Who is she and where does she hang out?"

"She's a saloon girl. Hangs out at the Bon Ton Bar."

"Thanks." Johnny angled down the street to Orme's place. Looking in he saw Adam Sawyer still busily probing for sundown alibis. He whistled, then beckoned as the sheriff looked his way.

Sawyer frowned at the interruption. He came out to the walk. "Better look up a woman named Mamie Griggs," Johnny said. "She just bought a gauze bandage."

"I told you," Sawyer said sternly, "to wait for me at Frankie's."

Johnny grinned. "I got restless. This Mamie's a fancy girl. She hangs out at the Bon Ton."

Sawyer strode half a block up the board walk. In his tight-fitting black coat, he made a somber figure against lamplight filtering from dives and cantinas. Any lurking outlaw could easily have shot him down. But fear had no part in the make-up of Adam Sawyer.

Johnny followed, leading his horse.

The Bon Ton was a cheap Mexican bar with rooms on the second floor. Someone was playing a harmonica inside. "Wait here," the sheriff said, and pushed the door open. Johnny caught a quick glimpse of a bar with stools in front of it. Three men and two women were seated on the stools. Another couple was dancing. The door swung shut behind Sawyer and Johnny saw nothing more.

If the man they wanted was in there, he might escape by a rear exit. Johnny swung to his saddle and loped around the block. He turned into an alley and stopped directly back of the Bon Ton.

There was a lean-to shed elling from the building. Over it Johnny saw a lighted window. He stood on his saddle and from there climbed to the shed roof. It brought his eyes level with the lighted window.

Peering in, he saw a man and a woman. They were seated on a bed. The woman was winding a bandage around the man's right wrist. The man had a dark, scarred face and a bearded chin.

He was facing the window and his eyes caught Johnny's face pressed against the pane there. His free hand pulled a gun from his belt. He triggered a bullet which smashed glass just as Johnny ducked below the sill. A cry of alarm came from the woman. Johnny himself wore no belt gun. But there was a carbine in his saddle scabbard. He jumped from the roof and landed astride of the saddle.

As he whipped out the carbine, he heard the man dashing down steps to the barroom. Then Johnny heard two gunshots. Adam Sawyer, he supposed, was shooting it out with the man. A second later the man himself jumped out into the alley. Johnny covered him with the carbine. "Stop right there," he ordered.

The man had no gun in his hand. In the blackness of the alley he made only a dim silhouette. Only a wrapping of white at his wrist identified him. Suddenly he darted up the alley at a fast sprint. Johnny gave chase on his horse. Not wanting to shoot an unarmed man, he clubbed the carbine. At the alley's exit he caught up and crashed the stock down on the man's head.

Adam Sawyer came running and found them there. The bearded fugitive lay in a sprawl. Johnny had dismounted and was bending over him.

Sawyer rolled the man face up. He struck a match for a better look. "He's Diego Salvador. Thanks for knocking him over, young man."

"He potted at me through a window," Johnny said, "then beat it downstairs."

"As he came through the barroom," Sawyer added, "I traded shots with him. He missed me and my shot knocked the gun out of his hand. He's not much of a gunman. Usually fights with a knife."

Diego Salvador had a sprained wrist. Almost certainly he was the man who'd waylaid Johnny in a hotel room.

"I've no doubt he killed Frankie Valdez," Sawyer said. "But if I know this town," he predicted gloomily, "he'll have a dozen alibis. Every crook here always backs the others up. That's why I never could clean out the place."

The prediction was soon verified. Diego Salvador was handcuffed and jerked to his feet. Sawyer marched him first to confront customers at the Bon Ton, then to confront Orme at the Peso de Oro.

"He was at my bar from four o'clock till

sundown," Orme swore. "Then he left here with Mamie Griggs."

"We went to the Bon Ton," Mamie said. She shook her curls, dyed a brilliant red, and fixed a defiant stare on Sawyer. "A drunk there wanted to dance with me and Diego hit him. It broke Diego's wrist and I went out to get a bandage."

The Bon Ton bartender verified this. So did a sly, rattish customer named Jakie Kim. Adam Sawyer bit his lip and swore bitterly. They wasted an hour looking for the drunk. No one remembered who the drunk was. No one had seen Frankie Valdez since midafternoon. No one had heard anybody mention a pair of Linked Diamonds boots.

Sawyer looked up Constable Matínez. "I'll hold Salvador in the county jail a few days. But if we can't crack his alibi, in the end we'll have to turn him loose. Put him on a nag and bring him along."

It was long after midnight when Sawyer and Johnny rode back to Las Perdidas. Martínez followed them with the prisoner.

"One thing is certain," the sheriff muttered. "Diego Salvador did not take part in a Texas raid six years ago. At that time he was serving a term in the Colorado state prison. He was released only a year or so ago. Since then he's hung around Chico."

"Doing what?" Johnny asked.

"Whatever Syd Orme tells him to do. Orme

controls most of the vice in Chico. He owns the Bon Ton as well as the Peso de Oro. Keeps half a dozen cheap killers like Diego Salvador and Jakie Kim at his beck and call. My guess is Orme hired Diego to kill both you and Frankie Valdez."

"But not," Johnny insisted, "just to keep me from locating a pair of old boots. He could ditch the boots, or burn 'em, or toss 'em in the river."

Sawyer had to agree with that. He rode thoughtfully on for a few minutes, then offered: "The boots can have some indirect connection, just the same. Your asking about them scared somebody. He was afraid Frankie Valdez might talk. Not about the boots, but about something you'd bump into if you kept hunting for them. There's a hornet's nest somewhere, and I'll wager Orme's sitting on it. Right there in Chico. He was afraid you'd poke a finger into it, Johnny Diamond."

They rode into Perdidas and turned up Commercial. Johnny left Hackamore at the livery barn and walked to his hotel. In his room he bolted the door on the inside. Whoever had sent a man to kill him would, by all logic, send another on the same errand.

He slept till noon. Later he checked at the sheriff's office and learned that nothing new had developed in the Frankie Valdez case.

75

Flo was there. She wore a starched white shirt-waist and a skirt of Scotch plaid. Her hair was parted in the middle and drawn back severely along the sides of her head. If she'd just fluff it out a little, Johnny thought, she'd be right pretty. Almost as pretty as her cousin Felicia.

Today she was a bit subdued. "Maybe we're not quite fair to you," she conceded. "At least you stirred up something at Chico."

Johnny grinned at her. "Maybe if I'd keep stirrin' things up you'd begin to like me a little."

Her face clouded. "I wish you wouldn't. You'll just get yourself shot, or knifed in some dark alley. Father has sent a deputy over to Chico, and he'll handle everything there."

"I wasn't calculating," Johnny said, "on going to Chico. Not in the next day or two, anyway."

She looked relieved. "You'll be safer," she said, "right here in Las Perdidas."

"I wasn't calculatin' on stayin' here either. Thought I'd take a *pasear*, tomorrow, out to the Circle D."

"What for?"

"Thought I'd ask Rick Sherwood where he got a mousey, four-year-old with four white feet. The bronc he sold Cranston."

This drew a chilly response. "Suit yourself, Mr. Diamond. But if you think you'll find a stolen mare there, you're just plain stupid."

"No harm in asking, is there? I mean I can just

ride out there tomorrow and lay my cards on the table. Him bein' a fine, upstandin' citizen, like you say, he'd be glad to . . ."

"Tomorrow," Flo broke in, "you won't find him at home."

"Know where he'll be?"

"He won't be at the ranch. I know because we invited him to come to town and take dinner with us tomorrow evening. He sent word he can't come because he'll be busy shipping some cattle."

"Where does he ship from?"

"Thacker, I imagine. It's due north of his place and the nearest point on the railroad."

"Then if I bought a train ticket to Thacker, I could see him there. Maybe I'll do that." Johnny looked at her and smiled. "And I promise to be right polite."

He went out, and a block down the street ran into Buck Perry. "Do you happen to know," he asked the Lazy M man, "just when and where the Circle D is shipping some cattle?"

"Couldn't say," Perry answered. "But you could find out, easy enough, from the district freight agent here. Just ask if the Circle D ordered some cars spotted at Thacker. Thacker's thirty-odd miles up the line."

"What kind of an outfit are they, the Circle D?"

"A he-stuff outfit, mainly. They buy steer

77

calves at weanin' and when they get to beef age they ship 'em to Kaycee."

"I mean Sherwood himself," Johnny prodded. "And his crew."

Perry looked thoughtful for a moment. "Rick Sherwood himself's all right. He stands well on this range. But his crew's a bit on the tough side. Gunnies, mostly, and they don't mix much with other folks around here. Some of 'em I wouldn't want on my payroll. 'Specially the top rod out there, Alf Sansone. Just between you an' me, Sansone's a killer. They say he usta be a trigger-happy marshal at Abilene. More notches on his gun than you could count on ten fingers."

"How come," Johnny inquired, "a nice friendly fella like Sherwood'd have an outfit like that?"

"That's easy." Perry nodded toward the chain of high, rugged mesas. "So the mesa rustlers'll leave him alone. More outlaws than you could shake a stick at, up there. The Circle Ds shoot it out with 'em, every now and then."

Johnny nodded. He remembered meeting the Circle D riders chasing horse thieves south over Capulin Gap.

He went on to the Santa Fe depot and checked with the freight agent there. "Yes," the freight man said, "the Circle D asked us to spot six cattle cars tomorrow at Thacker. Steers for Kaycee.

They're to be picked up at noon by an eastbound extra."

"Is there a passenger train up that way in the morning?"

"Yep. Leaves here at ten and stops at Thacker at eleven-eighteen."

"I'll be on it," Johnny said.

CHAPTER VII

Just before ten in the morning he arrived at the depot and bought a round-trip ticket to Thacker. The train pulled in and he boarded the smoker. He settled back comfortably with a cigaret. No use punishing Hackamore by a long saddle trip to the Circle D. This way the horse could rest in a stall while Johnny rode the cushions to meet Sherwood at his shipping point up the line. And most likely the Sawyers were right. Sherwood would turn out to be on the level.

Just as the train was pulling out, another passenger sprinted across the platform and swung on. He boarded a coach back of the smoker. Val Cranston! But naturally Cranston would be making this same trip. Shipping law all over the west stipulated that no one could ship cattle by rail without first notifying the official brand inspector. The inspector must then be on hand at the shipping point, to check the brand or brands of the stock being loaded.

Johnny considered going back for a chat with Cranston, then decided he wouldn't. He could see Cranston at Thacker. Not that there was anything to see him about. This trip would just be routine official business for Cranston. The only man who could answer Johnny's question, about the origin of a certain mouse-colored Morgan, would be Rick Sherwood.

The train followed the north bank of the Picketwire for a few miles, to an irrigated vega below Chico. Here the rails and the river split, the river winding easterly down a sunflower valley and the rails heading northeast across a grease-wood prairie.

It was a local train, making stops at Earl and Tyronne. At 11.18 it stopped at Thacker and Johnny got off.

The only buildings there were a depot and a section house. Behind the latter, a Mexican woman was hanging out wash. A sleepy operator was tapping a telegraph key in the depot.

Far down a sidetrack Johnny saw shipping pens. A cattle chute led into them, and on a siding opposite the chute were spotted six empty cattle cars. The herd to be shipped hadn't yet arrived, for the pens were empty and no herders were in sight.

"What are *you* doing here?" The voice was Val Cranston's who disembarked just as the train moved on. It struck Johnny that there was an uneasy tone in it. The man stood there staring at an him with his mouth hanging open. He looked tense and strangely apprehensive.

"Heard Rick Sherwood's shipping today,"

Johnny said. "Thought I'd come up and see him." He rolled a cigaret and offered the makings.

Cranston waved them away. He started to say something, then clamped his lips and turned to look southward across the bare range. The Circle D lay in that direction, somewhere in the lower Picketwire valley.

On the south horizon Johnny could see a cloud of dust. That, no doubt, would be six carloads of Circle D steers being driven this way. It would take about two hundred steers to fill six cars. "We can wait for 'em at the pens," Johnny said, and headed down the siding toward the spotted cars.

Cranston did not at once follow. He went into the depot, perhaps to ask the operator about the soon due freight train. Freights often ran several hours late.

Johnny walked a quarter mile down the siding to the pens. The six cars had been spotted so that the most easterly car was directly opposite the loading chute. Johnny climbed up on the pen fence and sat there, gazing south. The dust cloud was still many miles away, beyond a rise in the prairie. They'd have to hurry, Johnny thought, if they got those steers here in time for the eastbound freight.

Then he saw a nearer dust cloud approaching swiftly, a single rider. In a little while the man drew up at the shipping pens. He was astride a rangy strawberry roan branded Circle D.

"Whatcha doin' here?" the man demanded. The tone was alert and hostile. He was a small man with flat, pinkish eyes. His head had the shape of a bullet and he wore crossed gunbelts. His lips made a tight cruel crease over a tobacco-stained chin.

"Sittin' on a fence," Johnny told him, "waitin' to see Sherwood."

The flat eyes looked glassy. They fixed on Johnny with more of a glare than a stare. The man twisted in his saddle to look south. The dust of a cattle drive was still beyond the rise of prairie. Twisting back toward Johnny the man asked, this time in a tone of taut caution, "Did you come with Cranston?"

"We rode out on a train together," Johnny said. "There he is now." He nodded toward the depot from which the brand inspector had just emerged.

The Circle D man spurred his strawberry roan to meet Cranston, who was now walking toward them down the siding.

Johnny observed curiously. He saw the two meet about halfway between the pens and the depot. A colloquy between them took less than a minute. Then the two-gunned cowboy went racing south, toward the still distant cattle drive.

Cranston came on to the pens and took a perch on the fence beside Johnny. Moist beads stood on his face, glistening under the deep sideburns there, and yet in some way he looked faintly relieved. His voice took an amiable turn. "We got a long time to wait," he said. "Operator tells me that freight's two-three hours late. Won't be here till midafternoon."

"When can we get a passenger back to Las Perdidas?"

"Five o'clock." Cranston produced two cigars and offered one to Johnny

"Thanks. I'd rather roll my own," Johnny said, and did so. "Who was that fella with all the artillery?"

"He's Ferd Smith of the Circle D. Sherwood sent him ahead to make sure the cars are spotted. I told him they could take their time, because the freight's gonna be late."

The name Ferd Smith rang a bell. Johnny vaguely recalled hearing it at San Ysidro. It had drifted to him while Sheriff Sawyer was checking alibis after the killing of José Pacheco. "I was shooting pool with Ferd Smith." There'd been two Circle D mounts, Johnny remembered, tied that day in front of the San Ysidro pool room.

Ferd Smith was now out of sight, and had no doubt rejoined the drive beyond the lift of prairie.

Time dragged, and it seemed to Johnny that the drive was mighty slow coming on. It seemed to make lots of dust but very little progress. The sun passed its zenith. And there was no place a man

84

could buy a lunch here. Nothing in sight but a depot and a section house. Back of the latter, nearly half a mile down the track, the Mexican woman was still hanging out wash.

It was after one o'clock before Johnny could make out details of the oncoming herd. Four men were driving it. They were approaching at a brisk pace now, the steers lowing, riders whirling ropes at their flanks.

Cranston got down and opened a pen gate. The cattle came on and were driven into the pens. Whiteface stuff, Johnny noted, all mature steers branded Circle D.

One of the riders was Rick Sherwood. After exchanging greetings with Cranston, he rode up to where Johnny was seated on a fence. "Hi, fella." The voice was pleasantly casual. "Met you at the Riveras, didn't I?" He hooked a leg over his saddle horn and licked a cigaret. Range dust covered him from head to foot.

He looked, Johnny thought, like a hard-working stockman. His slate-gray eyes met Johnny's with a steady gaze. His one gun had an ivory handle. He looked solid and virile, Johnny thought, and only the self-willed set of his lips and a deeply cleft chin kept him from being handsome.

"Just thought maybe you could help me," Johnny said. "I been tryin' to trace an old Texas mare. She was a mousey Morgan with four white stockings and a starred forehead. She'd be about fourteen years old now."

Sherwood's stare at him was expressionless. "Yeh?" he prompted.

"Thought maybe some trader sawed her off on you, five or six years ago. That could happen, easy enough, without your knowin' anything about where the mare came from."

Sherwood shook his head slowly. "Can't remember any mare like that. What made you think I had one?"

"I didn't think you had one," Johnny said. "But leads are scarce and I'm playin' 'em all. That mare had a colt every year and they were always marked just like she was. It's reasonable to figure she kept on havin' colts after my folks lost her. Cranston rides a four-year-old with her breed and markings. Says he bought it from you."

Sherwood showed no resentment. But his lean, handsome face took the look, Johnny thought, of a poker player suddenly confronted with a stiff, unexpected bet. "Sure," he said. "I remember that bronc I sold Val. And the mare that foaled him. She was a white-stockinged buckskin. Isn't that right, Alf?"

One of the other Circle D men had ridden up. Johnny had seen him before. He had shaggy hair and a cold, flat face. His name was Alf Sansone. Like Ferd Smith he was two-gunned and looked like a hard-bitten triggerman. "That's right,"

Sansone agreed. "A white-stockinged buckskin."

Johnny noticed, then, that each of the four Circle D mounts was lathered and blown. Not just tired and droopy, but lathered and blown.

Rick Sherwood was smiling now. Was there a hint of derision, Johnny wondered, in that smile? His response had completely stymied further inquiry. It was entirely possible for a buckskin mare to have a mousey colt. The sire of the colt would be unknown, and could be any stallion on the range.

The loading of cattle was in brisk progress. Thirty steers were hazed up the inclined chute into the first car, filling it to capacity. Then Alf Sansone and Ferd Smith climbed to car roofs, to release the wheel brake of each car. The track had a one percent downgrade toward Kansas, and when other men of the crew used pinch bars at the axles the string of cars rolled slowly along the siding. As the door of the second car came opposite the chute, brakes were clamped and the string stopped.

Another thirty steers went into the second car. The process was repeated twice more, until four cars were loaded.

Johnny, watching idly, felt a new stir of interest. For the fourth car absorbed the last steer. There were no cattle left for the last two cars.

Why had Sherwood ordered six cars when he was only bringing enough cattle to fill four?

During the loading Val Cranston had stood faithfully by the chute, checking the brand of each steer as it went into a car. Now he looked southwest down the main line and saw the smoke of an approaching freight. "There she comes, Rick," he shouted. "You just got 'em loaded in time."

Sherwood turned to one of his men. "You ride the caboose to Kaycee, Sam. And see that you come back sober."

To Johnny he remarked carelessly: "Sorry I can't help you locate that old mare, fella. Chances are she's buzzard bait by now. Any time you come by the Circle D, stop in. So long, Val."

With Sansone and Smith he rode off south toward the Picketwire. One of them led the saddled horse of the man named Sam, who, having been detailed to chaperon the shipment to market, remained at the pens.

The freight rumbled in. Its engine was uncoupled and backed in upon the siding, there to pick up four cars of cattle and make them part of the train.

Johnny walked thoughtfully toward the depot. A wisp of memory tangled with a dozen other strands in his mind and hung there. Something about the murder of that San Ysidro blacksmith, José Pacheco. Finally he pinned it down. During the inquiry at San Ysidro, Buck Perry had asked if Pacheco had a family. Only a married daughter, they said, who lived at Thacker and whom Pacheco had visited the Sunday before his death.

The only woman here, as far as Johnny could see, was the section foreman's wife. She was still busy with her wash back of the section house. Johnny continued on past the depot and approached her.

"*Buenos días*, señora." He took off his hat and smiled. "I'm Johnny Diamond, a friend of Don Ronaldo Rivera."

She looked up at him with sad eyes. "Don Ronaldo is a good man, señor. Always he is kind to us *pobres*. He has paid for my poor father's funeral from which I have just returned."

Johnny gave a sympathetic nod. It was clear now that she was the daughter of the late José Pacheco. "Your father paid you a visit, didn't he? Sunday before last?"

She thought back. "Yes, señor, it was *el domingo pasado* that he was last here."

"A few cars of cattle were shipped out that day," Johnny suggested. "Just like today. Were they Circle D cattle?"

"I cannot say, señor. From here we cannot see the brands."

"But Circle D men were loading them?"

"*Si*, señor. My father walked up to the pens to see if they needed help. But they did not."

"Thanks, señora." A surge of excitement gripped Johnny as he left her and went to the depot.

"How many cars of cattle," he asked the operator, "were shipped from here Sunday before last?"

The man looked up the record of it. "Seven," he said. "Circle D stuff."

A hunch hit Johnny. It was something he felt stubbornly sure of, but couldn't prove. If true, it offered a motive for José Pacheco's murder. Also it would explain something else. Why Rick Sherwood, after ordering six cattle cars today, had filled only four of them!

It would even explain the blown and lathered horses. Mounts which had kept the easy pace of a cattle drive from the Picketwire shouldn't be winded. But if they'd stopped just before arriving, racing frantically and furiously among the cattle to cut out and turn back a third of them, the horses would be blown and lathered.

The four cars now having been shunted into the train, the freight pulled out for Kansas City. As the caboose went by, Sam of the Circle D stood on its rear platform. His eyes narrowed to a baleful stare as he saw Johnny at the depot. *It spilled their apple cart,* Johnny thought, *my being here!* He turned to look significantly at the two empties still spotted at the pens.

The plan, Johnny could hardly doubt, had been to fill those cars with brands other than Circle D.

CHAPTER VIII

When the west-bound local came along Johnny boarded it with Val Cranston. He sat beside the brand inspector all the way to Las Perdidas, talking about anything except cattle. It wouldn't do to voice his suspicions. Because if they were correct, Cranston was bound to be in it with Sherwood.

"You been around this range long?" Johnny asked casually.

Cranston leaned back, elevating his boots to the opposite seat. "Only about three years," he said. "Before that I was a weighmaster at the Denver stockyards."

Johnny had no doubt it was true. Cranston would hardly lie about anything so easily checked on. He didn't look like a ranch type. A Denver clerk's job would fit him much better. From there he could have advanced to a political appointment as brand inspector of this district.

Certainly the man couldn't have been one of three outlaws who'd gone raiding in Texas six years ago. But just as certainly he could more recently have been corrupted into falsifying brands at an isolated shipping point like Thacker.

The train was pulling into Las Perdidas when Cranston asked, "Rick explained about that mouse-colored horse of mine, I suppose?"

"Yeh," Johnny told him. "Out of a buckskin mare, he said."

He got off at the depot and walked up Commercial to his hotel. After supper he went out looking for Buck Perry. The Ysidro Creek cowman might or might not still be in town. Johnny wanted to confide in someone. Buck Perry would listen, if he could be found. But Sheriff Sawyer wouldn't. Sawyer would give him a quick brush-off. He'd be completely incredulous about any scheme of rustling in carload lots, hatched by Sherwood with the connivance of Cranston.

Johnny looked in at various saloons and failed to see Perry. He tried a hotel or two. It was dark by the time he headed back toward his own.

Then he became aware he was being followed. A smallish man wearing a sheepskin coat almost bumped into him twice. The collar of the coat was turned up over the ears, so that only a sly, narrow face peeped out. A face Johnny remembered seeing at Orme's bar in Chico.

Johnny circled down to Elm Street and stood watching a sidewalk dice game there. Glancing over his shoulder he saw the man again. Johnny strolled to the corner of Commercial and the man furtively followed.

There could be only one answer. Cranston was worried. He'd put a shadow on Johnny. Or maybe Sherwood had sent instructions by Cranston. They weren't sure whether or not Johnny had seen through that affair at Thacker. Were they watching to see if he made a report to the law?

Johnny had considered doing just that. But the law was Adam Sawyer and Sawyer wouldn't believe him. Sawyer was too opinionated. He was Sherwood's friend and might some day be Sherwood's father-in-law. Until Johnny had something more than a hunch, he'd sound stupid telling tales on Sherwood.

But it would be easy to make a test. And throw a scare into the man following him.

So Johnny turned into a cigar store and inquired where Adam Sawyer lived. At number 400 Piñon Lane, they told him, on the south side.

Johnny took that direction. Once he'd left the business district the streets were inky dark. He couldn't see anyone back of him. But faint footsteps half a block behind told that he was still being followed.

Piñon Lane was steep. The Sawyer residence, they'd told him, was a stone bungalow on a corner. Johnny stopped to light a cigaret. The steps back of him stopped too. They continued again as Johnny moved on.

He came to a corner bungalow of stone. A porch light was on there. The windows showed lamp glow, with the shades drawn. The sheriff and his daughter should have finished supper by now. Johnny remembered they'd invited Rick Sherwood to be their supper guest, and that he'd sent word he couldn't come.

Instead it was Johnny Diamond who came. He couldn't barge in with an unprovable theory about Sherwood and Cranston. They'd deride it and show him the door. Nevertheless he wanted to knock on that door and be admitted for a few minutes. Eyes were watching from the dark, the eyes of a spy probably sent by Cranston. Johnny wanted to impress and frighten Cranston, and in turn Sherwood. They'd assume he'd come here to accuse them and it might throw them off balance, jockeying them into some false move.

Why not simply go in and ask Sawyer for the latest about Diego Salvador. Salvador was being held in jail under suspicion of knifing Frankie Valdez. "Has he admitted anything yet?" Johnny could ask. A fair question, since Johnny himself had been assaulted by the same knife. Whatever the sheriff answered, Johnny would promptly take his leave.

But the spy outside would misinterpret the call, assuming that it concerned a suspicious circumstance at Thacker.

A smile quirked Johnny's lips as he mounted the Sawyer steps. The shot came just as he reached the porch level. It barked from the gloom of a cottonwood across the street, its bullet smashing into a porch post only inches from Johnny's head.

He dived to a crouched position back of the porch rail, expecting a second shot. He heard running feet, then silence. Not being armed himself, Johnny didn't consider giving chase. Anger boiled through him. Blast this town ordinance which made a man go defenseless here! It was humiliating to dodge and crouch back of a porch rail, while killers hunted him from the dark.

The house door opened and light from inside exposed Johnny kneeling there. In the open doorway stood Adam Sawyer. His questions cracked: "Did I hear a shot? What are you doing there, young man?"

"I was playin' tag with a slug," Johnny said.

Flo Sawyer appeared beside her father. She seemed curious rather than alarmed. And the sight of them, standing there looking at him like he might be some impudent intruder, made Johnny madder than ever. He got to his feet and said bitterly: "I was playin' blind-man's-buff with a bullet. Here's where it hit."

He thumbed toward a splintered hole in a porch post.

Sawyer stepped back into the parlor. He picked up a lamp and came out on the porch with it. Gravely he inspected a bullet hole in a post.

His lower lip pushed out and he gave a significant nod. "So Orme tried it again!" he muttered. "That makes twice he tried to get you, Johnny Diamond."

"Orme," Johnny snapped back, "had nothing to do with it this time. He wouldn't know I was at Thacker today. Only Cranston and the Circle Ds knew that." He added with a shrug: "But *you* wouldn't believe it! So what's the use?"

"I wouldn't believe what?" Sawyer demanded.

"That I know why José Pacheco was killed at San Ysidro. I didn't come here to tell you about it. But they thought I did. So they tried to mow me down."

Flo looked at him, her eyes big and round. *"They?"* she queried. "Whom do you mean?"

"Your boy friend," Johnny charged fiercely. He didn't care now whether he offended them or not. "Sherwood and his stooge, Cranston. They've been stealing this range blind. Pacheco got wind of it, so they had him gunned. Today I got another whiff, so they sicked a bullet on me too."

They stared at him, Adam dourly incredulous, Flo shocked to the pallor of marble. "That," Adam Sawyer said with a bite, "is the most absurd thing I ever heard."

Johnny turned brusquely and started down the steps. "I knew you'd talk that way. Sorry I bothered you. Goodnight."

But the sheriff caught his arm and whirled

him toward the open door. "I don't believe you, young man, but I'll listen to your story. You're confusing Orme with Sherwood, that's all. Somebody *did* try to kill you on my doorstep, and I insist on getting to the bottom of it."

"All you insist on," Johnny retorted, "is whitewashin' the guy you aimed to have here for dinner tonight. He couldn't come because he was too busy. Busy rustlin' a couple carloads of somebody's cattle."

"Nonsense!" Sawyer derided. "But come inside. I must hear how you arrived at this fantastic theory." Still gripping an arm, he propelled Johnny into his parlor and made him sit down. Flo closed the door and stood with her back against it, staring at Johnny as though he were some demented child.

"Now just what's this brainstorm of yours," the sheriff demanded, "about the Circle D stealing cattle? I happen to know that just the opposite is true. The Circle D carries on a relentless war against stock thieves. Outlaws who hang out in the mesas and drive Colorado stock down into New Mexico. Time and again the Circle D has chased such outlaws and brought the stock back."

That gave Johnny an idea and brought a grim grin to his lips. "Yeh, I saw 'em do that once up through Capulin Gap. They brought the stock back but they didn't catch any outlaws. Might be they framed that chase just for the looks of it.

Why? To fool you and their honest neighbors. Make you think the rustlin' is all southbound on the hoof, whereas really it goes eastbound on rails. It gives you a mesa outlaw prejudice, so you don't look for stolen cattle where they really are."

"And you," Sawyer challenged with stinging sarcasm, "know where they *really* are."

"Sure. They're packing-house beef by now. Shipped to Kaycee or Chicago and sold in the stockyards there. Some of 'em are in tin cans now, on grocery shelves all over the country."

Adam gave a sigh of impatience and sat down. He crossed his long legs and invited tolerantly: "Very well. Let's hear all of it, young man."

"I don't claim to know the details," Johnny admitted, "or how long it's been goin' on. Probably for three years."

The sheriff's head jerked back a little. He turned and met Flo's eyes. A half-startled look was in them. Then with a shrug Sawyer turned to face Johnny again. "You say three years, I suppose, because perhaps Buck Perry told you we've had more rustling complaints in the last three years than ever before. That is true. Go on, young man."

"No," Johnny corrected, "I guessed three years because that's how long Cranston's been brand inspector around here. He's in on the rustlin' himself. Not that he ever rides a horse except in a social way."

"How can you dare say that about Val?" This protest came in a tone of shock from Flo. "He's practically engaged to my cousin, Felicia Rivera."

"And Senator Rivera himself," Sawyer added, "got Cranston his appointment."

"At whose request?" Johnny questioned. "Sherwood's? The senator, they tell me, likes to accommodate his friends and neighbors. It's a laugh, when you stop to think about it. Sherwood wants to steal the senator's cattle. So he asks the senator to appoint Cranston brand inspector. 'Anything to oblige a friend,' says the senator. After which Val and Ricky steal the senator blind."

"You have evidence, of course?" Sawyer challenged, again with acrid irony.

"Nope," Johnny said. "Just a theory with a few pegs that fit. One peg that fits is José Pacheco. His daughter lives in the section house at Thacker. Sunday before last, Pacheco spent the weekend with her. Half a mile down the siding he saw the Circle D loadin' seven cars of cattle. So he walked down there and offered to help 'em. They said no thanks and he went back to the section house. That much we can prove."

"Everything else is a guess?"

"Not quite. But this much is. Pacheco noticed that some of those cattle had a Circle D brand, and some had a Bar L. He supposed it was a joint shipment, Rivera sendin' some of his own stuff to market along with some of Sherwood's. Then Pacheco went home to San Ysidro and started thinking. If it was a joint shipment, why hadn't Rivera sent a couple of his own vaqueros to help with the loading? It worried Pacheco. He decided to send a message to the senator and get a check on it. If it wasn't a joint shipment, it was a steal. So Pacheco began asking his customers if they'd take a message to Rivera. The Circle D got itchy and stopped him with a slug."

"Absurd on the face of it," Sawyer scoffed. "If cattle had been stolen from the senator a week ago Sunday, he would have reported it to the sheriff's office."

"How could he?" Johnny countered. "Rivera won't miss the cattle till roundup time. Then when the tally's short, everybody'll lay it on to mesa outlaws."

Sawyer asked coldly, "Is that all?"

"Nope. Today they tried the same steal again. Only I happened to show up at Thacker. Six cars were spotted and steers to fill 'em were on the way. But a Circle D gunnie named Ferd Smith rode ahead and spotted me. Cranston was on hand, as usual. He sent Smith back to the drive to warn 'em I was there. They couldn't very well gun me in broad daylight, with an operator in the depot and a woman at the section house. All they could do was cut out everything but Circle D stuff. They had to work fast, and it sure lathered their broncs. It left 'em just enough to fill four cars. Top of that, there was a lot of nervous looks and whispers and double talk. Cranston was scared stiff when he saw me get off the train."

"I don't believe it," Sawyer repeated.

"Neither do I," Flo echoed. "No one in his right mind could think that about Rick and Val."

"In that case," Johnny grinned, "I'm loco. Which still leaves a slug in your porch post."

"Fired," Sawyer insisted, "by an agent of Syd Orme. Did you see the man?"

"Only in the dark," Johnny said. "And not well enough to identify him in court. Little guy in a sheepherder's coat. Collar turned up about his ears. Big flappy hat. I admit he looked a little like one of those toughies I saw in Orme's bar. Just the same I'm bettin' Cranston sicked him on me to see where I went. When I came to a sheriff's house he let fly."

"You can't tie up decent citizens," Sawyer maintained, "with the riffraff of Chico. Cranston has no connection with Orme. The same goes for Sherwood. Both attempts on your life stemmed from your inquiry about Linked Diamonds boots at Chico."

Johnny shrugged. "Have it your way, sheriff. I'll be shovin' along now." He got up and went to the door. There he turned with a grin. "So long, folks. Hope I didn't upset you too much."

Flo opened the door for him. As he passed out

she followed him to the porch steps. "Where," she asked with a shade of anxiety, "are you going now?"

"To bed," Johnny said, "if I don't get bush-whacked on the way to the hotel."

"I mean tomorrow."

A glint came to Johnny's eyes. "Tomorrow I'll buckle on a gun. They won't let me wear it in town, so I'll hit for the range."

"But where?"

He met her eyes and smiled grimly. "If I told you, you might pass it on to your friend Sherwood next time he comes acourtin'. Then he could have someone slip up on me, some night when I'm asleep, and cut my throat."

Blood raced in an angry flood to her cheeks. "You're beastly!" she said. "I hope I never see you again."

Johnny left her and turned down the dark street, cautious and alert. A bullet was lurking for him. Either this night or some other. A bullet or a knife. A bullet from Sherwood or a knife from Orme.

CHAPTER IX

Neither came on his way to the hotel. He locked himself in his room, mulling over today and yesterday. Sherwood's pattern of crookery seemed clear enough. Mix stock of a neighbor with your own and ship it to market by rail. A thing which could only be done with the help of a brand inspector.

But now Sherwood was warned. He'd be careful not to make any more crooked shipments for a while. Which meant he'd boil over with resentment against a kid from Texas. Thacker, he'd assume, would be watched after this. He wouldn't dare repeat the operation.

What about Orme? Was he in any way connected with Sherwood? The patterns of motive at Chico were hazy and didn't seem to make sense. You inquire of a bootblack there about a pair of boots, and right away the bootblack gets killed. And right away you yourself get waylaid in your room. Nothing about that seemed remotely connected with stealing cattle. If a man at Chico had a pair of boots like that, he could claim he'd found them; or that he'd won them in a dice game. No sound reason for him to cover up by knifing Frankie Valdez.

When Johnny at last slipped into sleep, he had no plan at all.

In the morning he checked out of the hotel. At the livery barn he saddled Hackamore. The dun was in a mean temper this morning. He kicked a board off his stall in protest against leaving it. Johnny packed the bay pack mare and rode down East Main, leading her. A forty-five was belted around his waist now. He stopped at Griswold's Hardware Store for a box of shells.

Riding out of town he decided to check with the two friends he'd made so far on this range. Chuck Wiggins at the Rivera ranch; and Buck Perry on the San Ysidro. Maybe they could pass him a tip or some worthwhile advice.

The trail led over the Frijole hills, jutting out from Fisher's Mesa and thickly studded with piñons. Johnny kept alert every minute, on guard at every possible spot of ambush. He loosened the carbine in his saddle scabbard. Yet there could hardly be any immediate danger. His enemies wouldn't know that he was riding this way.

It was the road to San Ysidro. Also it was the road to both the Rivera ranch and the Circle D. To the right a steep slope ascended to Fisher's Mesa. Other mesas chained easterly from it: Horseshoe; Johnson's; Trinchera. To the left lay the broad level valley of the Picketwire.

Here, for a short way, was a ridge of piñons.

Before Johnny was halfway across it he heard, back of him on this same trail, the hoofbeats of a loping horse. He stopped, looked over his shoulder, then reined sharply around. A wryness curved his lips as the pursuer caught up with him.

He tipped his hat and smiled. "Mornin', Flo. You're out kinda early for a town girl."

She didn't smile back. Today she wore a jacket and riding pants, as when he'd first seen her. Her mount was blowing hard as she stopped it beside Johnny's. "I wanted to see you," she said, and then flushed with a memory of her words of last night: that she hoped never to see him again.

"How did you know I was headin' this way?"

"Trouble's this way," she said bitterly. "And you're sure to head for trouble."

"You mean the Circle D's this way. But I wasn't aimin' to go there, just now. First I figured to have a little confab with Chuck Wiggins and Buck Perry."

She looked at him hopelessly. "That's just what I was afraid of. You'll spread it all over the range that Rick Sherwood's been stealing cattle. Rick's sure to hear about it. And you know what that means, I suppose."

"You tell *me*."

"He'll do exactly what you'd do yourself. What any proud, red-blooded man would do. Rustler's a fighting word."

"He'll gun me, you mean?"

"He'll shoot you to ribbons," Flo predicted. "Or maybe you'll shoot him to ribbons. And all because you let your imagination run away with your tongue. Please don't be stupid." Her voice took a pleading tone. "Rick Sherwood never stole anything in his life. He's a solid, upright cattle-man. I guarantee it. Please stay away from him for just one week. I'll convince you, by that time, that you're wrong."

"How?" Johnny challenged.

"I can write to the Kansas City stockyards. I can ask what brands were in the seven cars shipped from Thacker a week ago Sunday. They'll tell me there was only one brand, Circle D."

Johnny shook his head. "Some day there'll be a law makin' 'em check brands at the receiving end. But there's no check like that now. Brands are inspected only at the shipping end. At the market end those seven cars were unloaded, weighed, and sold by the pound to the highest bidder. A day later they were beef. The hides were dumped in vats with thousands of other hides; nobody could say now which hide came in which shipment."

"Then," Flo proposed desperately, "we'll watch the next shipment at Thacker."

"Too late. The Circle D knows I'm hep to 'em. If they try that shipping trick again, it won't be at Thacker."

They heard hoofbeats approaching from the direction of Las Perdidas. Flo threw an apprehensive look in that direction. "It might be someone after you," she suggested. "Let's get off the road and let him pass."

Johnny didn't think so. His enemies could hardly know he'd come this way. But the girl insisted and they rode into the piñons a little way. In a few minutes a rider raced by, spurring a black pony. Johnny had a good look at his profile. The man had a slight build and a sly, sharp-angled face. A roll tied back of his saddle looked like a sheepskin coat.

"That's the guy, on a bet," Johnny said.

As Flo looked questioningly he explained: "I mean the guy who trailed me to your front steps last night. The one who flipped a slug. It was dark, so I can't swear to him in court. But I'd bet a saddle on it, just the same."

"He's Jakie Kim," Flo said with certainty.

"You've seen him before?"

She nodded. "Dad's had him in jail more than once. But we could never get a conviction. He ran a shell game for a while. Once he was held under suspicion for a pool-hall shooting at Chico."

"I got him placed now," Johnny said. "He was one of Diego Salvador's alibis at the Bon Ton bar, the other day."

The man had disappeared down the road now. "He's got a long ride ahead of him," Johnny brooded. "So chances are he'll stay all night and won't start back till tomorrow."

"Back from where?"

"From the Circle D. That's where he's headed, all right."

Flo flushed. "What," she asked coolly, "makes you think he's riding to the Circle D?"

"Common sense. Val Cranston sicked him on me last night, and he missed. So when he reports back to Val, Val gets worried. Bright and early this morning he sends Jakie Kim with a message to somebody. The way I figure it, the message oughta be somethin' like this: '*Cuidado*. Johnny from Texas went to see the sheriff last night. We tried to stop him but missed. What do we do now?' "

"That vivid imagination of yours!" Flo murmured scornfully. "There's not a chance in the world that little underworld rat's on his way to see Rick Sherwood."

"Let's bet on it," Johnny proposed with a grin. "If he goes straight to the Circle D, you owe me a date first night I'm in town. If he doesn't, I'll head straight back to Texas."

She gave him a straight look. "I'd take you up on that, Johnny Diamond, if there was any way to prove it."

"Provin' it's a cinch," Johnny said. "Let's ride on to the Riveras. Pick out any *mozo* you want. The *mayordomo* himself, if you like. Send him with a message to Sherwood. An invitation to dinner, seein' as he missed out on the last one on account of bein' busy rustlin' cattle." She froze at this but Johnny kept on. "The *mozo*'ll get there so late he'll have to stay all night at the bunk-shack. If Kim's there, he'll see the guy. If he isn't, I lose my bet."

"Why should I spy," Flo protested indignantly, "on a trusted friend?"

"You were goin' to send a letter to the Kaycee stockyards. That's spyin' on him. I'm offerin' you a nice polite way to spy. Just send a *mozo* over there on any errand you want. He'll either see Jakie there or he won't. One way makes me wrong, the other way makes me right. But of course if you're afraid . . ."

"Afraid I'll turn out to be wrong?" she cut in. "Of course I'm not. Just to show you up, I'll do it."

She spurred her pony down the road.

Johnny, leading a pack mare, couldn't catch up till she slowed to a walk. Thereafter they rode silently together, easterly toward the Rivera ranch. Flo with her chin high, Johnny with a brooding smile. It would make a neat trap, he thought, to catch Sherwood in a lie. For later the man would deny a visit from Jakie Kim. Yet if an honest *mozo* reported back to Flo that he'd seen the man there . . .

Johnny looked at Flo and suddenly felt a

desperate eagerness to convince her. Convincing her meant at least that she'd never marry Sherwood. And Johnny's own stock should soar, both with the girl and her father.

"I won't say a word about this," he promised, "to anyone but Chuck Wiggins and Buck Perry. And I'll tell them to keep it under their hats."

"You couldn't tell Uncle Ronald," she said, "even if you wanted to. The legislature's in session again and he went back to Denver."

"I'll just stop at the bunkhouse long enough to see Chuck. Then I'll go on to Perry's."

"You'll keep away from the Circle D?" Her face was anxious again.

"Like they were poison," he promised.

They crossed Frijole arroyo, topped another piñon rise and dropped into the valley of Grosella Creek. The Rivera meadows made a purple ribbon there.

After crossing a wooden bridge they turned through a gate into the ranch street. Johnny stopped at the bunkhouse. "Say howdy to Felicia for me," he said. "And don't forget our date, next time I'm in town."

Flo rode severely on without answering. Johnny watched her dismount at the main house.

He himself went into the bunkshack and found Chuck Wiggins there. The redhead, dressed for the road, was stuffing his belongings into a duffel bag.

"Goin' somewhere?" Johnny inquired. "What's the matter? Felicia turn you down?"

"I was only hired," Wiggins explained gloomily, "to bust a string of broncs. Made the job last as long as I could. It's done now. Those broncs are so tame now even the cook can ride 'em."

"Where you headin'?"

"For the first payroll I can get on. Know anybody needs a good puncher?"

"Why don't you try Buck Perry's outfit, over on the San Ysidro?"

"As good a place as any," Wiggins said.

"Let's get started, then. I'm headed that way myself."

They went first to the cookshack for a lunch of pork and frijoles. "And cheer up," Johnny said. "I got some good news for you."

"About what?" Chuck asked.

"About your number one rival, Val Cranston. Unless I'm loco, he's been helpin' the Circle D steal steers."

Wiggins froze, spilling beans off his spoon as the baldness of the charge jolted him. "Who are you kidding?" he demanded.

"Nobody. Open your ears and listen." Johnny proceeded to outline his theory about Sherwood and Cranston. He linked it to the murder of Pacheco at San Ysidro, and to an attempt on his own life last night in Las Perdidas.

Wiggins, incredulous at first, nevertheless

weighed each point shrewdly and in the end added a few of his own. "It's a fact," he admitted, "that every outfit on this range has been tallyin' out short at all roundups for the last three years. We laid it to mesa outlaws. Nobody ever thought of the Circle Ds. But they're hard cases, all right. Kansas gunnies, most of 'em, who used to know Alf Sansone when he was marshal at Abilene."

"We'll hash it over," Johnny suggested, "with Buck Perry. If we can pin this deadwood on Cranston, it leaves you top man with Felicia."

"That Cranston guy," Wiggins scowled, "has sure been beatin' my time. Buildin' a fire under him'd suit me just fine."

After lunch he tied a roll back of his saddle. They set out down the San Ysidro road. With Johnny leading a lazy pack mare the pace was held to a running walk.

"Where," he asked, "does the Circle D run its range horses?"

"Wintertime," Chuck said, "they run out here in the open flats. But summers you'd find 'em up in the timber. And on those grassy benches sticking out from the mesas." He thumbed toward the chain of mesas on their right, black with pine and green with aspen, which reared like a mile-high natural wall along the New Mexico line.

"What's the best water hole up there?" Johnny asked.

Chuck pointed to a curve in the rimrock of

Horseshoe Mesa. "They's a big spring up there. Spouts right out of a rock and makes a pool. Old trapper's cabin right by it. It's on government land and nobody ever uses it. Plenty of range horses water there, this season. Why?"

Johnny had been looking over his shoulder. A buggy, driven by an elderly Mexican, was gaining on them.

"That one of the Rivera *mozos*?"

Wiggins looked back. "Yeh, it's old Miguel. He's number one *mozo* at the house."

"He'd do you a favor, wouldn't he?"

"Sure. Miguel and I been palsy-walsy, last few weeks. He'd do anything I say."

"Listen, Chuck. When he catches up we'll hold a little confab with him. And here's what you tell him." Johnny gave rapid instructions and Wiggins was fully coached when the buggy drew up by them.

"*Buenos días*, señores," said Miguel.

"Drivin' to the Circle D?" Chuck inquired, rolling two cigarets and tossing one to the *mozo*.

"*Sí*, señor. And *gracias*. Last week they send us over a dressed antelope. So now I take them ten gallons of chokecherry wine. With the compliments of the casa Rivera."

Johnny smiled. It meant that Flo, having enlisted the help of her cousin Felicia, was making good on her bargain. Only she'd figured out something less crude than a trumped-up

113

dinner invitation. A gift for a gift was the rule at every Spanish hacienda. Your neighbor sends you an antelope, you respond in due course with ten gallons of chokecherry wine.

"You'll spend the night there?" suggested Wiggins.

"But of course, señor. The sun will no longer shine by the time I arrive there. Early *mañana* I shall return."

Johnny broke in to inquire: "Miguel, how can I get up to a big spring under the rimrock of Horseshoe Mesa? Wild Turkey Water Hole, they call it."

"You ride up McBride Creek, señor, and take the right fork. Much brush is there and it is very steep . . ." Miguel went on to explain in detail the route to a high mountain spring.

"Thanks," Johnny said. "I aim to camp up there for a week or two. Want to look over the range mares that water there. I'm huntin' for an old mousey mare with four white stockings. An old Texas brand. Linked Diamonds."

Miguel looked puzzled "I have never seen such a brand, señor."

It was Chuck's turn now, and he'd been well-instructed by Johnny. "Listen, Miguel. This is important. At supper tonight in the Circle D bunkshack, you put out a little idle gossip. To the cook or any hands at the table with you. Just say you met a Texas cowboy on the road this

114

afternoon. Which is true. You recognized him as a recent guest of Senator Rivera. So you stopped to pass the time of day. Which is true *también.* Only you don't mention I was with him."

The *mozo* stared. "But why should I say this, señor?"

"Never mind why. Just say it. You remark that this Texas cowboy asked how to get up to Wild Turkey Water Hole. He'll camp there, he told you, for a week to see if a mousey mare waters there. For a whole week he'll be there alone, camping in the old cabin. Is that clear, Miguel?"

Miguel was still confused. But evidently the red-headed bronc-breaker carried a lot of weight with him. "Since I must speak only the truth, I will do it, señor." He drove on.

Wiggins, with Johnny leading the pack mare, followed at a slower pace. "I don't like it," the redhead muttered. "You're usin' your own skin to bait a trap with."

Johnny grinned. "And why not? When Sherwood sends someone up there to gun me, I'll be watchin' for him. It'll show his hand, Chuck."

They saw the buggy ahead leave the main road. It veered to the left on a trail pointing toward the Circle D, far to the northeast near the confluence of the San Ysidro and the Picketwire. Johnny and Chuck kept to the main road.

At San Ysidro plaza they turned downcreek a

few miles to Buck Perry's place, the Lazy M. It was a stout layout, crude compared to the Rivera rancho. Buildings were of logs and there was no family house at all. Perry, a bachelor, lived with his hands at a long, gabled bunkhouse.

There were four of these hands and Perry was eating supper with them when Wiggins came in with Johnny Diamond.

"Howdy," Perry greeted. "Set and help yourself to victuals. What's new in town, Johnny?"

He presented his crew: Slim McBride; Dyke Dixon; Ed Sopers and Juan Romero. Romero, apparently, doubled as cook. He was brown and chunky. The others were lean, sun-blackened men with range-wise eyes. Johnny liked the cut of them.

"Don't start callin' me loco," he began with a sober grin, "till I finish." Once more he gave out his hunches about Sherwood and Cranston.

There was a long brittle silence. Then Slim McBride gave a low whistle. Perry blinked and said: "Thacker, huh? They ordered six cars. But when they heard you was there, they only shipped four!"

Ed Sopers' eyes narrowed to shrewd slits. "They could work it, all right, if they had a crooked brand inspector to back 'em up."

"You say Cranston was jumpy?" Slim McBride put in.

"As nervous as a cat," Johnny said.

"He's had that job three years," Perry brooded. "Durin' which we been short about ten percent, every roundup."

Dyke Dixon said nothing at all. He simply went to a shelf and poked around in a litter there for a can of gun oil. Then he sat on a bunk and began oiling his gun.

CHAPTER X

Buck Perry, however, promptly vetoed Johnny's scheme for making human bait of himself at a rimrock water hole.

"If your guess is wrong," he summed up, "nothing'll happen. If it's right, bullets'll happen. And not just from one gun. I mean Sherwood might send his whole outfit up there. They'd burn you down, Johnny."

"I'll take a chance," Johnny said.

"No you won't," the veteran stockman decreed. Older than the others, he had a bigger bump of discretion. "We'll all go. Juan can bring all the horses back except yours, Johnny. The rest of us'll hide in that cabin. Then if the Circle D comes ashootin', let 'em come."

A minor issue worried Johnny. Jakie Kim. Sherwood might keep him under cover where

Miguel wouldn't see him. Johnny talked it over with Buck Perry.

Perry turned to Juan Romero. "Juan, get up a couple hours before daylight and ride to that clump o' cedars just this side of the Circle D gate. Watch to see if Jakie Kim comes outa that gate on his way back to town."

Johnny found a bunk and turned in. In the morning they let him sleep. When he awakened, Juan Romero had returned from his errand.

"Kim was there, *amigos*," Romero reported. "He rides out through the Circle D gate just after daybreak and goes toward Las Perdidas. Soon I see Miguel come out in his buggy, on his way home. I ask if he told the man about our friend Johnny camping at the mountain spring. Miguel says yes, he did."

"Did he see Jakie Kim there?" Johnny asked.

"No," Romero said. "They kept Jakie out of sight."

Johnny grinned. "Good thing you checked on him, then. Otherwise I'd lose a bet to Flo Sawyer."

Buck Perry assembled provisions for a week. Bedrolls were packed. Johnny kept under cover all day. An hour after dark all of them set out for Wild Turkey Water Hole.

They left the main road at McBride Creek and rode up it to the canyon between Johnson and Horseshoe mesas. From this they turned to the right up a steep, single-file trail. Ed Sopers took the lead. Juan Romero came last leading two pack horses. Brush slapped at Johnny's thighs and he wished he'd worn chaparajos. For an hour more they pushed on and up through the dark, climbing toward the sheer façade of a rimrock.

A late moon was out when the pines opened on to a grassy bench jutting from Horseshoe Mesa. A few cattle were bedded down there, making only black shapes. The bench sloped upward to pines again. Beyond the pines they came to an aspen park just under the rimrock.

Water gushed from a niche in the rock, making a small pool in an open acre of vega. Romero dismounted and lighted a lantern. Its glow showed horse tracks, cow tracks and deer tracks by the pool. A cabin of slab rock centered the little vega. Hail had battered out its windowpanes and its stovepipe chimney was red with rust. "Here we are," Perry announced.

Saddles and packs were taken inside. "Hobble Johnny's horse and mare and leave 'em right here," Perry directed. "Juan, you take all the other broncs back to the ranch. Keep busy with the chores for the next week. Anybody comes by, tell 'em the outfit's over on the Chuquaak lookin' fer strays."

Well before dawn Juan Romero had departed with all the stock except Johnny's.

"Looks like we're gonna be crowded," Slim

McBride remarked as he spread his bedroll on the floor. The cabin had only one room with a rusty iron stove in one corner. Six outstretched bedrolls left but small space to move about.

"But here we are," Perry said grimly. "And everybody stays inside except Johnny. They peek outa the woods, they see Johnny and Johnny's broncs. Nothin' else."

Rifles were loaded and leaned against the walls. Each man had at least one Colt's forty-five. The trap was set. Any crew of assassins who came here, expecting to find only Johnny Diamond, would meet a warm reception.

McBride took the first watch and the others tried for a little sleep. The lantern was out now. From his blankets in the dark, Johnny chuckled and Chuck Wiggins wanted to know why.

"I was thinking of Flo Sawyer," Johnny said. "Miguel's back at the rancho by now and he's told her Jakie Kim wasn't at the Circle D. So she thinks she's rid of me. She figures I'll have to head back to Texas."

"Was that the bet?"

"That was it." Johnny chuckled again, then slipped into sleep.

Before a day had passed he knew it would be a tedious wait. And maybe the Circle D wouldn't come at all. While the others kept cover, Johnny exposed himself deliberately on the cabin steps.

Occasionally he saw stock come to water at the pool. The entire mountainside seemed peaceful. Jaybirds chattered in the aspens.

He was more than nine thousand feet high here. Far below, reaching to the north and east horizons, stretched the Picketwire valley. A treeless valley, except for thin cottonwood lines where tributary creeks crossed it like veins in a leaf. But here on this high slope the timber was dense, banking steeply down from rimrock to plain. Grass grew lush in the timber and lusher still on the occasional benches jutting from the mountain. It made a fine summer stock range for all the valley ranches.

A salt trough lay near the pool. A dozen times during the day Johnny saw stock file from the timber to water there and to lick at the rocky chunks in the trough. Johnny saw Circle D brands, as well as Bar L and Lazy M. In the afternoon two small bands of horses came to the spring, snorting at sight of Johnny, yet drinking their fill before galloping back into timber. Johnny kept an alert eye for colors. But there was no old mouse-colored mare.

Inside the cabin the others were playing seven up. The only horses in sight were Johnny's, grazing hobbled in the open acre by the spring. By all external signs Johnny was the only one here.

Perry spoke to him through the half-open door.

"If you hear anyone comin', turn a back flip and get inside. You're a sittin' duck, out there."

"Most likely he'll come at night," Johnny guessed, "figurin' to catch me asleep."

"Not if Sherwood sends a whole gang of em'," Perry argued. "They'd just ride up in broad daylight and cut loose."

Johnny grinned. "I'll keep my eyes peeled, Buck."

Slim McBride opened some food cans and boiled some coffee. It was sundown and Johnny went inside. "What about those mesa outlaws I hear about?" he asked Perry. "Any chance they'd come by here?"

Perry didn't think so. "Mostly they stay on the New Mex side. And away west o' here. These mesas reach a hundred mile down the state line, all the way to the Culebras. Them fellas got ten million acres to hide in."

"A few of 'em don't need to hide," Ed Sopers put in. "Not alla time, anyway. I mean guys with no local warrants out fer 'em. You'll find 'em driftin' down into Taos and Cimarron, for a few quick drinks. If they see their pitchers on a post-office wall, they fade back to the tall timber."

"They lay off Las Perdidas, mostly," Dyke Dixon offered, "account of bein' scared of Adam Sawyer. But they'll take a chance at Chico, sometimes. I've seen 'em at Shotgun Orme's bar there."

"What do they live on?"

"Beef. Anybody's beef that comes along."

Rolled in his blankets that night, with Chuck Wiggins on watch for prowlers, Johnny considered the beef angle from the standpoint of hideaway outlaws. On a wholesale basis it didn't seem convincing. When they needed meat they could slaughter a steer or two. But to what possible market could they drive off any large bunch?

A wholesale rustler, it seemed to Johnny, would need a solid base to work from. He'd need men and horses plus a scheme for disposing of the loot. The Circle D was equipped like that.

A ten percent shortage at recent roundups! It made too many cattle for hideaway outlaws to get away with. The existence of such outlaws offered convenient scapegoats, and Sherwood could be making the most of it. Even to the extent of staging a fake chase now and then.

But proving it was something else. Rick Sherwood stood high on this range. He had the confidence of the county sheriff and Senator Ronaldo Rivera. He had a sincere girl like Flo Sawyer believing in him, admiring him and perhaps on the verge of becoming his wife.

"Look, Chuck," Johnny said to the man on guard. "Didn't you tell me Sherwood started out six years ago with nothin' but a dugout in a sand bank?"

"He sure did," Wiggins confirmed. "And look at

the spread he's got now! Somethin' funny about that, Johnny."

In the morning Johnny again exposed himself outside the cabin. He kept a forty-five in his belt and a saddle gun was never far from his hand. Slim McBride stood back of him just inside the open door.

"That's a sweet cow country down there, Slim," Johnny said, gazing out over the broad Picketwire valley.

"It sure is," McBride agreed. "See that green line off to the left? That's Grosella Creek. The Rivera place lays along it. Last year I homesteaded me a quarter section right down in the middle of the senator's lower pasture. Built me a cabin on it. Aim to settle down there some day."

"Didn't the senator object?"

"Nope. He's got a lot of government land fenced inside that pasture. He told me he'd be glad to have me livin' down there. He knows I won't rustle his horses. And he figgers I'll make a pretty good watchdog to keep other folks from doin' it."

This day passed like yesterday. No Circle D killers came to cut Johnny down. And by evening he began to see doubt on the face of Buck Perry. "If they're comin'," Perry fretted, "why don't they come? Maybe you got the wrong slant on this, Johnny."

Another night and day went by and nothing

happened. The Lazy M men began to look sheepish. "Here we are," Dixon drawled, "all dressed up fer a fight and nothin' to shoot at."

"One time," Ed Sopers remarked on the fourth day of the vigil, "we took a tenderfoot out snipe huntin'. Left him holdin' the bag. That's kinder the way I feel now."

"This was the day," Dixon remembered, "I was supposed to irrigate the meadow. It sure needs it, too."

Perry stoked his pipe moodily. "Tell you what, Dyke. You might as well ride down and do it. There'd still be five of us. That ought to be enough. Looks like we're wastin' our time up here, anyway."

"Ride what?" Dyke questioned. They'd sent all the Lazy M mounts back by Juan Romero. Hackamore and the bay pack mare were needed here to advertise Johnny's residence at the cabin.

Buck Perry solved it. "First time a bunch of Lazy M horses water at the spring, rope yourself a mount, Dyke."

Horses came to water at sundown. One was a little Lazy M mare with a colt by her side. Dyke tossed a loop over her. At dusk he disappeared down the trail, reducing the cabin garrison by one.

Another night slipped by and half of another day. Then, as Johnny was sunning himself on the cabin stoop, he heard shod hooves ascending through the timber. He called back over his shoulder: "*Cuidado*, you fellas. We got company."

A shuffle of boots in the cabin told him that four men were picking up carbines.

Whoever approached made no effort at secrecy. Hooves clicked boldly on the gravel trail. It might, Johnny thought, be vaqueros from the Rivera ranch on a routine ride through summer range.

Then the sounds of approach stopped. A minute of silence which followed seemed ominous. "They're peekin' out of the brush," Johnny guessed aloud, "to make sure I'm alone here."

Buck Perry spoke cautiously from a window. "They've had time to see you by now. Better step back inside."

Johnny rolled a cigaret, licked and lighted it. He turned back into the cabin but left the door open. Chuck Wiggins, with a rifle, was crouching below one window. Perry had a post at the other window. Slim McBride stood near the door with a saddle carbine. Ed Sopers had a forty-five in each hand and a fighting glint in his eyes. "Come on, you Circle Ds," he invited.

"There they are," Wiggins reported from his window. "Right out in the open now. Seven of 'em!"

Seven to five! But the oncomers would think only Johnny Diamond was here. It gave him an advantage. "Cover me," Johnny said, and exposed himself in the open door.

Seven horsemen were riding toward him across the untimbered acre of vega. Six seemed to be gringos and one a Mexican. The Mexican looked faintly familiar. A droopy hatbrim covered most of his face. Johnny had never seen any of the gringos before. But he'd met only a few of the Circle D crew. He could hardly doubt that these were Circle Ds. They all wore guns and had hard hostile faces. One of them had a stubble of black beard and came slightly in the lead.

They halted abreast about six paces in front of the cabin. The bearded man fixed an insolent stare on Johnny. "Your name Diamond?"

"That's right," Johnny admitted. "Who are *you?*"

"We're undertakers," the bearded man announced. A titter ran along his line of companions. "How you wanta be buried, kid? Face down or face up?"

A gun appeared in his hand and he leveled it to an aim on Johnny. Johnny ducked, but he didn't need to. A rifle shot came from Wiggins' window, echoed by a shrill curse from the bearded man. The forty-five bounced from his hand and blood spurted from his wrist.

McBride and Sopers came catapulting out, shooting. Shots boomed from six saddles and a slug burned skin at Johnny's neck. He was on his knees, now, tripping his own trigger. He saw rearing horses and smoke. Lead spurted from two windows and Buck Perry's voice cracked like a bullwhacker's whip: "Blast 'em, Chuck. Get that guy on the end."

The man on the end doubled over his saddle horn, then slithered to the ground. The rider next to him took a bullet from Slim McBride, but kept shooting. Ed Sopers, badly hit, stumbled and fell face down. Johnny tripped his trigger again and got only a click. He dropped his gun and picked up Sopers'. A man who stood behind his horse was pumping bullets into Perry's window. But Perry appeared at the open door with a rifle stock at his cheek. He swept it in an arc down the line of horses, firing six times. Every saddle was empty now. A man on all fours under his horse had a blood-smeared face. "Don't shoot!" he begged.

"Nothin' left to shoot at," Perry said grimly, and lowered his rifle.

Johnny got groggily to his feet. Powder smoke made a stench in his nostrils but the fight was over. Every man of the invaders was either down or dead.

CHAPTER XI

"Only trouble is," Buck Perry said soberly, "they ain't Circle Ds."

Johnny blinked at him. "Not Circle Ds? Who are they?"

"Townies from Chico. Looks like Sheriff Sawyer was right, Johnny. The Circle D ain't after you. It's Orme's crowd from Chico. Slim, see what you can do for Ed."

Ed Sopers had a bullet-smashed leg. The only other casualty on Johnny's side was the nick on his own neck. Blood from it drenched his shirt but he felt nothing. Orme's crowd! How could anyone but the Circle D have known he was here?

Of the seven attackers, three were dead and two wounded. The other pair had simply thrown down their guns in surrender. One of the dead men was a Mexican. Johnny took the droopy black hat from his head and saw that he was Diego Salvador. The man who, almost certainly, had tried to knife him at the hotel after killing Frankie Valdez. And yet who'd presented a perfect alibi from two barrooms at Chico. The sheriff had held him in jail under suspicion, but, lacking evidence, had apparently released him.

"Orme musta sent this gang to get you, Johnny," Perry insisted. "Looks like Sherwood didn't have a thing to do with it."

The leader, he with the black stubble of beard, had only a broken gun wrist. "Name's Dade," Slim announced. "I saw him dealin' blackjack at Chico one time. Here's two guys that ain't hit. What'll I do with 'em, boss?"

"Tie 'em up, Slim. Then fork a horse and ride for the sheriff. Give him the facts and don't hold back a thing. Tell him he'd better bring a buckboard and a coupla deputies."

When the prisoners were wrist-bound and the wounded were carried inside, Slim picked what looked like the fastest of the Chico horses. He smiled sardonically as he mounted. "Dyke Dixon's gonna be plenty peeved when he hears about this. Missin' out on a gunfight. So long, fellas." He spurred down the mountain, heading for Las Perdidas and Sheriff Sawyer.

Chuck Wiggins took three tarps from as many bedrolls and covered the dead men. Perry took a look at Sopers' leg. The bone was shattered above the knee. Pain twisted the cowboy's face but he made no complaint. "Could you hang on, Ed," Perry asked gently, "if we hoisted you to a saddle?"

Sopers nodded. Chuck selected another of the Chico mounts and Johnny helped him get Sopers astride of it. He was in no shape to hold

130

the reins. "Chuck," Perry directed, "you lead him down to the ranch, careful-like. Pick up old Doc Guttierez as you go through San Ysidro. And send Juan Romero back up here with our saddle stock."

When Chuck rode down the trail, leading Ed's mount, only Johnny and Buck Perry were left of the original cabin garrison. Perry spent the rest of the day quizzing prisoners.

"Who hired you to come up here and gun Johnny Diamond?"

"Nobody."

"Was it Orme?"

"No."

"Was it Sherwood?"

"No."

"Val Cranston?"

"Don't know him." In general the responses were sullen.

"Who the hell was it then?"

"We ain't got nothin' to say, mister."

Dade, the man with the stubbled chin, was the most unresponsive of all. Perry searched them, found nothing which could tie them to either Orme or Sherwood.

When dark came Johnny moved his blankets outside and made a campfire. He sat up late over it, with Buck Perry, ferreting for motives. "If the Circle D had showed up," Perry brooded, "everything would dovetail fine. But these

Chico toughies ball it all up. Go back to the start, Johnny, and give me the whole play."

So Johnny began with the raid in Texas, six years ago. His father and brothers murdered by three unknown raiders. The stock driven off, including an eight-year-old brood mare. A four-year-old with the same markings now in the possession of Val Cranston, and branded Circle D. Linked Diamonds boots carried away by one of those Texas raiders. Inquiry at Chico about those boots leading promptly to the murder of a bootblack there, and an attempt on Johnny's life. The incident at Thacker and its possible connection with the killing of José Pacheco at San Ysidro. The shot fired at Johnny on the Sawyer front porch, probably by one Jakie Kim who the next day rode hard to the Circle D.

"So we set a trap for the Circle D," Buck summed up, "and instead we ketch a netful o' gunnies from Chico. I guess maybe your hunch about Sherwood was all haywire, Johnny."

"Let's keep our fingers crossed on that," Johnny said.

Another night and day of waiting and then a buckboard came toiling up the steepness of the mountain. At its wheel rode Adam Sawyer, his gaunt Lincoln-like face dark and stern and molded in anger. Two deputies and a doctor came with him.

The flood-gates of wrath opened first on Johnny Diamond. "Who the hell appointed you sheriff in this county, young man?"

"Nobody," Johnny said. "I was just campin' here, peaceful-like, when some guys rode up with guns. They asked whether I wanted to be buried face up or face down. Then they began shooting. What would *you* do in a case like that, sheriff?"

"None of your impudence," Sawyer stormed. "Where are the bodies?"

A look at the dead men mollified him a little. "Humph! Diego Salvador. Pinkie Thompson. Jabe Meggs. The backwash of Chico. Trigger-men, all of them, guns for sale to the highest bidder. A good riddance, I'll admit, even if you weren't very legal about it."

He took Buck Perry aside and held a moody talk with him. Then he began grilling the prisoners. Their sullen defiance ruffled him again. "Patch 'em up, doc, and we'll haul 'em to town. They're under arrest for attempted murder."

He turned to Johnny with a grim mouth. "One good thing came out of this, after all, young man."

"What?" Johnny asked.

"It gets us rid of you," Sawyer snapped. "Soon as I use you as a witness, you head straight back to Texas. Unless you want to welsh on a bet you made with my daughter."

"A bet which I won," Johnny said.

"A bet you lost," Sawyer corrected severely.

133

"What makes you think so, sheriff?"

"Because Jakie Kim did *not* go to the Circle D. That was the bet, Flo tells me. He passed you on the road, riding east. You guessed he was on the way to Sherwood's and Flo was sure he wasn't."

"He showed up there, didn't he?"

"Not according to Rick Sherwood. Flo asked Rick about it and Rick said Jakie Kim has never set foot on the Circle D. More than that, a Bar L *mozo* named Miguel was there that night. He also says Kim wasn't there."

A rider leading saddled horses emerged from the timber. Johnny saw that he was Juan Romero of the Lazy M. Romero was arriving with the stock needed to take men and bedrolls back to Perry's ranch.

Johnny called to him. "Come over here, Juan."

The Spanish cowboy joined them. His saddle-colored face had chagrin on it. "I have shame, *Amigo* Johnny, that I was not here to help you in the fight."

"Tell the sheriff," Johnny prompted, "what you saw at daybreak the morning Miguel left the Circle D."

Juan faced Adam Sawyer. "I am watching from piñons, señor, near the Circle D gate. I see Jakie Kim come out and ride toward Las Perdidas. Soon then I see a buggy come out. Miguel is in it. I ask him if he has seen Kim at the bunkhouse and he says no."

Sawyer shrugged irritably. "Sherwood and Miguel say one thing, Romero, and you say another. Someone's lying."

A hard glint sparked Romero's eyes but his answer came softly. "Are you suggesting, Señor Sheriff, that it is *I* who lies?"

"Very well," Sawyer conceded, "let's just say someone's mistaken. Kim could have been on the ranch without Sherwood knowing it. It's a big place with ten or twelve cowhands. Not that it makes any great difference." He turned back to Johnny. "You can't positively identify Kim, I understand, as the man who shot at you from the dark in front of my house?"

"No," Johnny admitted. "But he's a pussyfootin' sniper. If his errand to the Circle D was on the level, why did Sherwood keep him under cover and then lie about him being there?"

Sawyer brooded darkly for a moment. Then he summoned one of his deputies and Buck Perry.

"See here, Buck," he said, "I'm tired of all these charges and counter-charges about the Circle D. Three attempts have been made on Johnny Diamond's life. One in a hotel room, one in front of my house, one here at this cabin. We know positively that the first and third attempts were hatched at Chico, probably by Syd Orme. Diego Salvador, now dead, was in on both of them. Diego was Orme's man. About the second attempt, on my front porch, we don't know.

Young Diamond here, on a flimsy hunch, tries to connect it with two reputable citizens, Cranston and Sherwood. So I'm going to bring the whole thing out in the open."

"How you aim to do that, sheriff?" Perry queried.

"By airing all testimony at an open hearing in my office. We'll set it for one o'clock day after tomorrow. I want everyone there whose name has been mentioned in connection with the several attempts on Johnny Diamond's life. That means every survivor who took part in this gunfight. It means Rick Sherwood and the crew who helped him load cattle at Thacker. It means Jakie Kim and Miguel, and even my own daughter because she saw Kim on his alleged trip toward the Circle D. Val Cranston must be there too. And Syd Orme from Chico. Is that clear?"

"Ed Sopers," Perry objected, "can't very well be there. He's got a busted leg."

"Very well. We'll excuse Sopers. But everyone else be there. One o'clock day after tomorrow at my courthouse office." Sawyer turned to the deputy. "Mason, find Sherwood and serve notice on him. Then pick up Kim and Orme. I'll see Cranston myself." To Johnny he said, "Maybe you won't be so glib, young man, when you stand face to face with those fellows."

"I'll be there," Johnny promised.

"So will the coroner. He can pick whatever witnesses he wants for the inquest over these three dead men. Now let's everybody get out of here."

The sheriff's crew loaded casualties and prisoners in the buckboard. Perry's men lashed their duffel on Johnny's bay pack mare. Johnny unhobbled his big dun horse and slipped on a hackamore. Soon they were trailing down the mountain.

Arriving at the Lazy M Johnny found that Ed Sopers' leg had been set by an old Spanish medico from San Ysidro. That night he sat up late with Perry's crew, speculating on what might be brought out at Sawyer's open hearing in town.

"It's got me in a tailspin," Perry admitted. "Ad used to be a lawyer. He thinks like a lawyer. Could be he's got the right slant on it after all."

"How," queried Ed Sopers from his bunk, "does Ad dope it?"

"He lays everything on Orme and his Chico gunnies. You can't blame him, either. The Circle D angle's thin, any way you look at it."

"I do not agree, señor." This in a calm, deferent tone from Juan Romero. "The Circle D has lied about Jakie Kim being there."

The crew took sides, only Romero and Wiggins leaning toward support of Johnny's theory. Wiggins was a member of the outfit now, having been signed on to ride for Perry at least during Sopers' convalescence. "Those ten percent roundup shortages," Chuck kept pointing out. "And Sherwood starting from a dugout in a sand bank only six years ago."

Johnny lay restless, that night, rehashing the evidence. Like Perry said, it was pretty thin. And entirely circumstantial.

Yet his mind clung tenaciously to four facts: 1. After ordering six cars at Thacker, Sherwood had only used four of them; 2. José Pacheco had been murdered right after witnessing a Circle D shipment at Thacker; 3. Cranston rode a Circle D horse with the exact markings of a Linked Diamonds mare; 4. Sherwood denied the arrival of a messenger named Jakie Kim.

None of it was conclusive. All of it was indirect. Against it stood Sherwood's high repute as a stockman. No jury would be impressed by it. Even Buck Perry had his fingers crossed. It just wasn't strong enough, Johnny admitted. He'd have to dig up something else.

In the morning he turned his bay mare loose in Perry's horse pasture. Hackamore wanted to stay there too, and showed temper when Johnny tossed on a saddle.

"I'm hittin' for town. See you fellas tomorrow at the sheriff's office."

"We'll be there," Perry promised. "And keep your eyes open as you ride in, Johnny. Plenty of dry gulches between here and town. What happened three times could happen again."

Johnny grinned. "I can take care of myself, Buck. So long."

He cantered up San Ysidro Creek and turned west on the main road. Clouds hung low this morning, obscuring the sun, and clustered in gray rolls against the mesa rimrocks. They made the steep upslope to his left dark and forbidding. To his right the level sea of grama stretched to infinity. A jackrabbit zigzagged down the trail ahead. Johnny rode alertly, eyes sweeping the horizons. This range was alive with men who were saving bullets for him. Any arroyo could hide a cocked rifle.

The first one was McBride Creek, and Johnny scouted his approach to it cautiously. A small bunch of Buck Perry's cows scattered as he rode down into its bed. A mile beyond he met a string of burros driven by a Mexican on foot, heading for San Ysidro.

A drop of rain spanked his face as he came to a rise from which he could see the purple ribbon of the Rivera meadows. The façades of the rancho's plaza stood placidly against the cottonwoods there. Johnny debated whether he should stop in for a while. A week ago the senator had been in Denver, but he might be home by now. And somehow Johnny felt a complete trust for the man.

He came opposite the gate and paused there, still uncertain. Felicia Rivera, he thought, would hardly welcome him now. She'd resent his indictment of Val Cranston. Chances were she had a romantic understanding with Cranston, or expected to have one soon. And who was Johnny Diamond? Just an upstart stranger who'd appeared suddenly from nowhere to turn her world upside down. She'd be courteous, no doubt, but coldly so.

Johnny looked up the long ranch street at the indolent life in sight there. A fat vaquero sat on the well coping, encouraging two roosters to fight. A chubby Mexican boy was teasing a milch calf. A woman was hanging red peppers in front of her jacal. The old peonage system existed here, Johnny sensed. A kindly and paternal form of slavery where the help was paid no wages in money, but could call at the bodega for beans or beef or calico or anything else it needed. When the master summoned, they obeyed. Hay hands went to the fields and vaqueros rode lazily to the roundups. A fandango every Saturday night, all the chokecherry wine they could drink, and a priest at the ranch church to say Mass for them. What more could a peon want?

Yet help like that, Johnny thought, could hardly be expected to be vigilant or aggressive against outlaws and rustlers. If a roundup tallied a ten percent shortage, they'd shrug and murmur:

"*Qué lástima, patrón!*" A perfect setup for Rick Sherwood, whenever he wanted to ship a few cars of Bar L beef from Thacker. Especially with the senator away most of the time attending sessions of the legislature.

The teased calf got away from the boy and came galloping, tail high, out through the gate. When the boy gave chase Johnny asked him, "Has Don Ronaldo reurned from Denver?"

"*Todovía no,*" the boy said.

And Johnny rode on toward town.

Shortly he topped a ridge of piñons and rode down into Frijole arroyo. Its bed was wide, deep, and flood-gutted, but almost dry now. Again Johnny scouted cautiously against a possible ambush.

No human was there. But a quarter mile up the bed Johnny saw a band of horses. They were watering there, and at sight of Johnny they went racing upstream where a bend in the bank obscured them.

But Johnny had glimpsed a spot of color. An animal colored like a field mouse and with four white stockings. It needed a closer look. Johnny spurred Hackamore up on the bank and loped mountainward along the arroyo. There was no great hurry about getting to town.

The horse bunch emerged from the creek bed and galloped toward scrub oak foothills. Johnny spurred to a hard run and gained on them. He could see it was a band of range mares led by a half-wild stallion. His pulse quickened when again he saw white stockings under mousey flanks. An old mare, he was almost certain of it now. She lagged a bit behind the others.

Johnny raced on, every other objective forgotten. He wanted a look at the mare's teeth. If she was fourteen years old, and branded Linked Diamonds, she was a mare stolen six years ago from his boyhood home. Her head was away from him and he couldn't see whether the forehead had a white star. But the white stockings were knee high. If he only had a rope . . .

Maybe he could cut her out. The band was now veering up-slope into scrub oak. There the stallion stopped, whirled about, snorting, while the mares raced on. The stallion might be a wild mustang for Johnny could see no brand on him. Against his defense, cutting out even an old once-tame mare wouldn't be easy.

They were only a hundred yards ahead, but brush nearly obscured them now. Then, far to his left, Johnny saw a small Mexican plaza. Three or four squalid adobes slumbering at the mouth of Frijole canyon.

Abandoning pursuit for the time being, Johnny loped toward that plaza. An ancient Mexican was mending a saddle at a shed there. "May I borrow a *reata*, señor?" Johnny asked him. "Here is ten pesos until I return it."

It was more cash than the old man had seen for a long time. He produced a hand-woven lariat.

Johnny coiled it over his saddle horn and rode back to the chase. He could hear the mares crashing through brush high up the slope.

They led him upward into pine and thence on into aspen. A dozen times he sighted them. They were heading toward a niche in the rimrock giving on to Fisher's Mesa. The old mare was lagging again. Johnny uncoiled his rope and made ready to throw. Brush cheated him. But he saw the old mare's flank. The hair was short, at this summer season, and his heart thumped as he made out a brand there. Linked Diamonds!

"She's our own stuff, Hackamore," Johnny exulted. "We'll catch her if it takes a week."

Age made it hard for the mare to keep up. Again the stallion doubled back, snorting, biting her flank, bullying her ahead with the others. Hackamore, under Johnny's weight, was all but winded himself. Johnny forced him to a spurt up the last steep climb. There he got within thirty feet of his quarry and made a desperate throw.

The loop missed by inches and the old mare plunged on into the rimrock brush. For a minute Johnny completely lost sight of the band. Sliding rock told him it was scampering up through a niche to the mesa. He recoiled his rope and grimly resumed the pursuit.

CHAPTER XII

An afternoon later, at one o'clock sharp, Sheriff Adam Sawyer opened a hearing at his courthouse office. The room was jammed and only a few of the witnesses found chairs. The fleshy hulk of Syd Orme overflowed one of them. Orme sat there, calm and derisive, his great hairy arms folded over the barrel of his chest, more like an amused spectator than a culprit.

His chins hung in bags and his eyes, sly slits of malice, leered as he greeted Rick Sherwood of the Circle D. "What's this I hear, Rick, about you rustlin' steers in carload lots?"

Sherwood, his raw wind-burned face tight with fury, ignored him. The matter at hand was common knowledge now. Its elements were too sensational to be kept hidden. The entire range knew that a young upstart from Texas had conjured up monstrous charges against the Circle D. Charges which involved also the integrity of Brand Inspector Val Cranston.

Cranston stood by with a confused look, a flush on his soft, plump cheeks. Or was the confusion assumed? Was he really frightened? His eyes evaded Flo Sawyer's when she looked at him.

Others present included five Circle D riders—those who had assisted in the last two loadings at Thacker. Survivors of the fight at the mountain cabin were there. And Jakie Kim. Perry was there with all the Lazy M crew except Ed Sopers. It wasn't an official hearing, but the coroner stood by to select witnesses for his own inquest later. Flo Sawyer sat at her father's desk, grave and business-like in her blue skirt and white shirtwaist, ready to take notes.

Adam Sawyer paced the floor. He looked impatiently at his watch. The key witness hadn't appeared yet and his truancy annoyed the sheriff. What was keeping Johnny Diamond? According to Buck Perry, he'd left the Lazy M a day ahead of the others.

The sheriff strode to a window and scowled out at the street. A long line of saddle horses were tethered at racks there. But not the hackamored dun of Johnny Diamond.

"While we wait for him," Sawyer announced as he turned back to the roomful of men, "let's clear up the Jakie Kim angle. Jakie, my daughter saw you riding east toward San Ysidro. It was eight days ago. Where were you going?"

The answer came glibly from Kim. "To McBride Creek, sheriff."

"Where on McBride Creek?"

"A sheepherder named Pedro has a shack there. About a mile off the road. That's where I went."

"What for?"

The rattish face took a sly look. "He owes me some money. I went there to collect."

"Can you prove it?"

The little man grimaced. "Don't reckon I can," he admitted. "Pedro wasn't home. So I camped all night at his shack and the next day rode back to town."

"You didn't go to the Circle D?"

"Heck no. What would I go there for, sheriff?"

"He lies, señor." It was the voice of Juan Romero breaking in. "I myself saw him come from the Circle D gate."

A chorus of denials burst from the Circle D men present. They all swore that Kim had never been to the Circle D.

Sawyer looked questioningly at Rick Sherwood. "If he was there," Sherwood said stiffly, "I never saw him."

Miguel the Bar L *mozo* offered his bit. "I myself am there that night, señor. And I do not see this man."

Sawyer frowned darkly at Romero. "*You* say he was there. But seven men say he wasn't."

Buck Perry took a loyal stand beside his Spanish cowboy. "Juan's worked for me a long time, Ad, and I never knew him to tell anything but the truth."

Tension grew. The Lazy Ms looked coldly at the Circle Ds. The Circle Ds glared back. None of them, at the moment, wore guns. Obeying a local ordinance they'd checked their guns immediately upon arriving in town.

Sawyer faced Kim again. "Why did you follow Johnny Diamond to my house, nine evenings ago?"

"I didn't."

"Someone took a shot at him there. He thinks it was you."

Kim gave a pale smile and licked a split upper lip. "Thinkin' ain't provin', sheriff."

"He thinks you lit out for the Circle D, next morning, with a message from Cranston to Sherwood."

"He's just loco, sheriff."

Sawyer nodded. "On that score I think he is too. I think you're Orme's man, not Cranston's. But when he shows up, we'll let him speak for himself."

Again Sawyer looked from the window, his eyes searching the street for Johnny Diamond. "Why the devil," he complained bitterly, "can't that boy show up?"

A man with a cold, granite face spoke up. He was Alf Sansone of the Circle D. "That's easy, sheriff. The kid talks big behind our backs. Sayin' it to us face to face is somethin' else, and he ain't got the guts fer it. So he ducked out."

A growl of agreement ran through the Circle Ds. But Buck Perry shook his head. "He ain't the duckin'-out kind, Ad. Only way I can figger it, he must've got himself drygulched on the way to town. Some Chico gunny could pick him off, easy enough, while he was crossin' an arroyo."

An involuntary cry escaped Flo Sawyer. It drew the eyes of a dozen men, including her father's. "It happened three times, dad," she said in a tone of distress. "Why don't we send someone back over the road to look for him? I'm afraid . . ." She broke off, biting her lip as she met the gaze of Rick Sherwood.

"He's old enough," Sawyer snapped, "to look out for himself. Anyway we'll give him another hour to get here." He turned savagely to Syd Orme. "Just why," he demanded, "did you send a gang of killers up to that mountain cabin?"

Orme chuckled derisively. "What makes you think I did, sheriff?"

"*Someone* did. They were all Chico gunmen. One of them was your man Diego Salvador."

"Diego was just a customer of mine," the fat man asserted. "Same as everybody else in Chico."

Sawyer harangued him for several blistering minutes. Here he was on firmer ground, for Orme had been one of Salvador's alibis in the first attempt on Johnny's life. "That dive of yours," he shouted, "has always been a hangout for thieves and cutthroats. Some day I'll put a rope around your fat neck, Syd Orme."

148

"Not without more to go on," Orme jeered back, "than you got now."

Sawyer shifted his attack to the black-stubbled gunman, Dade, who'd led the attack on the cabin. "If Orme didn't send you up there, why did you go?"

Although Dade's answer didn't convince a single man in the room, it couldn't be disproved. "We had a few drinks, sheriff. We heard this brash kid was up there and we figgered to have a little fun with him. Didn't mean him any harm. Then all of a sudden the Lazy M jumps out on us and starts throwin' lead."

"Who told you young Diamond was up there?"

"Don't know his name. Some *hombre* we met at a water hole."

That was Dade's story and he stuck to it.

Sawyer turned with a sardonic apology to Rick Sherwood. "Rick, we mustn't be too hard on young Diamond. At Chico he probed into guilt. No doubt of it. Guilt of his father's murder in Texas six years ago. He asked about a pair of Linked Diamonds boots and right away the lid blew off. Knives and bullets started coming his way. His only mistake is trying to connect *you* with it. The truth is that all the guilt belongs right at Chico."

"Not all of it, sheriff." The voice was Johnny Diamond's. They looked up and saw him standing in the doorway. His face and shirt were scratched as though he'd been dragged through buckthorn brush.

"Where," Sawyer demanded sharply, "have you been?"

"Rounding up proof," Johnny said. He looked straight at Rick Sherwood. "And I've got it."

"Proof?" Sherwood echoed. His cleft chin quivered. "Of what?"

"That you're a two-timin' horse thief," Johnny said.

The Circle D man stiffened. His muscles flexed as though to make a dive for Johnny. Veins of blue fury stood out on his neck.

Sawyer stepped quickly in between them. "Watch out, young man," he warned. "I've seen men killed for saying that. What horse are you talking about?"

"Come out to the front walk," Johnny invited, "and I'll show you." He left the room and walked down the hall, spurs clinking on the board floor.

Adam Sawyer stared for a moment, then followed. Buck Perry went next, his crew tagging along. Flo left her desk and ran after them. Sherwood and the Circle Ds went next. Then Val Cranston. And Jakie Kim. And Miguel. Last of all Syd Orme raised his bulk from the chair and lumbered after the procession.

Only the prisoners being held for assault on the mountain cabin, and two deputies in charge of them, remained in the office. Even these crowded to windows, staring curiously out at the exhibit on display by Johnny Diamond.

They could see Buck Perry on the front walk, standing between Chuck Wiggins and Slim McBride. A little to the left stood Rick Sherwood, flanked by Alf Sansone and Ferd Smith. The others were all there, the black-shocked, homely head of Sawyer looming above all others.

Lined up at the hitchracks were the saddle horses on which witnesses had arrived for the hearing. But one animal wasn't saddled and it was to this one Johnny Diamond drew attention.

"Most of you," Johnny was saying, "are stockmen. Couple of you look at her teeth and tell us how old she is."

Buck Perry stepped forward. He put his hands on the jaw of an old mouse-colored mare and forced her teeth open. The mare was tied to the rack by the lead rope with which Johnny had led her in from the range.

Everyone gaped while Perry inspected the teeth. No one more avidly than a slim, spectacled man with a notebook in hand. He was Frank Sully, editor of the *Picketwire Daily Roundup*, and his presence obviously annoyed Adam Sawyer. Sawyer had excluded him from the private and semi-confidential inquiry inside, but no one could keep a news hawk away from an exhibition on the street.

"She's around fourteen year old," Perry announced.

"Look at her brand," Johnny invited.

The brand, though old and hair-grown, was easily read by all. It was Linked Diamonds, matching the design around the tops of Johnny's boots. Frank Sully scribbled eagerly in his notebook.

"Cranston," Johnny inquired, "you don't mind if I offsaddle your bronc, do you?"

He'd tied the mare directly beside the mount on which Val Cranston had ridden to the hearing. Without waiting for a response, and while Cranston gaped in confusion, Johnny stripped saddle and blanket from the back of a four-year-old gelding. The animal's brand was clearly seen to be Circle D.

Johnny faced his audience with a challenge. "Like I said, you men are stockmen. If you met these two broncs in the Maine woods, what would you say? You'd say they were mare and foal, wouldn't you? Look at their breeding. Both Morgans. Look at their markings, hair by hair."

Everybody looked. Each beast was the color of a field mouse with four knee-high white stockings. Each had a white star in its forehead. The mare eight years older than the horse; each nevertheless had the same shape of head and slant of eye. Long-tailed, both of them.

There they stood, flank to flank, under the eyes of men who knew horses.

Even Adam Sawyer was impressed. Yet he was a lawyer and he knew the law of the range. He stated it succinctly to Johnny Diamond. "You don't identify the parentage of livestock, young man, by family resemblance. Two things, and two only, are admissible in fixing the ownership of a horse. Its brand, if the horse is past weaning age. If the horse is under weaning age, then ownership is determined by the brand of the mare it follows. Since this colt is four years old, you're about three years too late, Johnny Diamond."

Legally, no one could deny him. No court in the land would award the mousey gelding to the mousey mare.

Yet—there they stood, matching each other hair by hair. Johnny read conviction in more eyes than Buck Perry's.

His own big dun, Hackamore, was tied at the same rack. Johnny unhitched him and mounted. "The mare," he said, "was stolen by whoever killed my father six years ago. Read the brand on her colt, sheriff, and draw your own conclusion."

His gaze went to Rick Sherwood. Sherwood stood frozen, his face flushed to a dark red and his hands clenched. It was Alf Sansone who started for Johnny, livid, and it was the strong right arm of Adam Sawyer which swept him back. "Keep your shirts on, you Circle Ds. First man who starts a fight gets tossed in jail."

Back of them all, on the courthouse lawn, stood Flo Sawyer. A tight dread on her face spoke knowledge of two facts: sudden and wholesale death could erupt here at any minute; and the rage of the Circle Ds didn't mean they were guilty. Innocent men, no less than the guilty, would resent with the last bullet in their guns the implication just offered by Johnny Diamond.

Only a wise town ordinance, Flo knew, checked an immediate holocaust on this spot. No one but the sheriff was armed. But tomorrow, on the open range, it would be different. Trigger fingers were itching and chips were on shoulders. A pinch of salt, after today, would be worth more than Johnny's life.

CHAPTER XIII

He saw Flo there and smiled, touching a hand to his hatbrim. Then he spoke to Buck Perry. "Buck, I'll leave this old mare at the livery barn. Would you mind takin' her home with you? You can turn her loose in your pasture."

As Perry nodded, Jakie Kim let out a yelp. The little hoodlum jumped back to the walk, slapping a hand to his cheek. He had crowded up too close to the hitchrack and Johnny's dun horse, never friendly with strangers, had taken a nip at him. Kim cursed the horse, and a guffaw came from Syd Orme.

Johnny's voice rose above it. "Anyone wants me, I'll be at the hotel." He took the old mare's lead rope and rode down High Street, leading her toward the livery barn.

Then he got a break. One he hadn't expected. Ten yards away the old mare turned her head, looked back at Cranston's horse and gave a low whimpering whinny. A whinny in response came from the four-year-old. As though mare and foal had recognized each other three years after weaning, each now offering a protest at being separated again.

Johnny rode on, and the crowd on the walk stared after him. Sawyer, with a let-down look on his face, seemed on the point of calling him back. Johnny Diamond, scheduled to be the key witness, had withheld his main punch. He'd said nothing at all about crooked cattle shipments from Thacker. He'd made no charge that the Circle D had inspired an attack on a mountain cabin. He'd done nothing at all except bring in an old mare and tie her beside a horse branded Circle D, now owned by Val Cranston.

Cranston, with a stunned look, was now restoring a saddle to that horse. The Circle Ds were still glaring balefully after Johnny Diamond.

It was then that the lawyer in Adam Sawyer made him feel his first grudging admiration for Johnny. The boy had made his case stronger, not weaker, by omitting the intangibles. By sticking to a visible fact, that two equines looked alike and were, in all probability, mare and foal.

"The hearing," Sawyer announced in a tired voice, "is dismissed."

By then, around the corner on Commercial, Johnny was unsaddling at the livery barn. He took his saddle roll from the cantle and carried it to the hotel. They gave him the same room he'd had before.

In it he bathed and shaved. His face stung from brush scratches, after a long chase across the mesas. That band of horses had led him almost to Wootten Pass, keeping him out all night and making him hours late for today's hearing.

The shave and a cigaret made him feel better. He thought back over the courthouse scene, wondering how much of an impression he'd made. He remembered Flo on the lawn there and the stark distress on her face. For whom had she been distressed? Rick Sherwood? Would she still believe in the man?

A buckskin, Sherwood claimed, was the mother of Cranston's horse. Could Sherwood produce that buckskin? Whether he could or not, his entire crew would back him up. For if the man had made crooked shipments from Thacker, his ranch hands had to be in on it. No shipper could conceal an operation like that from his own men.

Toughies, according to Wiggins and Perry. Their toughness explained by the Circle Ds' need to arm itself against mesa rustlers. Conveniently logical, Johnny thought with a smile. He couldn't dismiss the fact that they'd lied about Kim's overnight stay there. And only the Circle Ds could have known about Johnny being at a mountain cabin. Miguel had planted such information at the Circle D and nowhere else.

Yet the raiders who'd come were Orme's gang at Chico. Was there a hidden tie-up between Sherwood and Orme?

Johnny sat on the bed and rolled another cigaret. He was lighting it when someone knocked on the door.

He opened it and found Alf Sansone standing there. A barber had trimmed away the man's shagginess. But his cold, flat face had blotches on it and his eyes were bloodshot. Liquor was strong on his breath. He was still obeying the town ordinance and wore no visible gun.

"You talk a lot, kid." His voice was steady enough and Johnny braced for a fight.

"It's a free country," Johnny said.

"Not here in town," Sansone corrected. "They won't even let a man wear his gun. If they did, I'd've drilled you right there on the courthouse walk."

"Some other day, then?" Johnny suggested pleasantly.

"You get it," he was warned, "the first time you ride out on the range."

"You'll tend to it personally?" Johnny asked him. He looked at the man's cruel mouth and a thought came to him. Alf Sansone, more than anyone else he'd met here, looked the part of a ruthless killer. He might even be one of the three raiders of the Lampasas massacre, six years ago.

"Personally," Sansone promised with an accented malice. "I'll fill you full of lead and leave you for the buzzards."

"You'll put pennies on my eyes," Johnny suggested, "and then steal my boots?" He glanced significantly down at his own Linked Diamonds boots.

A mistake, because it left an opening. Sansone drove a fast punch to his chin. Johnny was knocked halfway across the room and his head struck a bed post. He fell senseless on the floor there.

Dusk had fallen when a two-horse cab drew up in front of the Toltec Hotel. Its fare had just disembarked from a train.

He was a small thin gentleman with a goatee. His suit was sprucely tailored. He wore a center-creased velour hat and a cigarito was compressed between his lips. *Gracias, senador.*

158

The cabman accepted his tip with a deferent bow.

As the fare entered the hotel and approached the desk, the face of the clerk there showed the same deference. "We are honored, Don Ronaldo. *Bien venida.*" He whirled the registry book and extended a quill pen.

Senator Rivera shook his head. His narrow, aristocratic face had a preoccupied look. "I come only," he announced, "to see a guest of yours. One Johnny Diamond."

"He's in room two-o-six, senator. I'll call him."

"Never mind, if you please. I will go up to his room myself." Rivera started for the steps, but midway there he saw a newsboy who'd just entered with papers to sell.

It was an extra edition of the *Picketwire Roundup*, hot off the press. A glaring headline caught the senator's eye. He bought a paper and sat down in a lobby chair.

At the legislature in Denver, rumors had reached him about a sensation in his own district. One which seemed to involve the honor of a close friend and neighbor. It had troubled the senator. Was not Rick Sherwood a suitor for the favor of his own niece, Flo Sawyer? And was not the other name mentioned, Val Cranston, one of his own appointees? More than that, only a month ago Señor Cranston had made clear his intentions toward Felicia Rivera.

So the senator had rushed homeward by the first train.

Anxiously skimming through the sensation printed in this paper, he briefed himself on details. His face registered shock. He puffed furiously at his cigarito. The whole thing was here. Editor Frank Sully had skilfully pumped information from every possible source. Some of the points were clear facts, attested to by the sheriff himself. There'd been three attempts on the life of Johnny Diamond. Johnny's family had been wiped out six years ago by three unknown raiders, who'd stolen an old mare and a pair of boots. Today the mare had turned up at the local courthouse, with an alleged colt bearing the brand of Circle D.

On debatable points the account was cautious. "The young Texan alleges that . . ." "His rather fantastic theory is . . ." Under such cover was presented the idea of Sherwood stealing cattle, in car lots, with the connivance of a brand inspector.

"*Carramba!*" muttered Don Ronaldo.

His faith in Rick Sherwood remained unshaken. Of Cranston he wasn't so sure. And after all it was Cranston who wanted to marry his own daughter.

Retaining his dignity only with a supreme effort, Don Ronaldo dropped his paper and went marching up the stairs. When he came to room 206 he found its door wide open.

Inside he saw Johnny Diamond lying on the floor. The senator stood staring for a moment. The young gringo, he thought, was dead. This, the fourth attempt on his life, seemed to have been successful.

Then Rivera stooped and put a hand over Johnny's heart. There was a beat of life. No blood was in sight, so there'd been neither a knifing or a shooting. The senator poured water from a china pitcher into a bowl, soaked a towel in it and swabbed the victim's head. A lump there indicated a blow.

Johnny opened his eyes. A pallid smile reassured Rivera. "I will call a doctor, señor."

"Don't bother," Johnny murmured. "I'm all right. No use makin' a fuss about it." He staggered to his feet and sat on the bed.

"You have been fighting, señor?"

Johnny grimaced. "You might call it that. There was only one punch and the other guy threw it. Guess he musta knocked me against that bed post." He caressed a lump on the back of his head.

"Who was he?" the senator demanded.

"Rides for the Circle D. Fella named Sansone. He's top rod out there, I hear."

Distress lined Rivera's face. He closed the door and made Johnny lie down. He himself took a chair and lighted a cigarito.

"By the newspaper, señor, I see you have insulted the Circle D. Perhaps one cannot blame them if they are mad when you call them rustlers."

"Reckon you're right," Johnny conceded. "Anybody talked like that about me, I'd get mad myself. Just the same I'm not takin' anything back."

"I have read what has happened here. Is there anything you wish to add?"

"I came here," Johnny told him, "looking for an old mare and a pair of boots. Boots like these." He pointed to his own. "I found the mare. But I haven't turned up the boots yet."

Rivera questioned him at length, drawing out a few details which hadn't been covered by the news story. Dusk dimmed the room and he lighted a lamp.

"I have great trust," he said broodingly, "for Rick Sherwood. But there is one small thing which gives me doubt about Señor Cranston."

By now the throbbing in Johnny's head had worn away. He sat up and looked shrewdly at Rivera. "Betcha I can guess, senator. Sherwood asked you to get the appointment for Cranston, three years ago. So you got it just to accommodate a neighbor."

"That much is true," Rivera admitted. "But in politics such matters are often done that way. Sometimes the appointment is wise, sometimes unwise. If Cranston is unworthy I do not believe Rick Sherwood knew about it, or meant to profit by it. It is something else which disturbs me, señor."

"Call me Johnny."

"*Muy Bien*, Johnny." Don Ronaldo's face clouded again. "It is about Ernesto. Have they told you of Ernesto?"

For a moment Johnny couldn't remember. Then it came to him that Chuck Wiggins had mentioned a young Indian, a foster son of the senator, who was now a renegade hiding from the law.

"What about him?" Johnny asked.

The subject was clearly painful to Rivera. "It is a matter I never speak of," he murmured, "and it has brought much shame and sorrow to our house. But now we must face it, bravely. We must find Ernesto. We must learn what it is that he knows about Señor Cranston."

"You mean he has something on Cranston?"

"There is reason to think so, Johnny. It is a thing so delicate that I cannot mention it to my good friend and brother-in-law, the sheriff. For if I send the sheriff to see Ernesto, duty would demand that he arrest him for murder." Don Ronaldo thumped away the snipe of his cigarito and stared bitterly into space.

Johnny felt sorry for him. This *hacendado* was a proud man and the humiliation of Ernesto's disgrace must have been a hard pill to swallow.

"You know where he is, senator?"

"No, I have not seen or heard from him since he became a fugitive nearly a year ago. But there is a possibility he may be at a certain place on a certain day." A pleading came into Rivera's tone. "Would you go there with me, Señor Johnny?"

"Sure," Johnny agreed promptly, "But where?"

"To a place called el Canyon de los Muertos."

A sinister name, Johnny thought. The Canyon of the Dead! "Is it far from here?"

Rivera shook his head and brought out another cigarito. His hand shook a little as he lighted it. "I tell you this only," he admitted, "because I need you to go with me there. And because if you are right about Cranston, you will have great zeal in helping me find Ernesto."

"I'll keep my mouth shut about it," Johnny promised.

"What I tell you first," Rivera said sadly, "is known to everyone. The great battle of long ago in a deep, dead-end canyon near San Ysidro. The vaqueros of my rancho, and of other ranches of the valley, were on one side; on the other side were Indians who had raided our ponies and our cattle. We trapped them in that canyon and every Indian raider was killed. So also was a squaw with them. But we found her papoose alive there, hidden in the brush. A boy baby which I took home to my ranch. I adopted him legally and he grew up as my son, Ernesto."

Johnny nodded. Chuck Wiggins had told him that much.

"He caused me much grief," Rivera went on.

164

"He rebelled at discipline and would not go to school. As a boy he often rode into the mountains and was gone for weeks we knew not where. Then he would be home again, telling us nothing, as stolid as his forefathers. Sometimes he rode to town to drink and throw dice in the bars. One virtue he had: he was devoted to his foster sister Felicia. And she still loves him very much."

"He learned about the Canyon of the Dead?"

"We could not keep it from him, Johnny. And it drew him apart from us. Sometimes I think it made him hate all of us except Felicia. With her he was like a Spanish gentleman. With others he was like a sullen Indian nursing a great wrong. On the sixteenth anniversary of the fight in el Canyon de los Muertos, he rode there and camped where we'd buried the dead of his people. Which of the graves covered his father and his mother he did not know. But he built a great pyre of stones, like a shrine. And on top of it he made a fire of black smoke, kept it burning from sunrise to sunset, and stood there by it, arms folded, like a stern sentinel.

"Again a year later he went there and did the same. Each year he went there to watch and to grieve and to build his fire on the stones. The twenty-first anniversary, Señor Johnny, will be day after tomorrow. So I think he will go there again."

"Likely he will," Johnny agreed soberly. "But would he let us ride up to him?"

"He will not fire his rifle at me, who raised him from infancy. Nor at you, if you are with me and hold up your right hand with the palm forward. That will mean you come as a friend, promising not to deliver him to a sheriff."

"And what do we say to him?"

"We ask him what made him think, one time, that Señor Cranston was unworthy to be a guest of his sister."

"When was that?"

"It was like this, Johnny. The first time Cranston called on Felicia, I chatted with them a while, then left Felicia to entertain him in the sala. In a few minutes Ernesto came in and stared coldly at the guest. Felicia presented him to Cranston. Ernesto said to Felicia: 'I have mislaid my serape, sister. Could you find it for me?' Felicia laughed, because this was not unusual. As a housekeeper who knew where everything was, she was always picking up after her men. She left the sala and in a little while came back with Ernesto's serape. Ernesto bowed and withdrew. And so, quite promptly, did Cranston. Señor Cranston, it seemed, was not feeling well. He went out to his horse and rode away."

A gleam came to Johnny's eyes. "You think Ernesto sent Felicia out of the room so he'd be alone with Cranston? And then he told Cranston to clear out."

"We did not think so then," Rivera said. "But

166

looking back now, I remember that Cranston did not return to call on Felicia for many months. Not until Ernesto had killed a man with a knife, fighting in a cantina over a woman. He became a fugitive then, and promptly Cranston came to our house again. He has come many times since, hoping to marry Felicia."

Johnny could see daylight now. His own suggestions that Cranston might be a crook had brought to Rivera's mind the conduct of Ernesto that evening in the sala. If Ernesto had had reason to consider Cranston unworthy of his sister, he would have acted just so. His strain of Spanish culture would forbid him from making a row with a guest, and offending Felicia; but his fierce Indian eyes could have thrown a prodigious scare into Cranston.

"Very well," Johnny said. "So we meet Ernesto day after tomorrow, and ask him why."

"*Sí*, Señor Johnny. *Pasado mañana*. In el Canyon de los Muertos."

CHAPTER XIV

It was agreed that Johnny should wait till after dark, tomorrow, before riding out to the Rivera rancho. The range was full of Circle Ds, to say nothing of snipers from Chico, and any one of them would have a bullet with Johnny's name on it. Johnny could arrive by midnight at the Bar L, rest a few hours, and at daybreak leave with Rivera for the canyon.

"We will speak of it to no one," the senator warned.

Johnny grinned. "It's a cinch I won't tell the Circle Ds."

"I do not agree with you," Rivera protested, "about Rick Sherwood. Many years I have known him. Always I have found him a *muy bueno* caballero. The guilt lies at Chico, all of it. Except perhaps Cranston is involved some way. Orme yes, Cranston perhaps, but not Sherwood."

"Have it your own way," Johnny said.

Rivera left him. He kept a mount at the livery barn and would ride immediately to his ranch. Johnny would follow twenty-four hours later.

Now he went down to the hotel dining room and had supper. As he emerged into the lobby the clerk handed him a note. Johnny opened it and saw a girl's handwriting:

Will you come to our house? Father and I must see you at once.

Flo Sawyer

Well, Johnny thought, *she owes me a date. I won that bet, didn't I?*

Then another idea wiped the smile from his face. It could be a trap. Maybe Flo hadn't written the note. He wasn't familiar with her writing. There were lots of Jakie Kims on this range. One of them could frame a saloon woman to write this note and be waiting with a rifle near the Sawyer front yard.

Johnny spoke to the clerk. "Who delivered this note?"

"A Mexican boy. Never saw him before."

"Could he be a *mozo* of the Sawyers?"

"Mebbe so; mebbe not."

Not taking any chances, Johnny left the hotel by an alley exit and made a wide detour. When he approached the Sawyer house it was from the rear and by way of a plum orchard there. A kitchen window was lighted. Through it he saw Flo Sawyer. She wore an apron and was washing dishes at a sink.

If the message was a decoy, the decoyer would expect him to approach from the street. An ambusher would be lurking in the dark there with a cocked gun. Unarmed, Johnny could see no sense in playing hide and seek with a bullet. He moved quietly on through the orchard to the Sawyer kitchen door and knocked there.

Flo opened it. When she saw Johnny, the astonishment on her face was all the answer he needed. Clearly she wasn't expecting him.

"My father isn't home." She said it without warmth and did not invite him in.

"When he comes back, give him this." Johnny handed her the message. "Some boy brought it to the hotel a little while ago."

She looked at the handwriting of a woman and grasped at once what it meant. Her own name had been used to lure Johnny up a dark street. Fright crossed her face and she drew Johnny into the kitchen, quickly closing the door. "I didn't write it," she said.

"That's what I figured. So I came in the back way. Just thought you ought to know. I'll be going now."

But she barred his way and locked the door. Then she pulled down the window shade. "They'll kill you," she said helplessly.

"They?"

"Orme's men, of course. The Chico gang. Men like Jakie Kim who do anything Orme tells them."

"You wouldn't nominate Rick Sherwood, would you?"

"Of course not. Don't be stupid. I talked with Rick just after the hearing broke up. He explained everything."

She went into the front room, beckoning Johnny to follow. The parlor was unlighted and they stood at a window there, looking out at the lawn and the street.

No life was in sight. But there were shrubs on the lawn, elms along the parking, weeds and brush in a vacant lot across the way. Plenty of cover for a sniper. Johnny felt Flo's shoulder shudder against his own. "You must stay here," she said, "till father comes home. He's at the courthouse."

Nothing could suit Johnny better. Standing by her in the dark gave him a strange thrill. It came to him with something of a shock, and he knew he wanted her to like him. "He explained about the mare and colt," she said, taking up where she'd left off.

Johnny didn't want to talk about mares and colts. Quarreling with her about Sherwood wouldn't get him anywhere.

"He admitted to me frankly," she went on, "that the old mare you brought in might have foaled the colt he sold Cranston. But he told me he'd never seen or heard of that mare before. He owns hundreds of horses, many of them mares running loose on the range which he only sees once a year. Three years ago the roundup brought in a buckskin mare who'd obviously borne a colt, but the colt wasn't with her. They thought maybe wolves had killed it during the winter. But six months later they found a yearling colt, unbranded, running with Circle D horses. They gave credit to the buckskin mare and thought nothing more about it. This afternoon he admitted, like the fair generous man he is, that perhaps he'd been mistaken."

"Mighty big of him," Johnny said. She drew slightly away from him and he knew he'd used the wrong tone. Her profile, in the dimness, was severe again. He noticed now that her nose and chin and forehead had classic lines, strong, intellectual, like the sculptured likeness of a Greek goddess.

Her gaze was still searching the street, the weeds and the brush beyond. Nothing could be seen or heard out there. To the left the street reared to a steep dead end in the timber of a mountainside. And high above this loomed the horn at the end of Fisher's Mesa, like a giant saddle, black against the moon.

To the right the winking lights of Las Perdidas. The Lost Ones! "Why do they call it that?" Johnny asked.

"More than two hundred years ago," she told him, "a band of Spanish explorers pushed this far north from Monterrey, in Mexico, and made a settlement here. But a great flood came down the river and drowned most of them. So the survivors called the river el Purgatoire. We gringos can't pronounce that, so we call it the Picketwire. Las Perdidas has the same meaning. Place of the Lost Ones."

"I'm sort of lost out here myself," Johnny said.

At her quick, questioning look he added: "I mean you've had it in for me, Flo, right from the start. You made it plenty plain you don't want me around."

"It's the motive which brought you here," she said, not sternly, but gently, and in a tone of self-justification. "Revenge. Revenge is ugly. Long ago someone did a great wrong to your people. So you dedicate your life to vengeance. It's not you I don't like, Johnny Diamond, but the drive back of you."

His lips formed a retort but he didn't speak it. For he knew she'd spoken the truth. He *had* come here to find and to kill three men. Until now it had never occurred to him that he could do anything less.

"And that's why you stay here," Flo said. "To find and to kill."

Boldness came to Johnny He said earnestly, "I got another reason to stay here now."

"What?" she asked him.

"You."

He said it simply and drew a quick response. It came not in words but in the abruptness with which she crossed to a lamp, lighted it, then lowered the window shade so that light would not show to the street. Her face wore a high flush. "Sit down, Johnny Diamond."

He chose the divan, hoping she'd sit beside him. But she preferred a straight-backed chair well away from him.

"My father and I," she said, "have talked about you a good deal. He's a very wise man, my father. He's a student of character, and he has taught me many things."

"What, for instance?"

"Character, he says, grows from the seed bed of motive. A crusade against injustice is a good motive, providing one concentrates on injustice suffered by others, and by society in general. If one broods on injustice to himself, he becomes narrow and mean and dangerous."

Johnny tried to digest it. "You mean if I was all hopped up about somebody else's family bein' wiped out, 'stead of my own, it'd be all right?"

"It would be impersonal, in that case. There'd be no self-pity in it. And so it could give a noble impulse, instead of one bristling with hate." A pleading came into her tone. "Think of it this way, Johnny Diamond. There've been millions of cruel injustices ever since the world began. Yours is only one. If you stuff your brain and heart with just that one, it warps you. You lose all perspective. You may suspect the wrong people and end up killing innocent men. My father said this to me one time: pity for others will make you wise; pity for yourself will make you stupid."

An odd thought came to Johnny. Ernesto Rivera! An entire clan of Indians wiped out, in the Canyon of the Dead, including both the father and the mother of Ernesto! What would happen if he, Johnny Diamond, were to concentrate on that tragedy instead of his own? Would he think clearer? Could he look at the whole thing without personal prejudice, and thus without rancor?

Johnny didn't speak his thought. Yet something printed on his face made Flo look at him with a new interest. She laughed an apology. "I must sound stupid myself, preaching to you." They heard footsteps on the walk outside. "That will be father coming home."

Adam Sawyer opened the door and stepped into the parlor. He saw Johnny and grimaced dourly. "I thought we'd had enough of you, young man, for one day."

"So did I." Johnny grinned.

"This brought him here, dad." Flo handed him the decoy message.

Reading it brought dark fury to the sheriff's face. He couldn't doubt that some cheap woman of the saloons, some pawn of Orme's, had written it and signed his daughter's name. "I didn't want to get your porch post all shot fulla holes again," Johnny said, "so I came in the back way."

"Wait here." Adam Sawyer swept back the skirt of his long black coat and drew a forty-five. With it he stepped outside.

From a window they saw him cross the street and patrol the brushy lot over there. He returned and circled the house. When he came back in he sank wearily into a chair. "I'm willing to bet," he muttered, "that they posted a sniper out there. Just like that other time. But he's gone now. You better go home yourself, young man."

Flo insisted that Johnny leave by the orchard, the way he had come. She let him out the kitchen door and walked to the orchard gate with him. "Where are you going now, Johnny?" Her face was anxious.

"To the hotel and to bed."

"I mean tomorrow?"

"I'll hang around town and rest up. Had to sleep out last night, chasin' that old mare."

"And day after tomorrow?"

Pasado mañana! He remembered Ronaldo Rivera's last word, and the tryst for day after tomorrow. At the Canyon of the Dead! But he'd promised the senator he wouldn't tell.

"Out on the range," Johnny said. He looked at her and added shyly: "And I'll give you my word, Flo, I won't ride my own troubles. I'll put 'em aside and cogitate about somebody else's. Somebody I've never even seen."

She smiled and said, "Goodbye, Johnny."

" 'Bye, Flo." Somehow it sounded final, and perhaps forever, because both of them knew what waited for Johnny on the range. Killers waited there, and next time they might not miss.

Dread of it was printed clearly on Flo's face and it made Johnny bold. He took her face gently between his hands and kissed her mouth.

Then he faded into the gloom of the orchard.

CHAPTER XV

At the hotel, he slept till noon, awaking refreshed and with a clear head. His face in the mirror, as he shaved, looked different. Some of the stern bitterness was gone from his lips. He smiled, giving credit to Flo. He'd keep his promise to her. He'd stop nursing his own grudges, at least long enough to think about Ernesto Rivera's.

What did he know about Ernesto? Only what two men had told him: Chuck Wiggins and Senator Rivera. Had they left out anything?

After lunch Johnny went to the offices of the *Picketwire Roundup*. Editor Frank Sully, wearing a green eye-shade and with sleeves rolled to the elbows, was at his desk. He recognized Johnny as the key figure in yesterday's sensational inquiry. "Anything new?" he asked eagerly.

"Not a thing," Johnny said. "Right now I'm lookin' up somethin' else. 'Bout 'leven months ago you had a knife killing in town. They say Ernesto Rivera and some guy quarreled over a woman. Could I see your file on it?"

Sully gave him a curious look, then nodded. "An open-and-shut case, with plenty of witnesses. That Indian high-tailed for the hills and he's been hiding out ever since." He went into the file room and came back with an issue nearly a year old.

The item was on page one. Johnny read it. The affair had taken place in a beer garden back of the Buenas Noches on Water Street. A three-way dive, the paper called it, meaning liquor, girls and dice. Ernesto had been drinking with one of the house girls, Winnie Quinn. About midnight a man named Eddie Falcon had joined them. In a quarrel over Winnie Quinn, Ernesto had stabbed Falcon through the heart. There was no evidence that Falcon had been armed. A dozen customers had seen the stabbing. Ernesto had fled town and was wanted for the crime.

Nothing here, Johnny thought, which could help him any. But maybe he could get more details from the woman, Winnie Quinn.

"Does she still work at that joint?" he asked the editor.

"Couldn't say," Sully said with a shrug. Then he

smiled. "But I got a printer who's pretty much of a rounder. Wait and I'll ask him."

He went into the press room. Presently he reappeared. "Yeh, Winnie's still there. Not only that, but she owns the joint now. It's down by the tracks. Caters to switchmen and yard clerks."

Johnny left the office with an idea clicking. Winnie Quinn, a cheap gyp-joint steerer, had suddenly become prosperous. Prosperous enough to buy out her employer.

Another thought jolted Johnny. If she owned a saloon, she paid taxes. She'd need to apply for a license. Her signature would be on file at the city hall.

Johnny hurried up to High Street and turned in at the courthouse. The city offices occupied a corner of the first floor. Johnny looked up the license clerk. "Did the Buenas Noches on Water Street," he inquired, "renew its license this year?"

"Must have," the clerk said, "or we'd've closed the joint up. Wait a minute and I'll make sure."

He stepped to a file and took from it a signed application. "Yeh," he reported. "Here it is. Winnie Quinn applied for a renewal and it was okayed. What's the matter?"

Johnny had snatched the application from his hand. "Let's show this to the sheriff, mister. He'll be interested."

The clerk followed him down the hall to the office of Adam Sawyer. The sheriff and Flo were

179

both there. "It's the same handwriting," Johnny announced jubilantly. "Take a look."

He dropped the signed application on Sawyer's desk. The sheriff looked at it. Then he produced last night's decoy note and his eyes narrowed shrewdly.

"It's the same handwriting," he agreed. "Means she works for Orme. Winnie Quinn, huh? Seems like she was mixed up in a case about a year ago."

"She was, sheriff. The Ernesto Rivera case. I checked up on it in a news file."

Sawyer stared at him. "What made you do that?"

Johnny looked at Flo with a grin. "A tip from Flo. She told me to quit ridin' my own peeves and start thinkin' about other people's. So I picked on Ernesto. His folks got wiped out, same as mine did. And look what I turned up?"

"You turned up," Sawyer conceded soberly, "the fact that the woman who decoyed you to a dark street last night is the same woman Ernesto and a man were quarreling over, a year ago, when Ernesto killed the man with a knife."

"That's the way it *looked*," Johnny said.

"That's the way it *was*," Sawyer corrected. "A dozen witnesses, several of them unimpeachable, saw the blow struck."

"Think it over," Johnny advised. "Winnie Quinn, hired as a decoy whenever they want a dangerous witness put out of the way. Maybe you'll get the same slant on it I have. If you do, maybe you'll drop that charge against Ernesto Rivera."

"If we only could!" exclaimed Flo. A wistful hope filled her eyes. It made Johnny remember that the fugitive was her foster cousin. The adopted son of her Uncle Ronald. And legally a nephew of the sheriff himself.

A glimmer of understanding was already dawning on the lean, bony face of Adam Sawyer. His fingers drummed on the desk. "Humph! A decoy used by Orme! We'll pick her up, young man, and give her a going over."

"So long, folks." Johnny waved jauntily to Flo and left them. Given this lead, they could be depended on to follow through.

He went to his hotel and kept out of sight there until after dark. A moon was showing on the east horizon when he took a walk down to Water Street, beyond the Santa Fe tracks on the north side of the river. The Buenas Noches was easily found there, but Johnny did not go in. He reconnoitred for a look at the beer garden at the rear. The scene of Ernesto's crime. It was a hedge-bound plot with tables spotted among tubbed shrubs, dimly lighted by hanging lanterns. Painted women were drinking with male customers, mostly railroad men, coaxing them to a dance floor inside. One look was enough for Johnny.

Half an hour later he was at the livery barn

tossing a saddle on Hackamore. He'd checked his gun here upon arriving in town. Now he belted it on. A carbine was in the saddle scabbard and he made sure no one had tampered with it.

Cantering out of town he used High Street instead of East Main. Those who wanted him dead didn't know he'd be abroad tonight but there was no use taking chances. At the town limits he stopped to read a sign on a piñon tree. It was a copy of the local ordinance decreeing that all who entered must check their guns and not reclaim them until ready to ride out again.

Beyond that sign Johnny paralleled the road, keeping to the piñons, until he'd crossed the Frijole hills and was down on the open flats. Here only a sparse growth of greasewood could provide ambush for a sniper. A full moon silhouetted Johnny. "They're layin' for us, Hackamore. The Circle Ds. Or Orme's gang. Or both."

A moving shadow in the sage made him snatch carbine from scabbard. But it was only a coyote stalking a rabbit.

He detoured at the Frijole Creek crossing and did the same at all other arroyos. On a low divide beyond he again kept to the piñons, well off the trail.

It slowed his progress and it was midnight when the Grosella Creek cottonwoods loomed ahead. Johnny crossed just below the wooden bridge, making his way through a wild plum thicket there. He rode on to the Rivera gate. Adobes along the ranch street were dark. A sheep dog came out of the barn and barked. Lamp glow showed at a window of the master's house and Johnny dismounted there.

To his surprise, it was Felicia who admitted him. Her oval, olive face looked excited, and he sensed at once that the senator had told her where he was going. "He is waiting for you, señor." She ushered Johnny to the sala.

Don Ronaldo was there, booted and spurred, standing by the hearth with a wine cup in hand. He filled another one for Johnny. Gravely he exchanged greetings and then glanced at his daughter. "She is going with us, señor."

"And why shouldn't I?" the Spanish girl said in a tense tone. "He is my own brother."

Her father summoned Miguel, instructing him to feed Johnny's horse and to have the mount saddled again at the first streak of dawn. "You yourself must sleep a few hours, my friend."

"Not," Johnny said, "till I tell you some good news."

Felicia looked at him curiously, "About what, señor?"

"About Ernesto. The way I figure it, maybe he's not guilty. Listen and hear why." Johnny told them about the decoy message last night, written in the hand of Winnie Quinn.

"So she's an agent of the enemy. The same enemy had it in for Ernesto. Assuming Ernesto had something on Val Cranston." Johnny looked at Felicia and saw her flush crimson. Since she was riding with them at dawn, her father must have told her why. The basic strategy of the excursion assumed that Ernesto had ordered Cranston from the house on the occasion of the man's first call here; and that Cranston, because of some guilt known to Ernesto, had been afraid to come back until after Ernesto's retreat to the hills.

"For a name," Johnny resumed, "call the enemy Orme. Say that Orme's house of cards will fall down if Cranston's guilt becomes known. Once he sent a knifer named Salvador to kill me. My hunch is he sent a knifer named Eddie Falcon to kill Ernesto. The skit could go something like this: Winnie Quinn inveigles Ernesto into buying her a drink in a dim beer garden. Other customers are there, minding their own business. Falcon slips up, maybe back of a hedge, to stab Ernesto. But Ernesto's too quick. He has Indian eyes and ears. He dodges the blow and pulls a knife from his own boot. Fighting for his life he kills Falcon. The customers see the end of the fight, but not the beginning. Ernesto is with a woman, so they assume the two men quarreled over her. As they crowd up, Winnie gets rid of Falcon's knife. Which leaves the only one in sight, Ernesto's."

"*Qué terrible!*" gasped Felicia. Yet relief mingled with the horror on her face. The same reactions ruled the senator. "If that is true," he murmured fervently, "then much of the shame is gone from my house. Are you sure about this Quinn woman?"

"Only that they used her to decoy me," Johnny said. "But if they used her that way once, they'd do it twice. What's more, she collected a big chunk of money right after Ernesto's fight. Enough to buy the Buenas Noches."

Don Ronaldo lighted a cigarito. He puffed it furiously, pacing the sala. "We must see Ernesto," he muttered impatiently, "and ask what it is he knows about Cranston."

"The truth of it," Felicia said, "he will tell to me. To the sister who loves him."

That was the consideration, Johnny presumed, which had made Rivera consent to take her along with them. Ernesto had always been devoted to her. She had more influence with him than anyone else. If only men approached him he might run away, or be hostile, or even fire his rifle as a warning to keep off. But his sullen suspicion would melt at sight of Felicia.

"We've got nothing to go on," Johnny warned them, "except three things. The fake note yesterday proves Winnie's in with them. And Ernesto had something on Cranston. And Winnie collected a big fee for something."

"But Val Cranston," Felicia protested, "has always been so . . . so mild and well-mannered. I can't imagine him killing anyone."

"He strikes me the same way," Johnny agreed. "So let's say he never killed anyone. Maybe he never did anything worse than petty theft or a forged check. Something small like that. But if it comes out it could uncover something big. Open a door to a lot of crookery higher up. So the higher-up guys send a knifer to get Ernesto."

After Don Ronaldo showed Johnny to a room, he lay awake there trying to imagine what Cranston's dereliction, petty or otherwise, might have been. It could not, he decided, have been the falsifying of brands at Thacker. At least Ernesto couldn't have known about that. For many of the stolen cattle had come from this ranch. If Ernesto had even faintly suspected anything like that, he certainly would have told Don Ronaldo.

Johnny fell asleep and it seemed scarcely a minute till Miguel awakened him. It was still dark outside. The senator and his daughter were waiting for him at a pre-dawn breakfast in the dining sala.

They were dressed for the saddle. Felicia in a trailing riding skirt. Any town girl, and most ranch girls, would have worn pants. But not this maid of old Spain reared in the conservative culture of the Riveras.

A faint light tinted the east when they rode out through the gate. They turned to the right, toward

San Ysidro, but Johnny knew they'd veer mountain-ward short of that plaza. He rode at Felicia's left, Don Ronaldo at her right. Miguel came back of them, leading a saddled horse.

"In case Ernesto is not mounted," Rivera explained.

Felicia added simply, "We shall bring him home with us, señor, if what you think is true."

"I believe it *is* true," murmured the senator. "So why should he hide like a renegade? If the sheriff says he must stand trial, I will bring in the greatest lawyers to defend him."

They crossed the Rio Seco wash and spurred on, faster now, and the top rim of the sun was showing when they forded McBride Creek. Johnny didn't worry about snipers. He reasoned that the Circle Ds would hardly dare waylay him in the presence of Ronaldo and Felicia Rivera. He smiled grimly, wondering what they'd think if they saw this dawn excursion.

A few miles further on Rivera left the road and led them obliquely across grama sod toward an upslope to Johnson's Mesa. Presently Johnny saw a deep gash in that slope, a narrow, rocky defile cut there by ancient floods. "El Canyon de los Muertos!" Rivera announced.

Canyon of the Dead! Twenty-one years ago, this very day, a battle had been fought there. In the infancy of Ernesto. Would he, the single survivor of his race, again remember?

The imminence of it subdued Don Ronaldo, and Felicia, and even Johnny Diamond.

They came to the narrow entrance of the gorge and turned up it. Scrub oak grew here and there was no trail. Nor any reason for one because the gorge had no outlet at the top end. Because of its somber tradition, men rarely entered this deep and blind slash in a mountainside.

Halfway up it they reined to an abrupt stop. "Ernesto! He is here!" exclaimed Rivera in an awed tone, and pointed.

Ahead of them, near the top of, the canyon, Johnny saw a column of gray smoke. It could only have one source. A fire of mourning which Ernesto built each year here. A salute to the spirits of his warrior forebears.

CHAPTER XVI

Don Ronaldo beckoned and they continued on through the oaken brush. The gorge widened a little. For an acre of space its floor was bare and on the bareness stood a monument of rocks. Atop of it a fire burned. Green boughs covered the fire, half smothering it and sending a dun smoke to the sky.

A saddled pony was tied near by. But they could see nothing of Ernesto.

"Perhaps," the senator whispered, "he heard us and is watching." He raised his right arm and held an open palm forward. Johnny did the same. But it was Felicia who spurred ahead.

"Ernesto!" she called eagerly. "*Hermano mío. It is I, Felicidad.*"

She loped straight to the rock monument and arrived there in advance of her father.

Then Johnny heard her scream. She swayed in the saddle, shocked white by what she saw just beyond the rocks. With Rivera he raced to her side and they all saw Ernesto.

The young Indian lay on his back, arms outflung, and he seemed to be dead. Blood which drenched his jacket was still fresh. "*Por Dios!*" cried Don Ronaldo. He dismounted to kneel by Ernesto. Felicia slid from her saddle and joined him there.

For the moment Johnny did not intrude. His eyes searched both ways along the gorge and to high shoulders on either side. Perfect screen for a sniper could have been found anywhere. It was cruelly clear, now, that someone else had known of Ernesto's ritual here each year.

Someone who, not more than an hour ago, had sent a bullet of death through Ernesto.

Then Felicia's pleading voice told Johnny that the Indian still had a breath of life. He dismounted, hat off, and stood gravely behind the kneeling father and sister. All around them were small, grassless mounds, where casualties of battle had been buried a generation ago. Graves of warriors dead and gone! And now Ernesto!

A rifle bullet had passed completely through him, piercing a lung. A quick examination told them there wasn't even a faint chance for the man to survive. For an hour, at the most, he might linger on. Don Ronaldo held a flask to his lips. Felicia sat sobbing on the ground, Ernesto's head pillowed in her lap.

His eyes were open. He knew them. But when he tried to speak, blood from the pierced lung choked him. "Who did this thing, son of mine?" Rivera demanded bitterly, in Spanish.

Ernesto could only shake his head. He did not know.

And Ronaldo Rivera, realizing he couldn't save a life, made a stern effort to save honor. He must prove here that Ernesto did not wear the guilt of murder.

"Attend closely, my son." He spoke in rapid Spanish. "We believe you were not fighting over a woman. You were attacked by a hired assassin and you struck only to save your life. Is it true?"

Ernesto could not reply in words. But his head nodded a clear affirmative.

"Then why," Don Ronaldo asked softly, "did you run away?"

Ernesto answered only with a bitter look at his monument of rocks, and at the commemoration fire smoldering on it. The senator looked sadly up at Johnny Diamond. "What he tries to tell us," he translated, "is that there is no justice for an Indian. He will not trust the laws of a race which destroyed his people."

And Ernesto confirmed it with a nod.

"We believe too," Don Ronaldo said to him, "that you knew evil in the past of one Val Cranston. You considered him unworthy to attend your sister. So you ordered him from our house."

Again an affirmative gesture from the dying man. Johnny saw it. The *mozo* Miguel was there now and saw it too.

"Does this evil also concern one Rick Sherwood?" The inquiry brought pain to the senator's sensitive face; yet he made it in the interest of justice.

This time Ernesto shook his head. A distinct negative. It was the same when Rivera asked if the matter concerned one Sydney Orme of Chico.

"Do you know of any accomplice, other than Cranston himself?"

Again a negative from Ernesto.

"Who told you about this evil in the life of Cranston?"

Ernesto's lips moved. He was making a desperate effort. Those about him listened carefully and caught two faint phrases: *"Un extranjero . . . un comprador de lana . . ."*

That was all. A stranger . . . a buyer of wool! The effort exhausted Ernesto; Felicia, bending over him in tears, refused to permit any more questions. It would be futile in any case. In a very few minutes Ernesto would breathe his last.

Not to intrude further on the mourning of a family, Johnny remounted his horse. His eyes searched the gorge for the most likely spot from which the fatal shot could have been fired.

The walls were steep, the one on the north barren, the one on the south spotted here and there with clumps of scrub oak. Johnny spurred Hackamore up that steepness, looking for sign at each possible cover.

In a little while he found it. An empty shell from a forty-four rifle. It lay in an oak thicket only a hundred yards from the gray smoke fire built at dawn today by Ernesto Rivera. Beyond the thicket Johnny saw where a shod horse had been tethered. Plain tracks marked the sniper's retreat. They angled upward over a shoulder and disappeared in the general direction of San Ysidro.

Johnny picked up the empty shell and rode back to the group huddled about Ernesto.

"He is dead," Don Ronaldo reported to him bitterly.

Johnny showed him the empty shell. "This is

what did it," he said grimly. "If you don't need me here I'll see if I can follow his tracks. At least I can see if he rode to the . . ."

He checked an impulse to mention the Circle D. If a Sherwood hand had done this, the man would probably ride straight home.

"We do not need you here, *Amigo* Johnny." The senator stood with bared head looking down at the body of his foster-son. "Miguel will help me take him to the rancho. He shall be buried with honor in the churchyard there."

"He told you nothing more?"

"*Nada más*," murmured Ronaldo.

Felicia looked up with tear-blurred eyes. "We thank you for coming with us, señor." She turned to her father and added fiercely, "We must go to Uncle Adam and demand the arrest of Val Cranston."

Johnny left them and rode upslope to where he'd found the rifle shell. The killer couldn't have more than a two-hour start. He picked up the tracks of a shod horse and followed them over the gorge shoulder.

Beyond, the tracks veered directly north, away from the mountain and toward the Picketwire valley. They led Johnny to bunch grass flats below. The hoofprints were dim here, and Johnny missed many of them. But because they took a beeline now he could always pick them up again. Soon he saw that they were heading neither for San Ysidro nor for the Circle D.

They crossed the road about halfway between San Ysidro and McBride Creek. Further on they passed a huge ant hill where the ground was sandy and bare for a ten-foot circle. Here the hoofmarks were especially distinct and Johnny dismounted for a close scrutiny.

The shoe of the right hind hoof, he saw, had a protruding nail. It made a tiny hole in the sand about a quarter inch deep. Later, at another bare sandy spot, Johnny made doubly sure of it. And two miles beyond, where the tracks crossed McBride Creek, he picked up another item to identify the horse ahead.

McBride Creek was only a trickle here, and on its far bank the ground was boggy. The left fore-leg of the fugitive's mount had sunk in to the knee. It was a bluish, gummy mud and only the left foreleg had sunk in that deeply. The mud would cling to the hair, Johnny thought, until the animal was washed and curried.

The beeline of the trail continued on, north-westerly. Johnny followed it, generally not faster than a walk, so that it was well past noon when the tracks brought him to the Picketwire River. The fugitive had crossed here in shallow riffles. Some of the blue mud would be washed off a foreleg, but not all of it. On the other side, the tracks turned upriver toward the town of Chico.

Orme! Not the Circle D but Sydney Orme,

Johnny concluded, had dispatched a killer to waylay Ernesto. Everything seemed to lead straight to Orme.

Was Orme the brains of the entire conspiracy? Were Sherwood and Cranston merely pawns of the fat vice king at Chico? Johnny followed on, with a late afternoon sun in his eyes. Sand along the river bank made the tracks easy to read. The other man's horse had become tired at this point, and its pace had been a running walk.

The last words of Ernesto came back to Johnny. "A stranger . . . buyer of wool . . ."

From such a source had Ernesto learned about something shady in the past of Val Cranston. Something unconnected, according to the information, with either Sherwood or Orme. A wool buyer. . . .

Suddenly it clicked in Johnny's memory. The wife of the Chico bootblack, Frankie Valdez! She'd deserted Frankie to elope with a wool buyer. The fact had come out during the inquiry after Frankie's murder by an unknown knife-man, probably Diego Salvador.

Johnny summoned back what the Chico constable, Martínez, had told him about the runaway wife. She'd gone to Taos, it seemed, with a wool buyer who had there deserted her. Destitute, the woman had then sought a sordid livelihood on the Street of Suffering and Bitterness, in Las Vegas.

Johnny jogged on, his mind piecing out the

possibilities. Frankie could have known something about Val Cranston. He could have let it slip to his wife. She, later, could have passed it on to her lover, the wool buyer. Who, after deserting her, might talk about it carelessly in his cups at some saloon or dance dive. And there young Ernesto Rivera, a frequenter of such dives, could hear it. A matter which wouldn't interest Ernesto at all, until one evening perhaps months later he found the man concerned, Val Cranston, paying court to his sister.

Bluntly Ernesto would tell Cranston he was unworthy of Felicia, ordering him to get out of the house and not come back.

The general pattern of it, in the light of Ernesto's last words, seemed at least probable.

The trail continued on up the river, past ragged patches of sunflowers, directly toward Chico. An irrigation ditch took off from the river and Johnny splashed through it, again worrying lest the same splashing had washed clean the left foreleg of the mount ahead. The sun had disappeared, now, back of the snowy sierra of the Culebras, fifty-odd miles upriver.

It was hazy twilight when Johnny rode into the squalid streets of Chico plaza. In the dust there he lost the tracks of his quarry among a myriad of other hoofprints. But on the main street a jaded black horse, with a forty-four rifle in its saddle scabbard, caught his eye. It was tied in front of Sydney Orme's triple-threat emporium of liquor, women and dice.

The mount drew Johnny's attention because it resembled another he'd seen one time. On the road out of Perdidas when he and Flo Sawyer had withdrawn into piñons to let a rider pass. Jakie Kim on the way to the Circle D. Jakie had been riding a lean-flanked black much like this one.

Johnny dismounted by it. He looked closely at the left foreleg. A bluish, gummy mud clung to it, from hoof to knee. Johnny picked up the animal's right hind leg and doubled it back, squatting in the pose a blacksmith takes when he shoes a horse. In the right hind shoe of this one he saw a loose nail. It lacked a quarter inch of being driven completely in.

This, beyond question, was the mount he'd followed from the Canyon of the Dead.

Kim's horse. The man had come here, Johnny guessed, to collect for a job of work. He wondered how much they paid Jakie for each sniping.

A peon was lounging on the walk. "You know Jakie Kim?" Johnny asked him.

The man nodded.

"Seen him lately?"

The peon jerked his head toward the latticed doors of Orme's place. Johnny pushed them open and stepped inside.

He saw five customers. Orme's white-jacketed bulk loomed back of the bar.

Two customers were tossing dice at a rear table. Two others were sipping beer in a booth near the front. The fifth was Jakie Kim. Kim stood at mid-bar, his back to it, his elbows hooked on it. A forty-five hung from his belt. His small sly eyes flickered at Johnny's entrance.

"Hello, Kim," Johnny said. "That black bronc out there. Is it yours?"

There would be no use for Kim to deny it. At least fifty people would know the horse was his own. "Sure," he admitted. "What about it?"

"He's come a long way," Johnny said. "You'd ought to give him a rubdown and a feed, after a ride like that."

Kim stiffened. His right hand inched a little toward his gun butt. Back of him Johnny could see Orme eyeing him with an alert craftiness, both hands below bar level. A shotgun would be within his reach, because men called him Shotgun Orme. The rattle of dice to the left stopped, as did a hum of talk from the pair sipping beer in a booth. All toughies, Johnny sensed, and ready to obey any signal from Orme.

"After a ride like what?" Kim challenged. He was like a charged wire, his gun hip swiveled toward Johnny and his gun hand cocked like a steel spring.

Johnny knew now that he shouldn't have come in here alone. If he accused Kim, he'd have to shoot his way out. And they were six to one.

CHAPTER XVII

He couldn't watch them all. If he took his eyes off Kim, Kim could beat him to a draw. He knew that Kim alone wouldn't have stood up to him. The man's present defiance was like that of a coyote, ready to snap and slash only because of a pack back of him.

He himself was at a disadvantage because no authority to arrest Kim was vested in him. He had no official deputyship. These rats could kill him and then claim it was a personal fight between himself and Kim. They'd name Johnny the aggressor. And they'd swear Kim had been there all day, and so couldn't possibly have ridden to the Canyon of the Dead.

Maybe he could cow them by using a big name. A name to conjure with, on this range, was Senator Ronaldo Rivera. A political power of the first magnitude, Rivera, and these barroom thugs might think twice if he brought the senator into it.

"A ride like Don Ronaldo took this morning," Johnny said. "To a gorge in a flank of Johnson Mesa. I was with him. So were his daughter and a *mozo*."

If it frightened them, the effect was opposite to that which Johnny had hoped for. A beer bottle came flying from a booth. It caught the side of Johnny's head and unbalanced him. And gained the needed split second for Jakie Kim. Kim's gun came out roaring. Its bullet would have brained Johnny had the bottle blow not knocked him a little to one side. His head was still thumping from it and his draw was awkward. Through the smoke of Kim's first shot he saw the man aim deliberately for another.

Beyond Kim he saw a startled change come over Sydney Orme's face. A forty-five boomed and Johnny for a moment thought it was Kim's. How could Kim miss him twice? A frozen look on the fat, hog-jowled face of Syd Orme, turned now toward swinging doors at the entrance, made Johnny look that way himself.

A man had just entered and there was a smoking gun in his hand. At the same instant Johnny became aware that Jakie Kim was collapsing in a lump on the bar rail. The intruder had cut loose, not at Johnny, but at Kim. "Hands up, all of you!" the man yelled. His gun covered the room. "That means you too, Orme."

Johnny blinked. He could hardly believe it. He looked at the man who'd saved his life. A tall handsome man with a cleft chin. Rick Sherwood of the Circle D!

Orme, who'd been on the point of pulling a shotgun from under the bar, now had his hairy hands ear high. So did the four table customers. Johnny had his own gun out but there was no need for it. The fight was over, brought to a deadly end by Rick Sherwood.

Kim lay motionless on the floor. A red hole between the eyes meant that he'd never snipe again.

Sherwood spoke amiably, almost comradely, to Johnny Diamond. "What were they gunnin' you for, fella?"

"I tracked Kim here," Johnny explained, "from a canyon where he drygulched Ernesto Rivera."

Sherwood glanced sharply at Orme. "You know anything about it, Orme?"

Orme licked puffy lips. His hands were still up. "Not a thing," he croaked. "Kim was just a customer here. Couldn't say where he's been today."

The four surviving customers backed sullenly to a wall. Sherwood shot questions at them. None of them would admit having thrown the bottle. "Like I said," Orme repeated with a sallow smile. "Kim come in alone and didn't say where he'd been. Then this Texas kid comes in and Kim goes on the prod. About what I didn't know. I was just grabbin' for a shotgun to stop a fight when you stopped it yerself. Thanks, fella."

He leaned forward and peered over the bar at the dead Kim.

"Call your constable," Sherwood directed, "and give him the dope on it. Maybe he can find out who tossed the bottle. Me, I'm reportin' straight to Sheriff Sawyer. Want to come along, Diamond?"

Johnny nodded and backed out to the front walk. Rick Sherwood followed him. "Thanks," Johnny said, "for saving my life."

The Circle D man shrugged. "Nothin' else I could do. Couldn't very well stand by and watch 'em fill you full of holes. Let's go."

His horse was tied beside Johnny's. Dusk was graying the plaza as they rode out of it and forded the river. They turned up the south bank toward Las Perdidas.

"You say he drygulched Ernesto?" Sherwood brooded. "How come you found out about it?"

Johnny told him about the dawn excursion with the Rivera family. But he omitted the dying Indian's testimony about a wool buyer. Neither did he mention the motive for the excursion or make any mention of Cranston.

For Johnny still had his fingers crossed about Sherwood. True, the man had just saved his life at the expense of Jakie Kim's. Still it contradicted all of Johnny's past reasoning. Everything till now had suggested treacherous collusion between Cranston and the Circle D. Could Sherwood have intervened at Orme's bar just for the effect on

Adam and Flo Sawyer? He was a persistent suitor of Flo's. Johnny's intimations had put him under a cloud. Wouldn't he now regain all lost ground, and more? Who could accuse Sherwood now of being in with the Orme ring? As for Jakie Kim, the ring would now look on him as a discarded tool. Getting rid of Kim would be an asset rather than a loss. Also it would save the men higher up from paying a fee for the murder of Ernesto.

In no case would they have dared to use Kim again. Kim had failed twice to ambush Johnny Diamond; and while he'd succeeded in the case of Ernesto he'd been tracked from the crime straight to Orme's bar. Had he murdered Johnny there, he most certainly would have compromised others than himself. To save his neck Kim might even have turned state's evidence, implicating those who'd hired his guns.

Johnny glanced sidewise at the tall, personable rancher at his stirrup. Sherwood looked relaxed and anything but hostile. The soft night light made his profile seem earnest, clean-cut, frank. It was hard to believe he could have been involved with the likes of Orme and Kim and Diego Salvador. Harder still to believe that, six years ago, he could have been one of three Texas raiders.

"I owe you apologies," the man said with a convincing grimace, "on two counts."

"Meaning which?" Johnny prompted.

"About Kim showing up at my ranch that night. I said he wasn't there. One of Perry's men said he was." Sherwood laughed mirthlessly. "And was my face red today when I found out I'd been wrong!"

"So Kim *was* there, after all?"

"That's right. I got a big outfit, Johnny. Some of 'em aren't exactly what you'd call Sunday Schoolers. Hard eggs, I mean. I let Alf Sansone hire a few like that to give us a little more fire power against rustlers. One of these gunnies was a gink named Ferd Smith. Turns out now Smith used to run around with Kim, back in Kansas. They had some unfinished business. No tellin' what it was. Somethin' personal between 'em, and maybe on the shady side, because when Kim rode out to see Smith about it Smith kept him out of sight from the rest of us. Today I found out about it and was my face red! I tied a can onto Ferd Smith."

Pretty neat, Johnny thought. Digging up a scapegoat like that. Still, it might be true. "How come you happened by Chico," Johnny asked, "just in time to walk in on a gunfight?"

Again Sherwood grimaced. "Soon as I found out about Ferd Smith, I headed upriver to see Adam Sawyer. Nothing else I could do. I'd told Sawyer Kim wasn't there. Knowin' now that he was, only thing I can do is ride in and admit it to the sheriff. Got as far as Chico and stopped for a drink. And there I found Kim gunning you at a bar."

Conveniently coincidental, Johnny thought. Sherwood walking in at just that particular time. It wouldn't be, though, if Sherwood had had an appointment with Kim there. A pay-off appointment! Kim standing there with his elbows hooked on the bar, waiting . . . waiting for blood money due for the killing of Ernesto.

"You mentioned *two* counts," Johnny prompted.

"That old mousey mare you rounded up. I got to thinkin'. She sure does look like the colt I sold Cranston. For forty bucks. Maybe that old mare foaled the colt and maybe not. We'll never know. Not worth arguing about, I say. So that's another reason I rode to town. To find you and hand you the price of the colt." Sherwood took forty dollars from his wallet and offered it to Johnny.

He's piling it on, Johnny thought. *Gilding himself like a lily.* He hesitated a moment, then accepted the money. To refuse it would mean an admission that he himself doubted the colt's origin. What baffled him now was the neat way in which Sherwood had dissolved the cloud hanging over him. He'd made himself look generous, warm, punctiliously honest. All of which would score big with Flo Sawyer.

They rode into East Main and jogged by a line of darkened shops. Most of the lighted night spots were on West Main or down by the railroad tracks. Turning to the left on Commercial, Johnny stopped at Grinstead's livery barn. Hackamore had traveled an eighty-mile circle and needed his oats.

Sherwood continued on toward the Sawyer cottage. It was half an hour later when Johnny himself arrived there on foot.

Flo admitted him. Her face had shock on it, which meant that Sherwood had already relayed the report about Ernesto. Adam Sawyer, chewing an unlighted stogie, was pacing the floor. Sherwood, looking relaxed and handsome, sat with a glass of wine in hand.

"Rick," Flo said quietly, "has told us everything."

Not everything, Johnny wanted to say, but didn't. Sherwood couldn't have relayed Ernesto's tip about a wool buyer. And Johnny decided to say nothing about it himself. Senator Rivera would, presumably, when he reported to his brother-in-law tomorrow.

"He sure showed up just in time," Johnny admitted with a dry smile. "That Kim guy was just about to burn me with a slug."

Mild rebuke was in the look Flo gave him. It said quite eloquently: "And aren't you ashamed of yourself, Johnny Diamond! Imagining all those wild things about Rick! And now he saved your life!"

Sherwood had even told them about Kim's

secret tryst with Ferd Smith at the Circle D, and about his surrender in the mare-and-colt controversy. Johnny could see it had put him on a pedestal with Flo. Honesty and generosity were the qualities she most admired in a man.

The sheriff was still pacing. "I can't understand," he muttered, "why anyone would want to kill Ernesto."

Johnny could have told him. All he said was: "Maybe the senator'll have an idea or two about that. He'll be in to see you."

Rivera would demand the arrest of Cranston. But if Johnny brought Cranston's name into it, and if Cranston was involved with Sherwood, Sherwood would warn the man. No telling what might happen then. They might even send someone to deal with the wool buyer mentioned by Ernesto. It was a risk not to be taken. He, Johnny Diamond, must get to the wool buyer first.

"Did you pick up Winnie Quinn?" Johnny asked. He watched sharply and it seemed to him that Sherwood stiffened a little.

Sawyer nodded. "I've got her in jail. But she's buttoned her lip. Won't give out a thing. All I can charge her with is a minor forgery. Signing Flo's name to a message."

"What message?" Sherwood asked. His tone seemed uneasy although no one noticed it but Johnny.

Flo herself explained to Sherwood about the decoy message. "Ernesto was involved with her, remember? It must have something to do with what happened today. It's all so horrible . . . poor Ernesto!" Her face clouded. She and Felicia and Ernesto had been children together.

An idea came to Johnny. About Winnie Quinn. But it would need thinking about. And it was something he didn't want to mention in front of Sherwood. Sherwood, with Flo seated loyally by him on the sofa, was riding high now. The girl's manner toward him seemed almost repentantly tender. As though Johnny's accusations had implanted some vague doubts of which she was now ashamed.

"What happened today," Adam Sawyer said with a snap of conviction, "proves I was right all along. All the dirty tracks lead to Orme. Orme and his crew of drygulching thugs. He's been too slippery for me. But in the end I'll nail him."

Johnny's cue was to agree. He should admit he'd been wrong about Sherwood. When he didn't, his silence drew another mute rebuke from Flo. From then on she cooled toward Johnny and warmed toward Sherwood. Johnny thought of night before last, when he'd kissed her lips at the orchard gate. Maybe she remembered it too, and resented him all the more for it. *She thinks I'm an ungrateful wretch. She thinks I ought to be humble and beg Sherwood's pardon, and eat everything I ever said about him. But I won't. Because I still think it's true.*

He'd arrived with the idea of winning a sit-out race with Sherwood. Of outstaying the man, and then having Flo all to himself. He could see now it wouldn't work. The Circle D man wore the halo tonight, and was far more welcome here than Johnny.

"I guess I'll be ambling," Johnny said.

Adam Sawyer went to the door with him. Flo said goodbye without rising.

Johnny walked thoughtfully to the hotel, planning tomorrow. At the desk he inquired when the first Santa Fe train went south in the morning.

The answer was six A.M., and when the train left Johnny was on it. He had a round-trip ticket to Las Vegas, New Mexico.

A pusher engine helped on the long climb to Wootten Pass. At Willow Springs, at the foot of the grade on the New Mexico side, Johnny got off for breakfast. Then on down the brown short grass range through Wagon Mound and Watrous. It was noon when Johnny got off at Las Vegas.

A Mexican porter was wrangling baggage on the depot platform. "Where," Johnny asked him, "can I find La Calle de la Amargura?"

The porter was a man of probity. "Do not go there, young man," he warned. "It is a place of sin and sorrow."

"Don't worry. I only want to look up a witness."

"It is a street in Old Town." The porter gave explicit directions.

This being New Town, Johnny took a hack which conveyed him across the Gallinas River to a district which had been old long before the coming of the railroad. Its avenue of flat-roofed adobe shops had once been the main artery of the Santa Fe Trail. Wagons and ponies lined it. The hack had to wait for a six-yoke bullock team to pass before it could cross to a plaza beyond.

The hack whirled around the plaza and turned up a narrow, dusty street leading to the more disreputable part of town. Another turn and the hack stopped. "Here you are, señor." Johnny paid his fare and got out.

He was on a street of uneven board walks and buzzing flies. The only shop there had a sign which announced: *TIENDA BARATA*. The rest of the buildings were dice joints, saloons and bawdy houses. Painted sirens peered from the windows. The cheapness of it depressed Johnny. And yet by startling contrast an ancient adobe church stood at the far end of the street, as though looking sadly down it; and the name on it was: The Church of Our Lady of Sorrows.

Johnny covered the bars first. Did anyone know where he could find a widow named Valdez?

It was a common name, they told him. Many Valdezes lived in Las Vegas.

"Her husband was called Frankie Valdez," Johnny said. "She left him and went off with a wool buyer. The wool buyer left her stranded in Taos and she came here."

That didn't help. "Lots of flossies got here by that route," a bartender told Johnny. "Chances are she uses another name now."

He had no better luck at the bawdy houses. "What is her first name?" a double-chinned proprietress asked Johnny. "On this street the women have no last names. Always they are Marie or Inez or Susanna."

Johnny didn't know. After canvassing the last joint he was ready to give up. Then he saw a white-haired priest emerge from the old church. Johnny went to him and told him everything he knew about the widow of Frankie Valdez.

The priest had intelligence and a good memory: "Recently a woman came here in grief," he said. "She had a newspaper in hand. It said her husband had been killed by a knife in Chico."

"That's the one."

"If you mean her no harm, my son, I will tell you where she is."

"All I want," Johnny assured him, "is information."

"She works not in the houses of ill fame," the priest said, "but for them. She bends over tubs, washing their linens. There." He pointed to a mud jacal facing an alley.

It was there, in squalid poverty, that Johnny found Dolores Valdez. She couldn't have been over thirty years old, but looked fifty. Her face was thin and lined and her eyes were black-circled. No longer could she be attractive to men. She stood at a washtub scrubbing the frilleries of shameless women.

"My only errand," Johnny said gently, "is to find and punish the men who killed your husband."

He took a chance that she'd want that. If she felt remorse for deserting Frankie, she'd sympathize with an effort to convict his murderers.

She gave only a dumb stare and Johnny realized she spoke no English. He repeated his statement in Spanish.

Promptly she responded in the same tongue. "You knew my Frankie?"

Johnny nodded. "Mine were the last boots he ever shined."

She dropped her scrub brush and led the way into the hut. It had a clean, swept floor and little else. There she faced Johnny and said, "How may I help you, señor?"

CHAPTER XVIII

It didn't take long then. "After the wool buyer left you," Johnny said, "he went to a cantina and had drinks. It loosened his tongue and he talked about a Señor Val Cranston. It was a matter, perhaps, that he learned from you, you having learned it from Frankie "

She thought back through the years. "All my husband ever said about Señor Cranston," she remembered, "concerned his cheating at the scales in Denver."

Johnny drew her out, bit by bit. It seemed that Cranston, prior to three years ago, had been employed as weigher by a live stock commission company at Denver. Incoming cattle were weighed in pen lots. Cranston had made a practice of overweighing certain pen lots. Since cattle were sold by the pound, the favored sellers got bigger checks than they deserved. The overcharge was split with Cranston. This had gone on till the stockyards people had established a double check on the weighings. Which had put an end to Cranston's petty graft there. Resigning his job, he'd later been appointed brand inspector for Las Perdidas County.

"Was Rick Sherwood one of the favored shippers?"

The woman didn't know.

"Is that all Frankie ever told you about Cranston?"

"That is all, señor."

"Did he ever tell you anything crooked about Syd Orme of Chico?"

"No, señor. Long ago, when we were first married, he worked as porter at Orme's bar. But he tells me nothing of what goes on there."

"You never heard him mention anything mysterious? Something hush-hush, I mean, in the doin's at Chico?"

"I can think of nothing, señor."

"Thanks," Johnny said. A genuine sympathy for this woman, stranded here in these sordid surroundings, stirred within him. He took a ten dollar bill from his wallet and dropped it on the burlaped packing box she used for a table. "Buy yourself a dress, señora."

She smiled gratefully. "You are kind, señor."

He went out and started up the alley. Before he'd taken a dozen steps she caught up with him. "I have just remembered one small thing, señor."

"What?" Johnny prompted.

"One time at Chico . . . four, five, maybe six years ago . . . I take my tubs to the shade of a cottonwood to wash clothes there. It is near the headgate of the *acequia* where it leaves the river. I am working there when my husband comes to me. He makes me move my tubs to another place. I ask him why and he says it is *mal suerte* to be under that alamo by the *acequia.* He says a dead man is buried there."

"What dead man?"

"I do not know, señor. Only that much Frankie has said to me."

Johnny took a cab back to New Town and at sunset boarded a Colorado-bound train. In the smoker he rolled a cigaret. He propped his legs, clad in their Linked Diamonds boots, on the opposite seat.

As the train rumbled northeast through Wagon Mound, his mind digested the information gleaned from Dolores Valdez. It certified to the crookery of Val Cranston. It would put Senator Rivera on firmer ground when he demanded Cranston's arrest. Still, Johnny felt disappointed. The woman had told him nothing which involved Sherwood or Orme.

A grave under a cottonwood could hardly excite him. Many men, in years past, must have died with their boots on at Chico. Makeshift graves, at any convenient spot, would be the rule rather than the exception. An ignorant peon like Frankie Valdez would be to a degree superstitious. He wouldn't want his wife to stand all day over the bones of a dead man.

The vital matter, Johnny thought, was not Cranston's crookery but the nature of it—the over-weighing of cattle to split a gain therefrom with a shipper. It involved collusion with a dishonest cowman . . . exactly the same type of guile which had later been used systematically, according to Johnny's theory, in the false checking of brands at Thacker. All in all it bolstered that theory. The appointment of Cranston as brand inspector, made through Senator Rivera at Sherwood's request, seemed to fill out a pattern. A double check at the stock-yards scales having stopped one form of thievery, Sherwood and Cranston had figured out another one. This time by shipments east from Thacker.

Should he discuss this with Sawyer? Johnny decided he wouldn't. At least not till he could tie a few threads. With Adam and Flo Sawyer, Sherwood was the fair-haired boy right now. Hadn't the man just waded into a gunfight to save Johnny's life at Chico?

A grimness shaded Johnny's lips as he tipped his hatbrim over his eyes, to shut out the smoker lights, and went to sleep.

The jolting of a pusher engine, being coupled on at Willow Springs, awakened him. He napped briefly again as the train toiled up Wootten Pass. Then a swifter hum from the fishplates as he coasted down into Las Perdidas. It was after midnight when Johnny got there.

At his hotel room he slept late. A headline caught his eye as he passed through the lobby on the way to breakfast. A boy was peddling the latest issue of the *Picketwire Roundup*. Johnny bought a copy and read it over his scrambled eggs and coffee.

The front page carried three stories, each a sensation. One announced the fatal sniping of Ernesto Rivera in the Canyon of the Dead. The story rated high because of the victim's relationship to a state senator.

The second story told about Johnny Diamond tracking the sniper to Chico where he, Johnny, would have been shot dead by the murderer except for the timely intervention of "a prominent stockman of the lower Sunflower Valley, Rick Sherwood of the Circle D." The story presented Sherwood in a heroic role. "In the light of recent insinuations against Sherwood," the account said, "the incident must surely heap coals of fire on the head of our well-meaning young friend from Texas."

Johnny grinned as his eyes shifted to the third sensation. CRANSTON DECAMPS, the lead line said. "On demand of Senator Ronaldo Rivera, Sheriff Sawyer called yesterday to question Cranston at his quarters on Park Avenue. Only to find that Cranston had left hastily for parts unknown. An exhaustive search has failed to uncover Cranston. His horse being at the livery barn, it is assumed he went away by train. He did not appear at Huerfano last night, where he was due to inspect brands on a shipment of cattle."

Johnny lingered long over the three news stories. The paper said that both the senator and the sheriff had been interviewed and had given out every known fact.

"Here you are, young man." The intruding voice was Frank Sully's, editor of this very sheet. "Spent all day yesterday looking for you. Where the heck have you been?"

"Just pasearin' around," Johnny said. He was determined to tell only Sawyer and Rivera about his trip to Las Vegas.

The editor sat down opposite Johnny. "I see you've read my latest scoops," he grinned. "I got 'em straight, didn't I?"

"Straight as a string," Johnny agreed.

"Anything to add?" Sully whipped out a notebook.

But Johnny disappointed him. "I got an idea or two," he admitted, "but I'd rather save 'em for the sheriff. If he wants to pass 'em on, it's okay with me."

"You can't see him today," Sully told him. "He and his daughter went out to the Bar L. Ernesto's funeral is being held there today. The Sawyers are in-laws, you know."

"I might find a deputy or two," Johnny ventured, "at Sawyer's office."

"Not today," Sully corrected. "All deputies are out beating the bushes for Cranston. Any idea where that fellow went?"

Johnny had a definite opinion on the matter; but he kept it to himself.

Sully gave him a sharp look. "I suppose you'll drop your feud with the Circle D," he suggested, "now that Sherwood went to bat for you at Chico."

"He's been right friendly lately," Johnny evaded, and let it go at that.

He went outside and strolled to the corner of Main and Commercial. Twisting a smoke in front of the cigar store there, he decided to mark time till Sawyer returned from Ernesto's funeral. Traffic of the town rattled by him. The air was full of dust and wheel sounds. Here and there groups of citizens huddled in low-voiced discussions of the recent sensations.

A Lazy M buckboard rolled in along East Main. Johnny knew it was a Perry rig because the driver had red hair and the face of Chuck Wiggins. Chuck hitched his team in front of Brandon's Hardware Store and Johnny crossed to join him on the walk there.

"Hi," Chuck greeted with a grin. "You sure stirred things up around here, fella. Anybody taken a shot at you yet, this mornin'?"

"If he did, he missed me," Johnny said.

"I just et all the dust between here and San Ysidro, Johnny. Let's hoist a couple."

They went into a saloon where Chuck ordered a rye highball. "A sarsaparilla for me," Johnny said.

They took the drinks to a booth. "I see where Cranston flew the coop," Chuck said. "You sure had that guy tagged right, Johnny."

Johnny looked speculatively at his friend. Chuck had a bright young mind. He wasn't handicapped, as were the Sawyers, with a prepossession of Rick Sherwood's upright innocence. "I'm goin' to sound you out, Chuck, to see if you think a hunch of mine makes sense. But keep it under your sombrero."

Chuck leaned forward, all ears. "Shoot, pal."

"My hunch," Johnny confided, "is that Syd Orme's a silent partner in the Circle D."

The redhead stared. Clearly the idea had never occurred to him. "Could be," he admitted. "Sherwood started six years ago with nothin' but a dugout in a sand bank. Then right sudden he gets to be a big cowman. Someone backed him. Maybe Orme, maybe someone else. Shoot again, pal."

"Kim was a tool of the Orme-Sherwood ring. A worn-out tool they couldn't use any more, after he'd let himself get tracked from Ernesto's murder. So they knocked him off, making it look like a heroic rescue of yours truly. *También* it saved payin' his fee."

Wiggins gulped on that one. But he came back for more. "Keep shootin', pal."

"The ring had another tool they didn't dare use any more. Cranston. The Thacker shipping racket was washed up, the minute I even suggested it. Everyone, even including Sherwood's friends, would be on the lookout for it after that. So Cranston, instead of an asset, became a liability. So why wouldn't they polish him off just like they did Kim?"

Chuck whistled softly. "You figger Cranston didn't run? They just plugged him and dumped him in the river!"

"It makes sense," Johnny insisted. "Nothing else does. A whisper from a dying Indian wasn't enough to make Cranston run."

"I'd buy it in a minute, Johnny, if I thought Orme's a silent partner in the Circle D."

"If you can turn up anything on that, Chuck, let me know. I got another angle to work on."

"I sure will," Wiggins promised. He had Lazy M errands in town and went out to get busy on them. Johnny sauntered to the hotel.

He was waiting in the sheriff's office, a morning later, when Adam Sawyer came in. Johnny was disappointed when Flo didn't appear.

The sheriff listened impassively as Johnny told about his interview with Dolores Valdez at Las Vegas. Then he pooched out a lower lip and nodded.

"Cranston!" he muttered. "So you were right

about him, young man. He's as crooked as a coiled sidewinder. Overweighing cattle at the Denver yards, huh? Still, I can't see why he'd be scared enough to run. The fraud was more than three years old. And with only hearsay gossip to back it up." Sawyer brooded over it. "You'd think he'd stand pat. 'Stead of that, he had a hearsay witness knocked off and then ran away himself."

"I doubt," Johnny offered, "that it happened that way."

"What do you mean?"

He'd run into a stone wall of prejudice, Johnny thought, if he mentioned Rick Sherwood. "I just think Cranston was small potatoes, sheriff. Like Winnie Quinn. By the way, you still got her locked up?"

"Yeh, and she's screaming to get out. Only thing I can charge her with is signing Flo's name to a message. If it was a decoy, the thing fizzled. Leaving me no solid case. So I guess I'll just hold her a few days and then let her go."

"Let's give her something to read," Johnny said. He brought from his pocket yesterday's copy of the local paper. "Mind sendin' this to her cell, sheriff?"

Sawyer gave a puzzled stare. "What for?"

"Just let her read it," Johnny urged, "and see what happens."

With a shrug Sawyer called in a deputy and

gave him the newspaper. "Take it to the Quinn woman," he directed. "Compliments of Mr. Diamond."

He turned back to Johnny. "What about this body? The one you say's buried by an *acequia* at Chico."

"I didn't say it's there. I said Frankie Valdez told his wife it's there."

"When did he tell her about it?"

Johnny thought back, trying to summon the woman's exact words. "Four . . . five . . . six years ago, she said."

Six years! The term of time might be significant. Johnny himself had come to this range on the trail of a crime six years old. True, that crime had occurred in Texas and this was Colorado. Yet somehow the information he'd gleaned from Dolores Valdez seemed now more important.

He got to his feet to suggest urgently, "Let's go dig it up, sheriff."

"What's the hurry?" Sawyer objected. "If it's been there four to six years, another few hours won't matter. You couldn't prove anything by it, after that long."

He agreed grumpily, however, at Johnny's insistence. Calling in a deputy he ordered horses.

An hour later Johnny was riding down the Picketwire toward Chico. Sawyer rode stiffly at his left, the deputy at his right. "You gave Winnie Quinn that paper?" Johnny asked.

223

The deputy nodded. "Left her readin' it, and she seemed right interested."

At Chico they looked up Constable Martínez. Martinez rounded up some digging tools and they went to the headgate of an irrigation ditch which diverged from the river just below town.

A single cottonwood grew near the headgate. "The Valdez woman," Johnny reminded them, "said it's under that tree."

They dismounted and Martínez passed out shovels. The space near the tree was littered with tin cans and ashes. Because of the shade and the convenient ditch water, many people had camped here. A rope swing hung from a branch of the tree. *Niños* of Chico were in the habit of playing here.

Johnny chunked his shovel blade into the ground at a dozen spots. The others did the same, each man taking a side of the tree. Being on the upper side of the ditch the soil was fairly dry. It was Pedro Martínez who struck a looseness of soil which, he was sure, meant that it had once been turned over.

The spot was about ten yards away from the bole of the cottonwood, on the side away from the ditch. Adam Sawyer joined the constable there and the two began spading out earth. "He's right," Sawyer agreed. "It's an old refilled hole."

Two feet down they found a human skull. Sawyer looked at it soberly. Four . . . five . . . six years, the woman had said. Nothing but bones would be left after that long.

Johnny and the deputy took a turn at the digging. The ribs of a skeleton, with strands of rotted leather hanging to the bones, came into view.

"Nothing we can make of it, though," Sawyer growled. "No way to tell who the man was, or how he died."

Two things were certain. The man had been buried coffin-less and fully dressed. He'd been interred hastily too, Johnny thought, else the grave would have been deeper.

Then he saw the boots. Or what remained of them, which were matched and mildewed shells of what had once been fine Morocco leather. Rusty spurs clung to them and they still encased the feet of the skeleton. Johnny dropped to his knees for a close look.

A sense of awe, then, left him dumb. A faint design was still readable around the valanced top of each boot. Linked Diamonds!

These were the boots which had been stripped from the feet of his murdered father, six years ago in Texas!

CHAPTER XIX

There could be no doubt. Even Adam Sawyer, comparing the boots with those worn by Johnny now, agreed solemnly.

"What do you make of it?" he muttered.

"One guess," Johnny said, "could be as good as another. Mine is that the three raiders came here to Chico where, maybe in a quarrel over the loot, two of 'em killed the third. So they planted him with his boots on under the nearest tree."

"And mine is," Sawyer brooded, "that only one of them came here and took the losing end of a gunfight. Some local hoodlum did it, maybe Shotgun Orme himself."

"He wasn't killed with a shotgun." Johnny pointed out a single bullet hole in the skull.

Sawyer examined all details and made notes. "Cover him up, Pedro," he instructed the constable. "I'll turn in a report to the D.A. and ask if he wants to follow through on it. Can't see what good it'd do, after six years."

He stepped into his saddle and rode dourly to Orme's saloon. Johnny was waiting on the walk there when Sawyer came out.

"Orme," he reported, "claims he doesn't know

a thing about it. He naturally would. If you want my idea on it, it's just another corpus delicti that turned up six years too late."

Yet Johnny, as they rode back toward Las Perdidas, knew a feeling of excited vindication. He'd come here looking for an old mare and a pair of boots. He was wasting his time, people had told him. The trail was too dim and too old. But now he'd found both the mare and the boots.

"One down, sheriff, and two to go."

"You mean," Sawyer challenged, "you think two of those old Texas raiders are still on this range?"

"That's my hunch, sheriff."

"They're not Orme and Cranston," Sawyer said with assurance. "Orme started that Chico saloon eight years ago and he's never left it for more'n a day or two at a time. He's too heavy in the saddle, anyway, to go raiding deep down in Texas. And I've checked on Cranston. Six years ago he was a weighmaster at Denver and he kept right on that job till he came here as brand inspector."

At the courthouse they found Flo waiting in her father's office. She was busily transcribing reports from various deputies who were out looking for Cranston. Johnny felt his pulse quicken when she looked up to smile at him. She wore a tailored blue suit with starched white cuffs. Her dark hair, usually drawn severely back

227

on either side, was fluffed out today in a wavy, crinkly effect which won Johnny's instant approval. "I've just heard," she said, "that you went to Las Vegas."

"Give her a complete report on it," Adam said. "And Flo, you'd better take notes for the record."

"First," Johnny said, "I've got another idea. It's about Winnie Quinn. She's in jail, you say, and yesterday she was screamin' to be turned loose."

The sheriff looked askance at him. "That's right. So what?"

Johnny twisted a cigaret thoughtfully. "I could be wrong," he admitted. "But it's worth a try. Why don't you go to her cell right now? Ask her if she still wants to get out?"

"Of course she does. Just what are you getting at, young man?"

"Why don't you humor me," Johnny wheedled, "and see if Winnie's changed her mind?"

Sawyer gave a shrug of tolerance. Abruptly he left the office, heading down a corridor toward an annex which housed the county jail.

Johnny turned back to Flo, launching into an account of his interview with Dolores Valdez. The girl took precise notes. "That poor woman!" she murmured, her face vividly sympathetic as Johnny described the alley hut in Las Vegas.

When he went on to tell about the find today at Chico, sympathy on Flo's face changed to

228

shock. "How horrible! And yet how perfectly amazing that you'd find those old boots!"

Johnny smiled somberly. "Funny how things work out, Flo. Two other people had grief as bad or worse than mine. Ernesto Rivera and Dolores Valdez. I begin chasing their troubles, and first thing you know I begin to see daylight on my own."

"It's always that way," Flo said warmly. "I'm so glad you . . ." The return of Adam Sawyer interrupted her. The sheriff had a baffled look.

"I can't understand it," he muttered.

"You saw Winnie Quinn?" Johnny prompted.

He nodded. "Yesterday she was yelling her head off to be turned loose. Now she wants to stay right there in her cell."

"She's had time," Johnny suggested, "to read the paper we gave her."

"What," Sawyer demanded, "could *that* have to do with it?"

"She was a stooge," Johnny reminded him, "of the boss crook, whoever he is. For a name let's call him Mr. Big. Mr. Big had two other stooges. Jakie Kim and Val Cranston. The paper says Kim got shot and Cranston disappeared."

The sheriff's mouth fell open. He gave a long penetrating stare. "You mean you think Winnie figures she'll be killed if . . ."

"If she's anywhere but safe in a cell," Johnny supplied. "And why not? Mr. Big used her at least twice, once to decoy Ernesto and once to decoy me. So he wouldn't dare use her again. After reading the paper, she knows what happened to Kim. And her guess about Cranston could be the same as mine. Which is that Cranston didn't do a run-out; he's full of slugs and buried somewhere."

Johnny looked at Flo. In the last half minute her manner toward him had changed. It was stiff and distant again. Only a little while ago he'd felt close to her. Now she seemed a million miles away.

"That," she said coldly, "would make sense if Orme had shot Kim. But he didn't. It was Rick Sherwood. He did it to save your life, remember?"

The old stone wall again. Why, Johnny wondered, couldn't he keep his mouth shut?

Flo got up and put on her street coat. She turned her back on Johnny and spoke to her father. "Rick happens to be in town, dad. He'll be stopping by to take me to lunch, any minute now."

She's layin' it on thick, Johnny thought. *I'm knee high to a duck and the other guy's ten feet tall.*

A clink of spurs came down the hall. Then Rick Sherwood breezed in, hat on the back of his head, cockily sure of his welcome. "Ready, Flo?" He saw Johnny and for half a second he stiffened a little. A flicker of caution came to his slate-gray eyes.

But only for an instant. Then he nodded amiably. "Hello, Diamond. Haven't seen you around lately. Anything new in the wind?"

"Nothing much," Johnny said. "What's stirrin' at the Circle D?"

"Hard work and plenty of it. Which reminds me, we're a bit short-handed since I had to fire Ferd Smith. Don't need a job punching cows, do you?"

It was a bold stroke, and Johnny could see that it scored with Flo. The man who had every reason to resent him had first saved his life and now was offering him a job.

You see? Flo didn't say it but she looked it.

Johnny managed a laugh. "You wouldn't want a corpse on your hands, would you, Sherwood? That's what I'd be, about ten seconds after I showed up at the Circle D. I've got Alf Sansone's word for it. I'd hate to misquote him. But near as I can recollect he said there's a Circle D slug waitin' for me on every trail in the county."

Sherwood shrugged and made light of it. "Look, fella. Alf had a chip on his shoulder, sure. He's sensitive, like all punchers. Like you are yourself. You implied the Circle D'd been stealing cattle and Alf naturally went on the prod about it. But I had a talk with the boys and toned 'em down. You just made a wrong guess, that's all, like we all do."

Butter, Johnny thought, *wouldn't melt in his*

231

mouth. The exasperating thing was that his line was going over big. Both with Flo and Adam Sawyer.

"Ride out to the Circle D any time you want to," Sherwood resumed, pouring it on, "and I'll personally guarantee not a single hand'll be raised against you. You'll be as safe as a tick in a yearling ewe. Ready, Flo?"

She turned for a last look at Johnny. This time her eyes said, "Aren't you ashamed of yourself, Johnny Diamond?"

She took Sherwood's arm and they disappeared down the corridor. Johnny turned with a grimace to her father. "How much would you bet on my chances, sheriff?"

Sawyer answered him gravely. "Not a plugged nickel, young man."

Strolling down East Main a few minutes later, Johnny saw a dust-covered buckboard whirl by. It turned north on Commercial toward the Santa Fe depot. But not before Johnny had recognized the occupants. Miguel of the Bar L was driving, with Senator Rivera on the seat by him.

A north-bound train was due. Presumably the senator, having attended his foster son's funeral yesterday, was returning to the legislature at Denver.

Johnny walked briskly down Commercial, crossed the river bridge there and found Rivera on the station platform. Miguel was taking bags out of the buckboard.

Since the train might come at any minute, Johnny cut the greetings short. "Somethin' you ought to know, senator." He gave a terse account of his excursion to Las Vegas, describing just how and where he'd found Dolores Valdez, and what he'd learned from her.

"*La pobrecita!*" murmured Don Ronaldo.

And Johnny honored him for it. The man's deepest interest went with a quick burst of pity for the condition of this woman who'd once lived in his district.

What the senator did next was spontaneous, and came from the goodness of his heart. Nevertheless it explained why he'd been re-elected term after term. And why he'd endeared himself for many years to a thousand poor peon voters all over the country.

He clapped his hands sharply and summoned Miguel. He thrust money into Miguel's hands. "You will put away the team, Miguel. Then you will take the first train to Las Vegas. You will find the widow of Frankie Valdez in an alley back of La Calle de la Amargura. You will bring her back with you on the train. You will drive her out to our hacienda and install her as a maid there. *La pobrecita!*"

That was all. Miguel understood and would be delighted to obey. A thousand other *pobres* would hear about it and murmur: "*Qué bondad! Qué caballero simpático, el senador!*"

What kindness! What a sympathetic gentleman, the senator! "We must vote for him again, *primo.*"

There'd been no hypocrisy about it, yet never in his life would Ronaldo Rivera need to worry about re-election.

The senator took a train north and Miguel, after putting up his team at Grinstead's livery barn, took one south. Johnny sauntered restlessly back to his hotel.

He decided to keep out of Flo's way for a few days. Maybe her father would turn up the bullet-riddled body of Val Cranston. Something like that might take Flo down a peg or two.

The evening paper gave him a new item about Winnie Quinn. She'd called a real estate agent to her cell and had commissioned him to dispose of her Water Street saloon and dance garden, The Buenas Noches, for whatever cash she could get.

When she got the cash, Johnny concluded, she'd accept her freedom and leave town on the first train. All her reactions indicated she was afraid of someone here.

Again Johnny slept late and it was midmorning when he went down to breakfast. Later he picked up a timetable. It told him that the first train on which Miguel could arrive back from Las Vegas was due at noon.

Would he bring the Valdez woman with him?

Mildly curious on that point, and with nothing else to do, Johnny at noontime strolled down to the depot. Presently a California-to-Chicago train pulled in. Yes, there they were, getting off a day coach.

The old *mozo* Miguel came up the platform shepherding Dolores Valdez. The woman looked tremulously excited. Her dark Latin eyes had a moistness and on her face was awe, wonder, gratitude, the look of a lost soul snatched suddenly from hell to heaven. To be a maid at the great Rivera hacienda! She still seemed hardly able to believe it.

"Hi," Johnny greeted. The woman, he noticed, had a new black skirt and a matching mantilla over her head. They gave her an appearance much less slattern than when he'd seen her last.

"How can I thank you, señor?" She said it in soft Spanish with something like worship in her eyes.

Johnny shrugged. "Don't thank me. Thank the senator."

"But it was you, señor, who found me. But for you he would not have known I was there."

A waitress came to the door of the depot eating-house and began beating a gong. "You folks had anything to eat?" Johnny asked.

When Miguel murmured a negative, Johnny herded them into the eating-house dining room. He sat down with them at a table there. A girl came and passed them menus.

Again Dolores Valdez could hardly believe it. Miracle of miracles! To be taken from a brothel alley and transported to the house of the great Senator Rivera! To be met by this handsome young gringo who sat at a table with her, treating her like an equal! Nothing would ever shake Dolores Valdez from a feeling of adoring gratitude for Johnny Diamond. Had he not given her the money to buy this beautiful new skirt and mantilla? What shame to have gone in rags to a hacienda of *los ricos*!

Johnny made them order the full-course dinner. He himself, having just breakfasted, wanted only pie and coffee. An item on the menu caught his eye. "Yum!" he said to the waitress. "Wild currant! My favorite dish, and I haven't had any since I left Texas. Just bring me a slab of that wild currant pie and some coffee."

Presently the waitress reappeared with the first course for Miguel and Dolores. Bowls of *cazuela gallina*. To Johnny, she said: "Sorry, mister. We're all out o' wild currant. Nothing left but raisin."

Johnny looked disappointed. "Skip it, then. Just some coffee."

It was of no importance, yet the widow of Frankie Valdez took it as a major tragedy. "*Qué lástima!*" she murmured. "Some day, señor," she added shyly, "I would like to make for you a pie of the wild currants. I know a place where they grow. When we were young, Frankie and I went there often on the feast days, to gather the gooseberries and the *capulíns* and the wild currants."

Johnny rolled a cigaret and sat chatting with them all through the dinner. Then he paid the check and left them, heading back toward his hotel.

The grateful voice of Dolores floated after him: "*Vaya con Dios*, señor."

CHAPTER XX

Editor Frank Sully was waiting for him in the Toltec lobby. He had a fat notebook and a poised pencil.

"We're doing a feature," he announced, "on those old boots you and the sheriff dug up at Chico. Just like the ones you got on now. What about 'em?"

"They were stolen from the feet of my father," Johnny said, "by the man who murdered him."

"Fill in a few details, won't you?"

Johnny was reluctant. Yet if he held anything

back, this man would print a hodge-podge of guesses. Better to get the thing as nearly straight as possible.

"We had a ranch near Lampasas. I was fourteen and away to school. I came home and found my father and brothers dead, the house burned and the stock driven off. Dad's wallet was gone. So were his boots."

Sully nodded. "I already picked up that much. Seems one of the killers had a sadistic sense of humor. He put what he thought were pennies on your father's eyes. You threw 'em away and found 'em six years later. One was a penny and the other was a beer check on a Colorado saloon. Tracks indicated three raiders. What do you figure they did with the loot?"

"I'd have to guess," Johnny said. "Chances are they sold the stock to some trail herd bound for Kansas. All but one old brood mare that wasn't easy to sell. Maybe that's why one of 'em put on dad's Linked Diamonds boots. The stock was branded Linked Diamonds. So it made whoever wore the boots look convincing as the owner of the stock."

The editor's eyes gleamed shrewdly. "I'll buy it that far. What next?"

"Likely the raiders made camp somewhere. One grabbed the poke of loot while the other two slept. The one with the Linked Diamonds boots. The other two woke up and trailed him.

Say they caught up with him at Chico, killed and buried him there. Maybe it happened that way and maybe it didn't."

Sully wrote rapidly in his notebook. "Anything to add?" he prodded.

Johnny smiled grimly. "Only what you and the sheriff already know. I found the old mare on this range. Plus one of her colts with a Circle D brand on him. And I found the boots in a six-year-old grave at Chico."

A morning later Johnny went up to Grinstead's livery for a look at Hackamore. The big dun was feeling his oats and needed exercise. Johnny's saddle hung on a rack near the stall. A coiled lariat on the horn reminded him of an obligation. The rope wasn't his. He'd merely borrowed it from a peon at a little plaza up at the head of Frijole arroyo.

Why not take a ride out that way and return the rope? Johnny felt restless anyway. He looped a hackamore over the dun's nose and tossed on a saddle. A hostler came by and gave a sour look. "That brute like to bit my ear off the other day. Why doncha shoot him?"

Johnny checked the loadings in his saddle rifle. At the barn office he picked up his belt and forty-five. "Be back by nightfall," he said.

Riding out East Main he made a jaunty, clean-cut figure. A young rangeman fully armed and ready for any challenge. From the shop doors and walks he was seen and discussed by many. Johnny Diamond was something of a celebrity by now. A hunter of men who was in turn hunted. The *Picketwire Roundup* had kept up a running story on Johnny. Everyone knew his theory implicating the Circle D. And that due to his inquiries on this range many men had died and one other, Val Cranston, had disappeared. That he'd been playing up to the sheriff's daughter who, in her turn, seemed to prefer Rick Sherwood. Than Johnny Diamond no juicier foil for gossip had ever appeared in Las Perdidas, Place of the Lost Ones on a river of the same name.

Johnny held the hackamore reins high as the big raw dun cantered out of town. Again he took to the piñons, paralleling the road wherever it offered close cover for a sniper. It was true that Sherwood had offered a palm branch. But was the man sincere?

From the low piñon hills he dropped down onto the sagebrush floor of Frijole valley. Buzzards feeding on a dead calf by the trail went flapping away at his approach. He turned up the right bank at Frijole arroyo, riding toward the wall of mesas heading it. Cedared hogbacks reached out like long green fingers from the mountain. Johnny kept about halfway between two of them. It was near here, he remembered, that he'd first sighted the mouse-colored mare and given chase.

The sun shone warmly. Johnny opened his jacket and loosened the collar of his shirt. Except for occasional pools the arroyo he followed was dry. He watered Hackamore at one of the pools. Johnny twisted a cigaret and rode on.

His hat jumped. And so did Johnny. He yanked the carbine from his saddle scabbard and hit the ground to his left. The hat was still on his head but he knew there was a hole through it. The shot had seemed to come from atop a cedar hogback about three hundred yards to his right.

Johnny rolled like a barrel till he was behind a sand hummock. A second shot splashed sand in his eyes. He hunched down, prone on the sod. His eyes, peering over the hummock, scanned the hogback for sign of the sniper.

Hackamore, reins dragging, ran a few paces further on and came to a stop.

A puff of smoke up there and another splash of sand near Johnny. He poked his carbine over the hummock and fired at the puff. He could hear his bullet split a cedar bough up there.

The sniper was on its very summit, well screened. There was small chance to hit him unless he advanced. He might do that, Johnny thought, by slipping down to the head of a gully. He could follow the gully to the main arroyo and in that way flank this hummock.

So Johnny decided to do the advancing himself. Crouching low, he ran to the arroyo and dropped into it. He went up it to the mouth of the gully. Still crouching, his head lower than the bank, he moved up the gully. Ten patient minutes took him to cedars on the slope of the hogback.

Gravel crunched under his boots as he climbed to the summit. But he had plenty of cedar screen now. At the top he could look far out over the plain beyond.

Nearly a mile away he made out a retreating horseman. The horse caught the sunlight and looked like a strawberry roan. It was moving at a lope and in a few minutes disappeared.

Johnny walked down the ridge a little way to the sniper's stand. He found three empty shells there. Forty-fours. They matched the three puffs of smoke.

He tramped down to the flat below and caught Hackamore. "He figured to get us with that first shot, Hack. Soon as we started shootin' back, he gave up."

Johnny rode on toward the mesas and came, soon, to the sleeping Mexican plaza. Here he had borrowed the lariat. The same elderly Mexican was sunning himself against the adobe wall of his shack.

"Thanks for the loan," Johnny said, returning the coil of rope.

The old man nodded graciously. "*No hay de qué*, señor."

Johnny looped a leg over his saddle horn. "Anybody pass here," he inquired, "forking a strawberry roan?"

"Not today, señor. But yesterday such a rider filled his canteen at my well."

"An *Americano*?"

"*Sí*, señor. A gringo vaquero like yourself. Once he has worked for the Circle D, but not now. His name, I think, is Fernando Smith."

Ferd Smith! Johnny rode thoughtfully back to the main valley trail. Sherwood was playing it smart, he admitted. Proclaiming publicly, in fact right in the sheriff's office, that he'd discharged Ferd Smith!

But Smith, Johnny was willing to bet, was still drawing pay from the Circle D. With a single roving assignment . . . the drygulching of Johnny Diamond.

If Smith succeeded, Sherwood would be in the clear. His halo would still fit. Not a Circle D man, but an ex-Circle D man, would be guilty. All the rest of the Circle Ds, apparently, were behaving themselves. "I'll guarantee they won't touch you," Sherwood had promised. And he would seem to have kept that promise even if Johnny were found shot dead by the rifle of Ferd Smith.

Johnny turned west on the main road and jogged incautiously back toward town. He was convinced there'd be no further attack today. Getting him was Ferd Smith's job, and he'd just seen Smith heading the other way. He wondered if Smith had shot Val Cranston. And José Pacheco at San Ysidro. Did Sherwood pay Smith by the month, or so much per kill?

Johnny hit the dust of East Main by late afternoon. He was passing Jameison's General Store when he saw Sheriff Sawyer emerge from it. Sawyer, looming tall and lean and saturnine in his long black coat, as usual looked much more like a Congressman than a sheriff. His dark, angular face had a harried look as he strode down the board walk.

Johnny drew up at the curb beside him. He didn't dismount, merely leaned forward like a tired rider with his hands folded over the saddle pummel. "Howdy, sheriff. Did you find Cranston yet?"

"Not yet," Sawyer admitted somberly. "But sheriffs and police all over the country are looking for him. He's sure to be picked up."

Johnny grinned. "He'll be *picked* up, I betcha, if he gets up at all. Any more deadwood on Orme?"

"Nothing we can prove, young man. But I'm certain he's at the bottom of the whole business. Some day I'll turn up evidence to hang him." Sawyer heaved a disgruntled sigh. "Then all our troubles'll be over."

"Hope so," Johnny said.

"Have *you* anything new to report?"

"Only this, sheriff." Johnny took off his hat and displayed two jagged holes where a bullet had passed through the crown.

Sawyer gaped. "Who," he demanded, "took a shot at you?"

"Guy on a strawberry roan," Johnny told him. "Goes by the name o' Ferd Smith. Used to work for the Circle D, I hear."

"You mean the man Rick Sherwood fired?"

"I mean," Johnny amended, "the man Sherwood *claims* he fired. So long, sheriff. My best to Flo."

He loped on to Grinstead's barn and put up his horse there.

CHAPTER XXI

Black clouds gathered around Fisher's Horn. A morning later Johnny wakened to hear rain splashing in the streets. By noon it was a torrent and he kept restlessly indoors.

He looked out at deserted walks. Water raced from gutter to gutter down Commercial. Occasionally a slicker-wrapped cowboy splashed by. Later Johnny heard a roar from the deep valley of the town. The Picketwire, River of Lost Ones, was on the rampage. Ditches would flood and many an alfalfa shock would blacken. Cattle would huddle, backs humped, on the lee of buttes and cedar brakes.

Where, Johnny wondered, in all this stormy world was Val Cranston? Was his body in the river? If so this flood might beach it on the sands below town. Or had he really taken flight, fearing exposure of his past perfidies, as held by Sheriff Sawyer?

For three days the rain penned Johnny in his hotel. All he could do was fret and wait. He absorbed daily the speculative editorials of the local paper, most of them about the missing brand inspector. Editor Sully clearly concurred with Sheriff Sawyer: that all guilt except Cranston's centered at Chico; that Syd Orme was in it up to his neck but had covered his tracks by assigning all the dirty work to men like Diego Salvador and Jakie Kim. Sherwood, they said, was just a practical cattleman with a few hard-boiled lead-throwers on his payroll as proper defense against mesa outlaws and rustlers.

The bullet hole through Johnny's hat leaked out and Sully, agreeing with Sawyer, had a ready explanation. "It seems," he wrote, "that one Ferd Smith, having been discharged for rowdyism by the Circle D, lost no time in getting himself a job at Chico."

The score against Cranston mounted when Sheriff Sawyer, making a quick trip to Denver, returned with a solid fact. There was no way to determine whether or not Cranston had over-weighed cattle there. But the records clearly gave the date on which a double check had been placed on the weighing. A date three years ago, and only a day later Cranston had quit his job. Psychologically at least it confirmed the charge passed along from Frankie Valdez to his wife to the wool buyer and finally to Ernesto Rivera. "It looks," Sully editorialized, "like Brother Cranston lost interest in that job the minute opportunity for graft was gone. Being a man of plausibility and persuasion, he then got on as brand inspector in our own community. But while it is true he got the appointment through Ronaldo Rivera on the recommendation of Rick Sherwood, it is absurd to suggest that either of those highly respected citizens could have known about his character."

Johnny had just digested this when a rain-soaked stockman came into the hotel lobby. He was Buck Perry of the Lazy M.

Perry bought a cigar and peeled out of his dripping slicker. "What's new on the San Ysidro?" Johnny asked him.

"Rain," Buck complained. "And right when our second cutting is in the shock. Everything else is all right. Ed Sopers' leg is on the mend. I've put Chuck Wiggins on regular on account Slim McBride's gonna quit right after the fall roundup."

"What's Slim quittin' for?"

Perry smiled. "Didn't you hear? Slim's gettin' married in November. Gal up in Denver. Slim's been sparkin' her for a couple years."

"How come," Johnny inquired, "it took him so long?"

The cowman lighted the cigar and pulled up a chair by Johnny's. "Her old man," he explained, "won't let her hitch up with an ordinary bunkhouse puncher. Says Slim has to have a place of his own. So 'bout a year ago Slim filed a homestead down on Grosella Crik and he's built a cabin on it. So now the gal's old man says okay, they can get married right after the fall roundup."

"I remember Slim tellin' me about that cabin," Johnny said.

Perry noticed the bullet holes in Johnny's hat. "So Orme's still got a man gunnin' for you!" he remarked dryly.

"Either Orme or Sherwood," Johnny countered.

The older man rubbed the stubble on his chin dubiously. "Maybe you're wrong about Sherwood, Johnny. Anyway those Circle Ds've sure been behavin' themselves lately. We made a quick tally of the Lazy M stuff and nothin' seems to be short. No complaints from the Bar L, either. You told Wiggins to poke around and see if Orme's a silent partner in the Circle D. So Chuck went over and spent a coupla days with 'em, like he was huntin' fer strays. He came back convinced that Sherwood's an ordinary independent stock-man, same as I am."

It made Johnny feel lonely and discouraged. Even his best friends seemed to be deserting him. They were all taking the Sawyer point of view. "I'll make a bet with you, Buck. That Ferd Smith's still on Sherwood's payroll."

Perry shook his head. "Don't let yourself get all hog-tied with prejudice, Johnny. Think back to how this thing started. You went to Chico and had Frankie Valdez shine your boots. You asked if he'd ever seen any boots like 'em. It got Frankie's wind up, because he knew about a dead man buried with boots like that. He scurried straight to Orme and told him you were hot on the trail. Orme got itchy and sent for Diego Salvador. 'Diego,' he says, 'Frankie Valdez knows too much and he talks too much. Get rid of him. And while you're at it, get rid of a Texas kid named Diamond.' Point is, Rick Sherwood couldn't possibly have been in on that. He was thirty miles away at his ranch."

"The bet still stands," Johnny said stubbornly. "Let's make it a new hat."

On the fourth day the rain petered out. But the tension in town didn't. On the contrary it grew by the hour. Johnny could feel it every time he walked down the street. Eyes followed him. Men huddled in subdued comment as he passed.

Johnny Diamond was a marked man, and everybody in Las Perdidas knew it. His name was written on a bullet, inscribed there by Sydney Orme.

An item in the paper caught Johnny's eye. Buck Perry, it said, was shipping a few cars of canners to Denver. Canners, he knew, were aging cows not likely to bear any more calves and so hardly worth wintering. According to the item, the shipment would go out the next day on the D & RG narrow gauge from Chico.

Johnny was lonesome. Chico being only a few miles down the river, here was a chance to see some of his friends from the Lazy M. Early in the morning he saddled Hackamore and took his six-gun out of check. "You'll likely need it," the liveryman remarked with an ominous wink at his holster, "if you're ridin' to Chico."

After days of restless inactivity, saddle leather between his knees felt good to Johnny. The air had a fresh, dustless taste and the ditches flowed full, pouring their tawny draughts out on the garden patches below town. Magpies chattered in the willows and all the range gave thanks for the rain.

Johnny cantered down the muddy bank and forded the riffles at Chico. The town sprawled there brown and ugly, just as he'd last seen it except that now the streets held mire instead of dust. The clatter of a switch engine and a bawling of cattle meant that the Lazy M shipment was already being loaded.

At the terminal yard on the edge of town Johnny found three narrow gauge stock cars spotted opposite a chute pen. The two men hazing cows up the chute were Chuck Wiggins and Slim McBride. A substitute inspector, appointed to replace the missing Val Cranston, was checking brands. Two of the cars were already loaded.

"Hi, Johnny," Slim McBride yelled. "This is off limits for you, ain't it?"

"I couldn't win an election over here," Johnny conceded with a grin. He dismounted and helped them load the last car.

A switch engine bunted the three cars to a freight train which was already made up. A caboose was coupled on and the freight was soon ready for its two hundred mile run north to Denver.

"Which one of you fellas," Johnny asked, "is gonna do the chaperonin'?"

"Me," Slim said, and climbed on the caboose. "Take care of my bronc, Chuck. I'll be seein' you in a week."

Shortly the string of little cars pulled out, Slim waving gayly from the caboose platform.

"How come," Johnny asked, "he's gonna stay up there a week?"

"His gal lives in Denver," Wiggins explained, "so Perry's givin' him a break. Buck told him to stay up there long as he wants to, just so he gets back for the fall roundup. Right after the roundup Slim's quittin' to get married."

"So I heard," Johnny said. "You headin' right back to the ranch?"

"Not till tomorrow," Chuck said. "Buck told me I can stay all night in Perdidas. Want to buy myself a new outfit for the roundup. Ready to ride?"

They mounted, Chuck leading Slim's horse, and slogged up the miry track-front street. It was past noon now. "Shall we eat here or at Perdidas?" Johnny asked.

"Perdidas," Chuck decided. "This place gives me the willies."

But at the intersection with the main saloon street Johnny reined to a sudden stop. "Look, Chuck. Do you see what I see?"

He was staring at the hitchrack in front of the most ambitious dive of the town, Syd Orme's place, the Peso de Oro.

"All I see," Wiggins said, "is a strawberry roan tied there."

Johnny took off his hat and showed the bullet holes in it. "Guy on a strawberry roan did it. Name of Ferd Smith."

Wiggins wasn't too much impressed. "They's lots of strawberry roans, Johnny. Maybe this ain't the same one."

"Only thing suspicious about it," Johnny

admitted, "is that it's hitched in front of Orme's. Let's go look at the brand."

They turned up the main street and dismounted at the Peso do Oro. "It's a Slash 7," Chuck said, pointing to the strawberry's right hip. "Which don't mean a thing. Slash 7's a big horse ranch down around Wagon Mound. They've sold and traded broncs all over the southwest. We got a Slash 7 or two at Perry's place, held by bill of sale."

Johnny was disappointed. He'd more than half expected to see a Circle D on the horse. "The man who tied him here, Chuck, oughta be inside. Let's go in and see if he's Ferd Smith. You know Smith by sight?"

"Sure. He rode spring roundup for the Circle D. You sure it was him took a pop atcha?"

"No," Johnny admitted. "The guy was almost a mile off by the time I sighted him. But his bronc looked like a strawberry. The day before that, Ferd Smith was forking a strawberry when he filled his canteen at Frijole plaza."

"I'll cover you," Chuck said, "in case he starts anything." He pushed the latticed doors back and stepped into the barroom.

Johnny followed, ready for trouble.

At once they saw that Ferd Smith wasn't there. Johnny would have recognized him, because Smith had been one of the men he'd watched load four cars of steers at Thacker.

The gross hulk of Syd Orme stood back of the bar. He was swabbing it with a rag. Oil glistened on his baldness, plastering the few strands of his hair. "Hi, gents," he greeted with an overdone affability. "Step up and have one on the house. Don't often see you gents over this way."

"No thanks," Johnny said.

At this lazy noon hour only two customers were in evidence. One was a bleary, bearded man with no visible weapon. The woman who sat drinking beer with him looked vaguely familiar. In a moment Johnny placed her. She was Mamie Griggs, the one who'd wrapped a bandage around Diego Salvador's sprained wrist.

Which meant she was a pawn of Orme's.

Wiggins spoke to the man with her. "That your strawberry roan outside?"

The man gave him a surly look. "It ain't, mister. Not that it's any of your business. Anything else you wanna know?"

Chuck turned to the bar. "Whose bronc is it, Orme?"

Orme's stare was vacant. "How would *I* know? I don't keep tabs on who ties what bronc out in the street. Why? Is it a stole hoss?"

"How long," Johnny inquired, "since you've seen Ferd Smith?"

Again the vacant stare. Yet Johnny could sense derision back of it. "Can't recollect knowin' any Ferd Smith," Orme said.

Stairs ascended to an upper floor. Also a door giving to an alley stood open. Johnny felt sure that Smith had been in here only a few minutes ago. Observing the approach of Johnny with a friend, the man could easily slip away by the alley.

"He's clammin' up on us, Johnny. Let's go." Wiggins led the way out to the front walk. "We can just hang around," he suggested, "and see who claims the bronc."

Standing on tiptoes, Johnny peered over the latticed doors. He was just in time to see Orme beckon Mamie Griggs to the bar. The woman listened to some whispered instruction. Immediately she left the barroom, almost bumping into Johnny as she stepped out on the walk.

Her high heels clicking on the boards, she moved briskly toward the next corner. Her errand seemed obvious.

"Let's tag along, Chuck." Up the walk they went, on the trail of Mamie Griggs.

"It's a cinch," Chuck said. "Ferd Smith ducked out the alley way. Orme knows we're watchin' his bronc, so he sends Mamie to warn Smith he'd better keep away from it."

When they turned the corner they saw the woman a block ahead of them, still walking fast. She looked back over her shoulder, then increased her pace. "Keep your gun limber," Chuck advised. "Might be she's just lurin' us past

255

some upstairs window where Smith's sittin' with a cocked rifle."

The humiliating truth dawned on them only when Mamie Griggs, after leading them four blocks away, doubled back to the Peso de Oro. They saw her re-enter the place, and they heard Orme's mocking laugh from within.

The strawberry roan was gone. Ferd Smith, clearly, had been inside all the time. Possibly hiding in a broom closet, perhaps crouched behind the bar. Chuck grimaced sheepishly. "We been taken fer a walk, pal. Let's get the hell outa here before they take us fer a ride."

CHAPTER XXII

They rode upriver to Las Perdidas and on Main Street there Chuck's face brightened. "All our luck ain't bad, Johnny. Look who's turnin' in at the drugstore."

Johnny saw them. The cousins, Flo Sawyer and Felicia Rivera. He hadn't known Felicia was in town.

Chuck dismounted eagerly. "And us wastin' time over at Chico! On your toes, cowboy. It ain't often we get a break like this."

Johnny caught up with him, not at all confident of his welcome. He remembered Flo's coolness at their last encounter.

"Lucky thing," Chuck chattered brightly, "we stopped long enough to wash our face and hands when we forded the river. Otherwise we'd smell like them cattle cars we just loaded."

He breezed into the drugstore with Johnny at his heels. The young ladies were pricing perfumery. Chuck pretended surprise at meeting them. "Well look who's here, Johnny! Our Sunday best girls!" He swept the sombrero from his fire-red hair. "Howdy, *lindas*. What about a round of ice cream? Johnny an' me are feelin' rich."

Felicia smiled graciously. "It will be a pleasure, señor."

"There you go!" Wiggins complained. "Callin' me names again. The right name's Chuck and I been lyin' awake nights dreamin' of yuh."

Johnny looked at Flo and grinned awkwardly. "He says it better than I can. But I've been kinda wakeful myself. Hopin' you're not mad at me, I mean."

She gave him a searching look. Then her face relaxed and she laughed. "Mad at you? Nonsense. I *could* like you, Johnny Diamond, if you just wouldn't say such awful things about my friends."

"I won't say another word about 'em," he promised solemnly.

They sat down at a table and Chuck gave the order. "This is what I call cozy," he exclaimed irrepressibly. "What about lettin' us two lonely cowboys come up to see yuh tonight? We was just envyin' Slim McBride because he . . ."

"I'm so sorry," Felicia broke in, "but tonight we have an engagement. The play called *Uncle Tom's Cabin* is at the opera house. That is why I came in. Uncle Adam and Mr. Sherwood are taking us."

"And tomorrow," Flo added, "Felicia's going back to the ranch. I'm going with her to spend a few days out there."

Chuck turned mournfully to Johnny "If that ain't just our luck!"

Felicia's next words brightened him again. "But why don't you come out to see us at the hacienda? Some evening late in the week, perhaps?"

"It's a date!" Chuck exclaimed. "Okay, Johnny?"

Johnny looked at Flo and said earnestly: "I'd sure like to come. Can we make it Friday?"

Flo seemed about to assent when a thought clouded her brow. "We could," she said hesitantly, "except for . . ."

"What?"

"That hole in your hat." Johnny's bullet-riddled hat lay on the table at his elbow. "It's sixteen miles to the ranch. You'd have to ride out there alone. And back again late at night."

Johnny flushed. "Don't worry about that sniper. Anyway I can't let him pen me up here in town."

"Sure you can't," Wiggins agreed. "Friday evening then. I'll meet you there at eight o'clock, Johnny."

"No," Felicia corrected. "You will arrive at six. For *comida*." Her Spanish hospitality wouldn't permit guests to ride sixteen miles, arriving tired and hungry, unless they also came for supper.

Flo looked anxiously at Johnny. "You'll be careful? I mean . . . father and I worry about you a good deal, naturally, after what's happened. That terrible Orme! He's always sending men to waylay you on the road."

Johnny's spirits took a bound. "Orme? We just saw him and he's getting right friendly. Offered to stand treats. Chuck and I'll show up at six Friday."

"You mentioned your friend Slim McBride," Felicia murmured. "Why do you envy him?"

"He's got a girl," Johnny said, "who likes him."

"They're gonna get married," Chuck put in, "right after roundup." He turned buoyantly to Johnny. "So cheer up, pal. If Slim can do it, so can we. Just give us time and a couple o' more moonlight dates. We'll see you at six Friday, *lindas*."

Chuck paid the check and they left the drugstore, leaving the girls to finish their shopping there.

That night they had gallery seats at the opera house. Looking down they could see the box which held Adam Sawyer, his daughter, his country niece, and his daughter's escort. Some of the afternoon lift oozed away from Johnny, then. Sherwood looked so personable and so solidly eligible there, whispering into the ear of Flo Sawyer. In war or in love, he'd be a hard man to beat.

That was Tuesday. Early Wednesday morning Chuck Wiggins, leading Slim McBride's horse, left for the Perry ranch on the San Ysidro. *"Hasta pasado mañana,"* were his last words to Johnny.

"I'll be there," Johnny promised.

He spent the day refurbishing his wardrobe, adding a green silk shirt. Thursday he polished his Linked Diamonds boots. Friday morning he went to the livery barn and personally curried Hackamore. When you went calling at the Rivera hacienda, you must at least look like a caballero. The holes in his hat fretted Johnny a little. But his purse was too flat to afford a new one. "We'd better get us a job somewhere, Hack."

Why not try getting on with Buck Perry for the roundup? He decided to go home with Wiggins after the date, and see if the Lazy M could use him as a hand.

At four in the afternoon he rode out of town, allowing himself two hours for the sixteen mile trip to the Rivera place. Wiggins would be leaving the Lazy M at about this same time, on this same road, but approaching the Bar L from the opposite direction.

Johnny's forty-five was in his holster and his carbine was in the saddle scabbard. There was always a chance of ambush. The man or men out to get him might even have heard about his *comida* date at the Riveras.

So again Johnny left the road, detouring through the piñons, paralleling the trail about a half mile on the upper side. It was the same detour he'd taken twice before.

He rode leisurely, a bit dreamily, his thoughts on Flo Sawyer and how she'd look against moonlight shimmering on the little patio lake. The senator was away at Denver. So no one would be there except himself and Chuck and the two girls. And the servants, of course. Then he remembered that one of the servants would be Dolores Valdez. He'd be glad to see her again.

Thinking pleasantly of these things, Johnny rode a trifle less cautiously than usual. It was five o'clock when he came to Frijole arroyo. He struck this deep wide wash just where he'd crossed it the last time, about a half mile above the road.

He paused for a moment on its brink, his eyes searching cedars on a hogback about three hundred yards away. A distant rifleman seemed the only possible hazard. It didn't occur to him that an enemy might be lurking in a crack of this very bank, posted there because Johnny had twice before used this crossing.

The whirr of a rope came just as he slid his horse down the steep bank into the arroyo's bed. It came from the right and slightly to his rear. He twisted sharply, reaching for his gun, but too late. The loop settled neatly over his shoulders and was jerked tight, pinioning his arms to his sides.

The same hard jerk pulled Johnny from the saddle. He landed with dazing force on the shale bed of the wash. Then he was aware of a man— Ferd Smith—covering him with a gun. Smith, wearing batwing chaps, stood there with his legs wide apart, keeping the rope taut and aiming a forty-five with his free hand. His small, apish face wore a grin of elation.

"A cinch!" he crowed. "I've looped me many a bull calf with a heap more trouble. Figgered you'd come this way."

Johnny sprawled with his arms pinioned. There wasn't a thing he could do. But why the capture? Why hadn't the man simply shot him out of the saddle?

"On your belly, mister," Ferd Smith commanded. "Face down to the shale."

With a gun on him, Johnny had to obey. Smith crawled toward him along the rope, keeping it tight. His hand darted down to snatch Johnny's gun.

Johnny, face to the ground, couldn't see him

now. He felt his hands being drawn behind his back. Then came a clink of metal, steel links clamping on each wrist. Handcuffs! "That Mex constable down at Chico—" Smith chuckled— "gets kinda careless sometimes. I snitched me two pair of 'em right out of his shack."

The rope was still tight, making Johnny doubly helpless. Hackamore was standing by. Ferd Smith dallied the rope around the saddle horn. Then he led the big dun up the arroyo, dragging Johnny like a sled. Twice Hackamore balked. Once he pawed out viciously with a forehoof. Ferd Smith dodged the hoof and cursed the horse amiably. He kept pulling on the lead rope, finally leading Hackamore around a bend in the bank where another horse stood tethered to a root.

A strawberry roan.

Having been dragged some fifty yards like a calf to a branding fire, Johnny felt burning bruises from head to foot. Nothing hurt, though, so badly as his pride. He abused himself bitterly. He'd let this sly little killer outmaneuver him completely.

Ferd Smith, still in high humor, loosened the rope. "You can set up now," he invited, "long as you don't get funny."

Johnny wriggled to a sitting posture. Disarmed and with hands cuffed behind his back, there was no chance either to fight or to escape. "Who are you working for?" he asked dully. "Orme or Sherwood?"

"Both." The admission came frankly and cheerfully from Ferd Smith.

It gave Johnny a gloomy sense of triumph. Not that it could do him any good now. But at least it proved he'd been right all along. Sherwood was in it with Orme. Sherwood, the fine caballero, the upstanding cattleman in whom the Sawyers and the Riveras had such complete confidence! It would be almost worth this defeat, Johnny thought, if Flo could hear that concession from Ferd Smith.

Flo, who at this very minute was expecting him as a dinner guest! What would she think when he didn't show up?

Squatting on his spurs, Ferd Smith rolled a cigaret. After lighting it he rolled another one. He lighted this one too, putting it between Johnny's lips. "Personally I ain't got a thing agin you, kid. This is business. A guy has to make a livin', you understand."

"You must make a nice thing out of it," Johnny said dryly. "How much do you get per kill?"

The man grinned. "I don't work for no chicken feed, like Salvador and Kim did. They's risks, you understand, and I gotta charge for 'em."

The gun hung loosely by its trigger guard from his finger. They were in an arroyo ten feet deep, well hidden from all distant views, and the man seemed in no hurry to get the business over with.

Johnny bit grimly on his cigaret. "What are you waiting for?" he asked bitterly.

"Nightfall," Ferd Smith explained. "The place I'm takin' you is below the road. We got to cross the road to get there. In daylight, someone might come along and see us."

It meant a brief respite but Johnny could see no hope in it. "Where 'bouts below the road? To Sherwood at the Circle D?"

Smith smiled slyly and shook his head.

"To Orme at Chico?"

The man chuckled. "Guess again, kid. It's the last place anyone'd ever look fer yuh."

"Where?"

But that was all Johnny could get out of him at the moment. The sun had now set behind the mountains and twilight dimmed the arroyo. Ferd Smith disposed of half a dozen more smokes, waiting patiently for dark.

Where, Johnny pondered, would be the last place anyone would look for him? And why didn't this man shoot him right here? Was he playing some double game of his own, needing a hostage for a better deal with Orme and Sherwood? Anyone looking for him would reason that Smith had taken him to the cover of mountain timber Perhaps to some cave up under the rimrock. Instead, he was to be taken to open country below the road. Johnny couldn't imagine a safe hiding place there.

Twilight faded to dusk and dusk to darkness.

"On your feet," Ferd Smith ordered, "and stand on that drift log."

Johnny stood up, hands manacled behind him, and stepped up on a log which some flood had left stranded in the arroyo. Ferd Smith led Johnny's horse to the log. "Step into the saddle, kid."

Johnny put his left foot in a stirrup and swung his right leg over the saddle. He was now mounted but without the use of his hands. To make sure he wouldn't dismount, Smith tied Johnny's belt securely to the saddle horn.

After which the man put a long lead rope on Hackamore and mounted his own strawberry roan. "We're on our way, kid."

He rode up out of the arroyo, leading the dun with Johnny astride of it. There were stars, but no moon had risen. Ferd Smith proceeded at a trot down the arroyo bank, toward the road leading from town to the Rivera ranch.

All Johnny knew about his destination was that they must cross that road. A road frequently traveled by day, although infrequently by night. He took his left foot out of the stirrup. Its boot had a spur. Johnny groped with it until the spur hooked in the mesh of the saddle's girth.

Then he drew his leg up slightly, pulling gently. The boot came part way off. The grip of the spur in the girth served like a bootjack, with which a man may pull off a boot without using his hands.

Johnny didn't let the boot slip more than half-way off. His eyes strained into the darkness, watching for the road. His captor was a rope-length ahead of him. No sound broke the silence of night except the hoof thuds of two trotting horses.

They came to the road and just as they crossed it Johnny slipped his left foot entirely out of the boot. He kicked it, dislodging the spur from the girth. The boot fell squarely between wagon ruts in the road. The sound of the fall was no greater than a hoof thud on rock or clod by one of the horses.

Ferd Smith, not even turning his head, rode on. Johnny followed astride Hackamore, his left leg bootless now. The forsaken boot, with a design of Linked Diamonds circling its top, lay neatly in the middle of the road—the San Ysidro road leading one way to Las Perdidas, and the other way to the ranches of Buck Perry and Ronaldo Rivera.

CHAPTER XXIII

Arriving from the east, Chuck Wiggins presented himself at the Rivera hacienda promptly at six o'clock. Miguel ushered him to the sala. Flo and Felicia, entrancing in their long, ruffled *comida* gowns, were waiting there.

"Hi," the redhead greeted as he breezed in. "Johnny showed up yet?"

"He will be here soon," Felicia assured him.

Flo looked at the clock and her face registered a faint worry. Johnny had been eager to come, she remembered, and it wasn't like him not to be prompt. She moved restlessly to a spinet piano and strummed the keys there.

Chuck chatted with Felicia. Minutes sped by and Johnny Diamond didn't appear. Flo got up and stood at a window. She gazed anxiously down a road which led from town.

"I can't understand," she worried. "Something may have happened to him. What do you think, Chuck?"

Wiggins was an optimist. "Shucks," he said. "Johnny's all right. Right good at taking care of himself, that boy is. Chances are somethin' came up in town. Some break in the Cranston case, maybe."

But Flo wasn't at all reassured. If something had detained Johnny, why hadn't he sent word he couldn't come?

At seven o'clock Felicia decided not to hold dinner any longer. She led them across the patio to the detached dining sala. Four places were laid at a table there.

A middle-aged Mexican maid in a white apron stood ready to serve. When only three sat down, she looked askance at her mistress.

Felicia smiled nervously. "I'm afraid he's not coming, Dolores. You may bring the *cazuela* now."

Dolores Valdez showed acute disappointment. "*Qué lástima!*" she sighed. "After I have made for him the *torta de grosella!*"

As she disappeared to the kitchen Felicia explained to Chuck Wiggins. "Our new maid has much gratitude and affection for your friend. It was he who found her living in poverty and distress at Las Vegas. He has changed her whole life, she thinks, and so he is her great hero."

"Where," Chuck asked, "does currant pie come in?"

"Once," Felicia said, "he has told her that he likes it very much. He ordered it when he bought her a luncheon at the depot. But alas they had none. So, today, when Dolores learns he will come for *comida*, she makes him a pie of wild currants."

"That's all right," Chuck said. "I'll eat his share myself."

Flo didn't taste her *cazuela*. She barely touched the other delicious courses brought in by Dolores. Assassins had been stalking Johnny Diamond ever since his arrival on this range. Were they busy again tonight?

All her impulse was to send Chuck Wiggins, or Miguel, on a fast ride to Las Perdidas. To inquire why Johnny didn't come. To make sure he was all right. But a girl simply couldn't do that. Flo Sawyer bit her lip in frustration. When you make a date with a young man and he doesn't appear, you don't dash out looking for him.

After dinner Flo again stood at a window. She stared at the darkness out there, cut thinly by starlight. She remembered a bullet hole in Johnny's hat. Another one in a porch post at her own house in town. A cold terror grew inside of her. Had the last one found the heart of Johnny Diamond?

In the same starlight Ferd Smith, leading Johnny's horse, came to a gate in a pasture fence. He dismounted, opened it, led the horses through. "We're almost there, kid."

Johnny, hands linked behind his back, sat helplessly astride Hackamore. As nearly as he could reckon they'd come about five miles since crossing the road. They'd angled northeast, toward Grosella Creek, and he knew that no land was fenced over this way except the meadows and pastures of Senator Rivera. This must be the big winter pasture of the Bar L, down-creek from the hacienda.

Ferd Smith closed the gate, remounted his strawberry roan. "Last place they'd ever look," he chuckled as he proceeded onward. In the darkness he hadn't yet observed that his prisoner wore only one boot.

A line of cottonwoods loomed ahead. That would be Grosella Creek, which watered this pasture. Slim McBride, Johnny recalled, had told him about it one time. The pasture had about eight thousand acres, partly owned in fee by Senator Rivera and parts of it still government land. Slim had filed a homestead in it with the senator's approval, because Slim's residence there would make the pasture less vulnerable to thieves.

In midpasture, near the creek brush, they came to a log cabin. It loomed like a black square box in the starlight. This, Johnny guessed, would be Slim McBride's homestead house. The one to which he planned to bring a bride soon after the next roundup.

"Last place they'd ever look," Ferd Smith repeated as he dismounted at the cabin. "Who'd ever figger I'd take you to the shack of one of your best friends, right plumb in the middle of a pasture owned by your best girl's uncle?"

"How do you know," Johnny asked him, "that McBride himself won't show up here?"

" 'Cause he went to Denver fer a week. I was in Chico the other day and I seen him leave with them three cars o' canners." Smith removed the tie which held Johnny's belt to the saddle horn. "Hop off, kid."

Johnny slid to the ground. With a gun at his ribs he was marched into the cabin. Ferd Smith lighted a candle.

It exposed the fact of a missing boot. "What happened to it?" the man demanded.

"Snagged it on a greasewood bush as we rode along," Johnny told him, "and it came off."

"How far back?"

Johnny shrugged. "Two-three miles, maybe."

The man didn't seem too much alarmed about it. A boot under a greasewood bush on the open range wasn't likely to be soon found.

"I been holin' up here fer a coupla days," Smith said, "gettin' things ready. Let's see. What'd I do with that other pair of cuffs?"

In a moment he produced a second pair of handcuffs from beneath a cot mattress. With these he clamped Johnny's bootless ankle to a spike he'd driven into the floor. Then he took an axe and pounded the spike flat, so that the link couldn't be freed without the use of a prying tool.

He drove a second spike into a log wall. His gun made Johnny face that wall. Ferd Smith then freed one wrist and linked the other to the wall spike. When the wall spike was flattened, Johnny stood there with one free leg and one free hand.

Ferd Smith removed all tools from his reach. He pushed a small table in front of Johnny and placed a chair so Johnny could sit down. Next he pulled off the prisoner's remaining boot.

"What's the idea?" Johnny asked him.

The man's eyes narrowed slyly. "When I show it to 'em, it'll prove I got you."

"Show it to Orme and Sherwood?"

"You said it. They been holdin' out on me, kid. Owe me fer two jobs, them buzzards do. Yours makes three. So I'm keepin' you fer a pet till they pay off."

"The two jobs they owe you for," Johnny suggested, "are José Pacheco and Val Cranston?"

Ferd Smith didn't deny it.

He just stood there looking cunning and malignant. He licked a cigaret and lighted it. Then he put a bucket of creek water and a loaf of stale bread on the table in front of Johnny. "Chances are you won't need it, kid. Chances are they'll pay off. If they do I'll come back and finish up."

"And if they don't?"

"I'll head fer Old Mex and send a card back to the sheriff tellin' where you are. He can turn you loose and then hang Orme and Sherwood."

"What about Alf Sansone?"

"Hang him too, if you wanta. The whole outfit's got it comin' to 'em, from Orme down."

"You mean Orme owns the Circle D?"

"A good size slice of it. He set Sherwood and Sansone up in the cow business six years ago, after they trailed Alex Pardee here from Texas and killed him in Orme's bar."

The puzzle pieces were beginning to fit, now. "It was Pardee's body I dug up at Chico?"

Smith nodded. He sucked his cigaret for a minute and then thumped away the snipe. An evil grin rode his face. "Don't get no hopes up, kid. Chances are them guys'll come across. If they do you'll see me again in the morning." A glitter in the man's eyes left no doubt as to what he'd do when he returned in the morning.

He blew out the candle and went out with Johnny's Linked Diamonds boot. Johnny heard him fighting Hackamore outside. Presumably he'd hide Hackamore in the creek thickets, riding his strawberry roan to the Circle D.

In the blackness of the cabin, Johnny jerked futilely at his irons. He was like a galley slave chained there, free only to move one arm and one leg. The ironic nearness of potential rescue maddened him. He couldn't be more than a half-dozen miles downcreek from the Rivera hacienda. Too far for a gunshot to be heard, even if he could fire one. At this very minute Chuck Wiggins was dining at that ranch-house, with Flo and Felicia. They'd wonder where he was. They might suspect he'd been ambushed on the road. But they'd never imagine he was in Slim McBride's cabin down the creek, right in the middle of a Bar L pasture.

The steel links cut cruelly at ankle and wrist, as Johnny fought vainly to break them. They bruised his flesh and crucified his spirit, yet his mind had never been clearer. Almost in exact detail, now, he could piece out the story of three renegade raiders in Texas.

Ferd Smith had given them names. Sherwood; Sansone; Pardee. Pardee, wearing the Linked Diamonds boots, had stolen the loot from the others and fled to Colorado. Sherwood and Sansone, in pursuit, had caught up with him in Orme's bar, killing him.

What then? Orme would snatch his shotgun from under the bar and cover the intruders. What's the idea, he'd demand, of gunning one of my customers? Because he stole money from us, they'd say. And Orme would see a chance to cut in. "Okay," he'd say, "we'll give the bar porter fifty bucks to bury the body and split the rest of it three ways."

The bar porter had been Frankie Valdez. So for a tip Frankie had buried the body, with its Linked Diamonds boots on, near the headgate of an *acequia*. No wonder he remembered the boots! Fearful and superstitious, no wonder he'd cautioned his wife against setting up her wash tub on that grave!

Other pieces of the jigsaw slipped into place, although more loosely. Orme had backed Sherwood in the establishment of a shoestring stock outfit which later became the Circle D. Sansone had drifted to Kansas, where for a year or so he'd been a trigger-happy marshal at Abilene. Hearing that Sherwood was prospering he'd rejoined him at the Circle D. Needing guns for a rustling program, Sansone had perhaps recruited some of the outlaw connections he'd made at Abilene. Orme, the backer and silent partner, had remained at his Chico bar. Three years ago they'd schemed to have a corrupt weighmaster named Cranston appointed brand inspector, so that they could ship car after car of their neighbors' cattle from Thacker.

But now that he'd figured it out, it only made Johnny feel the more hopelessly doomed. Except for some miracle of rescue, the secret was sure to die with him here. Sherwood wouldn't dare hold out on Ferd Smith. Paid off, Smith would certainly return to keep his bargain. A bullet through Johnny's heart.

Ferd Smith loped through the night, the hooves of his strawberry roan thudding on grama sod. They'd leave tracks, Smith knew, so he maneuvered to nullify them. The roan was unshod. So when he came to a band of grazing range mares he drove them ahead of him for a mile. He rode in among them, scattered them, then continued on toward the Circle D.

It would foil the Circle Ds if they tried to backtrack him to the prisoner. Sherwood was sure to think of doing just that. Here on the Picketwire, as everywhere else, there was no honor among thieves.

A Linked Diamonds boot was tied to a *látigo* of Smith's saddle. It was midnight when he rode through the Circle D gate, a mile or so up the San Ysidro from its confluence with the Picketwire. Ferd Smith galloped into the ranchyard. The bunkshack was dark, but lamplight glowed at a window of the main house.

With the boot in hand, Ferd Smith rapped at a door there.

Sherwood's voice summoned him to come in.

He found Sherwood playing stud poker with Alf Sansone. A brandy bottle stood between them. Sherwood wore a lounging robe and slippers. In comparison with Sansone he looked like a genteel clubman. Sansone's cold flat face had temper on it. He'd been drinking too much and the chips were all on Sherwood's side of the table.

Sherwood fixed a slate-gray stare on Ferd Smith. "I told you to stay away from here." His tone carried sharp rebuke.

Smith tossed a boot to him. "Take a look, Rick.

I got that Texas kid. Got him all wrapped up for a slug."

The phrasing startled Sherwood. "You mean you haven't gunned him yet?"

"Nope," Ferd Smith answered cheerfully. "And he won't get gunned till I'm paid off. Paid off not only for him, but for what you owe me on the Cranston job. And the half you still owe me on the Pacheco job. Comes to six thousand in all. Slip me, Rick." He held out an open palm.

Sansone jerked out a gun and stood up. "I'll slip you a chunk o' lead. Who do you think you are, anyway?"

Sherwood intervened cagily. "Sit down, Alf." He turned placatingly to Smith. "Where've you got him, Ferd?"

A mocking grin answered him. "Where his friends'll pick him up in a few days, unless I go back there and knock him off. Which I'll sure do if you quit stallin' and pay me off. He knows the works, that kid does. Enough to hang the pack of you a mile high."

Fear shadowed Sherwood's face. His chin, with the deep cleft in it, trembled a little. He poured himself a drink, then spoke coaxingly to Smith. "I don't keep that much money at the ranch, Ferd. Orme'll pay you off, soon as the job's done."

"He'll pay me off tonight," Smith decreed stubbornly, "or the job won't get done at all. Take it or leave it, you guys."

278

Again Sansone was on his feet, livid, finger crooked on a trigger. Again Sherwood made him sit down. Ferd Smith held a hole ace right now, and he knew it. This Linked Diamonds boot proved the man was holding its owner somewhere. Everything would blow up if the kid escaped to tell what he knew. War would erupt on the Picketwire, with every honest gun on the range turned against the Circle D.

"You win, Ferd." Sherwood's tone had complete capitulation in it. "Alf, toss a saddle on the fastest bronc in the corral. Fan the breeze for Chico and get Syd Orme. Tell him to bring along the cash for Ferd Smith. All of it."

Ferd Smith, reaching for the brandy, failed to see one of Sherwood's eyelids droop furtively. The wink was caught only by Alf Sansone.

CHAPTER XXIV

It was midnight too at the house of Don Ronaldo Rivera. Time for Chuck Wiggins to say goodnight to his hostesses and ride home to the Lazy M.

Yet something held Chuck there. The mounting apprehensions of Flo Sawyer, all through the evening, had been contagious. Both her cousin and Chuck Wiggins now shared them.

Why hadn't Johnny Diamond kept his date?

"If its okay with you," Chuck said at midnight, "I'll just bed down at the bunkshack. At the first crack o' dawn I'll light out for town. I got to find out why that kid didn't show up."

Flo stared at him, her face milk pale. "I shouldn't," she lamented, "have told him he could come!"

"You may stay in the guest room," Felicia invited.

But Chuck preferred the bunkhouse. He went there and found a bunk. He lay down without undressing, careful not to disturb the vaqueros in the other bunks. Sleep evaded him as he tried to think of some harmless reason which might have detained Johnny. Nothing made sense except an ambush on the trail. *He's nuts about Flo. All hell couldn't keep him from coming.*

He wondered if Flo knew that too. Had she read Johnny's heart in his eyes? Her own had held terror tonight. *She's that way about him too,* Chuck decided.

He knew it beyond doubt when at the first peep of daylight he went outside. Flo was emerging from the corral with two horses. She'd saddled them herself. Her own and Chuck's. She was dressed for hard riding, in denim pants and a leather jacket. "I'm going with you, Chuck."

"No sense in it," he argued. "You better stay right here."

But nothing could stop Flo from going. By her eyes he could see she hadn't slept. "It was my fault," she said wretchedly, "for telling him he could come."

Chuck had left his gunbelt looped over the saddle horn. He buckled it around his waist. The saddle scabbard held a carbine. Flo's saddle had one too. She looked grimly miserable as she mounted. "Let's get started," she urged impatiently, and spurred through the gate.

Wiggins caught up with her at the creek bridge. Light was still only a dim gray, with just a faint hint of pink showing at the east horizon.

Flo took a canteen from her saddle horn and passed it to Wiggins. It was warm to his touch, and what he upturned to his lips was hot coffee. "Thanks, Flo. You think of everything."

"I think of everything too late," she amended bitterly. "Before I said Johnny could come, I should have thought about poor José Pacheco. And Ernesto. And Val Cranston who disappeared. I should have remembered Diego Salvador. And all those other ruffians from Chico."

She spurred ahead again and Chuck had trouble keeping up. Not that his horse wasn't fast enough. But he needed to watch the road. It was a dirt road, ungraded, with deep ruts. Due to recent rains it wasn't dusty. Too many wheel marks and hoof-prints were in it for any single track to be identified. Nevertheless Chuck

Wiggins was a rangeman and a natural reader of sign. A recent conflict along this trail might have left sign.

They topped a low piñon ridge and dropped down into Frijole valley. The light was bright by now. It wasn't far from here, Chuck remembered, that a man on a strawberry roan had fired a bullet through Johnny's hat.

It was Flo who first saw the shiny black thing in the road. From a distance it looked like a bundle wrapped in dark paper. Chuck saw it and thought something had fallen from a wagon. They rode on toward it and could see that it was polished leather.

Flo gave a low cry. "It's a boot. It's Johnny's boot!"

Squarely in the middle of the road it lay. Wiggins saw the design around the top. It was Johnny's, all right. He leaned from the saddle and scooped it up. "But why," Flo wondered, "would he take off a boot?"

"He got this far," Chuck said grimly. His first thought was that Johnny had been shot out of his saddle right here. Then he saw that there was no near and convenient cover for a sniper. Anyone waiting to ambush Johnny would have picked a better place.

"But look, Flo. Two broncs crossed the road here at right angles. One shod and one unshod Single file. The shod horse went last."

Johnny's dun, they both knew, was shod. The ground near by showed no mark of conflict such as bloodstains or empty gun shells. If Johnny had been attacked here, he would have cut loose with a shot or two himself. The tracks looked like he'd crossed the road driving an unshod horse ahead of him, dropping one of his boots as he did so.

Except for the conspicuous boot, Chuck would have paid no attention to horse tracks crossing the road. Grazing range horses were always crossing from one side of the road to the other. But the boot meant something. It tightened Chuck Wiggins and made him like a steel spring. Flo was no less tense. She turned a harassed face to Wiggins. "Let's see where they go, Chuck."

The horse tracks led slightly east of north, across the flat and open greasewood range. Chuck followed them a little way, Flo keeping at his stirrup. The sod was still soft from the rains, making tracks easy to read. These continued in single file, the unshod horse ahead.

"The unshod horse," Flo suggested, "could be leading Johnny's."

"Okay," Chuck said. "You hit for town and get the sheriff."

"Not," she protested, "till I see where . . ." She didn't speak the rest of her thought. Chuck knew what it was, because his own was the same. Johnny, either dead or wounded, could have been laid across a saddle to be led far out into the sage, there to be dumped out of sight in some arroyo.

Maybe he'd had enough life left, while crossing the road, to drop a boot there.

So Chuck rode on down the line of tracks, bleakly expectant of the worst. But nothing he could say would make Flo Sawyer go back. She kept stubbornly with him. A mile brought them to a gully. Chuck peered into it fearfully, braced to see a bullet-riddled body there. But the tracks of two horses crossed the gully and kept on.

"They ain't headin' toward Chico," Chuck said, "nor straight north toward the river. They're anglin' northeast, kinda toward the Circle D."

The sun had rimmed the horizon and shone brightly in their eyes now. Mile after mile they kept on, until they sighted a fence ahead. "It's the fence," Flo said, "of Uncle Ronald's lower pasture."

The tracks led to a gate in it. When they got there, Chuck saw bootprints where a man had dismounted to open the gate. Someone else than Johnny, for Johnny only had one boot on. His left foot would make only a sock print.

Within the big pasture the tracks led on toward a creek bottom where a line of greenery angled northeasterly. Grosella Creek. The grass grew lush here, kept fresh for the wintering of cattle now summering on mountain range. "If he was headin' for the Circle D," Chuck muttered, "I can't see why he'd cut through this pasture. He could have stayed outside the fence and made a bee line for it."

"Look," Flo cried, pointing. "Isn't that Slim McBride's cabin?"

The cabin stood far down the bottom and snug against the creek thickets. The bark of its logs was fresh and unsealed. "Honeymoon Cabin," Felicia Rivera had called it, because everyone knew that Slim McBride would bring his bride here.

As the horse tracks led toward it Flo felt a glimmer of hope. It was hard for her to imagine anything sinister about that cabin. Surely outlaws would shun it, since it belonged to an honest cowboy and was in the middle of a state senator's pasture.

"Hurry, Chuck." Flo raced ahead. But Chuck caught up with her to advise caution.

"Might be," he brooded, "that somebody's in there with Johnny. Holdin' a gun on him, maybe. Let's slip up on it through the brush."

They veered to the creek. Here dense thickets along the bank screened them. Wild plum and *capulin*, and berries, with occasionally a tall cottonwood. "Heck," Chuck muttered. "We're only about six mile downcrik from the Bar L ranchhouse. Somethin' funny about this, Flo. Why would a Chico killer take anyone here?"

"I don't think he would either," Flo agreed.

They followed down the creek bank, pushing through brush, until they came opposite the cabin. And there they found further reassurance. Tethered in a thicket was one saddled horse, and one only. A hackamore haltered his head in place of a bridle. He was Johnny Diamond's big dun gelding.

The absence of a second horse suggested that only Johnny was in the cabin. Chuck looked the saddle over carefully. There was no blood on it. Chuck plucked the carbine from his scabbard and advanced toward the house. "You stay here, Flo."

He advanced cautiously, carbine at the ready, on a chance that a captor might be inside with Johnny. There was a window on this side, high up. He kept his eye on it. The cabin, its chimney smokeless, looked deserted. Its door was closed.

Chuck was almost there when he heard a step back of him. It was Flo. She too had taken a carbine from her saddle scabbard. "Get back in the brush," Chuck ordered roughly.

But she kept at his heels. She was there when Chuck Wiggins kicked the door open and looked inside.

They both saw Johnny Diamond. He was alone in there. Nothing seemed to be wrong with him. Seated at a table with water and bread in front of him, he looked almost comfortable. Sight of Chuck's red head brought a pale grin to his face. Then, beyond Chuck, he saw Flo Sawyer.

He shouted hoarsely to her. "You shouldn't've come here, Flo." He tried to stand up but a manacle on his ankle pulled him down.

"Oh, Johnny," Flo ran to him, all restraint to the winds. She put her hands humbly on his shoulders. "It's all my fault . . . I've been such a fool!" She took up his right hand and tried to pull the link from his wrist. Then tears of fury came to her eyes. "Don't just stand there, Chuck," she said fiercely. "Get it off of him. Who did it, Johnny?"

"Guy named Smith," Johnny said. "There's an axe around here somewhere, Chuck. You'll need it to loosen these spikes."

"Where did he go?" Chuck demanded.

"To the Circle D."

"What for?"

"For a pay-off. He used to do a credit business," Johnny added with a grin, "but now his terms are strictly cash. Get busy with that axe, cowboy."

Chuck couldn't at once find the axe. Ferd Smith might have taken it outside. Chuck went out and circled the cabin, looking for any stout prying tool to use on the spikes.

He came back with an old spade which Slim McBride had used to ditch the premises for drainage. "We haven't got too much time," Johnny warned. "That guy's likely to show up any minute."

"Watch for him, Flo," Wiggins directed. "And better close the door." He set to work with the blade of the spade trying to pry up the bent spike in the floor. Flo closed the cabin door. She stood then at a window, her eyes searching distance toward the Circle D.

"He left here about twelve hours ago," Johnny told them. "He could have got to the Circle D by midnight and he oughta be back by now. Unless he's not coming back at all."

The spike was stubborn. Mashed flat to the floor, Chuck could not readily get the spade blade under it. He tried the spike on the wall and had better luck. It came up a little way and the hand-cuff link slipped free. Johnny could now move both arms at will, although a manacle still dangled from his right wrist.

Chuck returned savagely to an attack on the floor spike. "Why mightn't he not come back, Johnny?"

"He said he won't if they don't pay him off. For three jobs. Pacheco, Cranston and me." Johnny stood up, stretching the stiffness from his arms.

A cry of alarm came from Flo at the window. "I see him! He's coming. Look!"

Wiggins joined her and looked out. A horseman

was loping toward the cabin on a strawberry roan. His approach was from the northeast, and directly across the open pasture. Ferd Smith, beyond any question, returning for the kill!

CHAPTER XXV

"Don't let him in," Flo cried frantically. She rushed to the door and was about to bolt it when Chuck stopped her.

"No," the redhead decided grimly. "Let him walk right in. He can't see our broncs in the brush. He thinks nobody's here but Johnny. Stand flat against the wall, Flo. Right there. We'll let that blood-hungry buzzard sashay right in."

Flo stood with her back to the wall at one side of the door. Chuck drew his forty-five and took a similar position on the other side. Anyone entering would be unable to see them until he was at least halfway through the doorway. "Sit down, Johnny, just like you were before."

Johnny sat down at the table, his left ankle still chained to the floor. He placed his right hand, with its dangling manacle, against the wall spike.

Flo held her breath. She could hear the beatings of her heart. She looked at Johnny and he smiled at her. Then she could hear the thudding hoof-beats of an approaching horse.

Ferd Smith drew up in front. Sweat on the strawberry roan evidenced a long fast ride. The man jerked a carbine from his saddle scabbard and dismounted. The cabin seemed just as he'd left it some thirteen hours ago.

He pushed its door open and stood on the threshold there. All he saw was his manacled prisoner, seated at a table with a look of bitter dejection.

"Sorry, kid." Ferd Smith raised the rifle and took aim. "Them guys came through. So what else can I do?"

Wiggins, clubbing his forty-five, crashed its barrel down on the man's head. Ferd Smith didn't know what hit him. His knees buckled. He toppled inward, stunned, on the cabin floor.

A grin curved the lips of Johnny Diamond. "Thanks, Chuck. Maybe I can do the same for you sometime."

Chuck dragged Ferd Smith a little further into the cabin so that Flo could close the door. "Oughta be handcuff keys on him," Chuck said. He kneeled to search the man.

From a coat pocket he brought out a roll of currency. It was fat enough to be six thousand dollars. "He collected, all right," Chuck confirmed.

Flo stood by, staring remorsefully at Johnny.

"He meant Sherwood and Orme, didn't he? They paid him! I've been so stupid, Johnny."

"No such thing," Johnny protested. "You've been smart as a whip, gettin' me out of this mess. Look in his pants, Chuck."

In a pocket of Ferd Smith's pants Wiggins found a small key. It fitted both pair of handcuffs and Johnny was soon free.

"They'll come in right handy," Chuck said, "to use on this Circle D killer. Roll him over, Johnny." They rolled Ferd Smith over on his back, clamping one pair of irons on wrists and the other on ankles. Then Chuck picked up a bucket and poured water on the man's face.

Smith opened his eyes, groaning, and looked up at them with a glazy stare. "I'll get the broncs," Chuck said, "and we'll pack him to town."

He opened the door and stepped outside. Instantly he was back in again, slamming the door and bolting it. "We got company," he announced to Johnny. "Grab a rifle."

Johnny picked up Ferd Smith's carbine and stepped to the east window. Flo crowded to his elbow and they looked out. Coming at a hard gallop, about a quarter mile away, were a dozen horsemen. Johnny recognized Rick Sherwood and Alf Sansone. Lagging back of them, and riding awkwardly, came a fat man with the double-chinned face of Sydney Orme.

Chuck snapped a shell into his rifle chamber.

He said hoarsely: "They can see a strawberry roan standin' outside. So they know Smith's in here. Reckon they followed him from the Circle D. They must be gunnin' for him, Johnny."

"They've come close enough," Johnny said. "Duck low, Flo." He smashed glass from the window and fired through it at the leading rider.

Instantly the entire band of them reined to a stop, one man slumping across his saddle horn and clutching at his mount's mane. The others scattered, some riding out of sight into the creek brush. Four of them veered out into the open pasture looking for cover there. Johnny fired again but his bullet didn't stop anyone. "They're surrounding us," he reported. "Looks like the whole Circle D outfit plus Orme."

"Likely they think it was Ferdie took those two shots at 'em," Chuck said.

The creekward side of the cabin had a door and a window. The east and west walls each had a window. But the north wall had no opening at all. All walls were of heavy spruce logs.

"Get in a corner, Flo," Johnny ordered, "and lie on the floor."

But she wouldn't. She was a sheriff's daughter and she'd brought a saddle rifle in here with her. She took it to the creekside window and peered out there. As a bullet splashed glass splinters on her cheek she dodged low behind the logs.

The nearest of the creek cottonwoods were

barely fifty yards away. From them came the shouting of Alf Sansone. "You ain't got a chance, Ferd. Toss your guns out."

"They still think," Johnny whispered, "that Smith's the only live man in here."

But only a minute later they learned better. Another yell came from the thickets. "Take a look, Alf. Here's three broncs. One of 'em's the big dun that Texas kid rides. He's got a hackamore on him. Another's a Lazy M and another's a Bar L."

Johnny fired at the voice sound. He heard men scatter through the thickets. "Come and get us," he shouted.

No answer came. Finding four people at the cabin, instead of only Ferd Smith and a dead prisoner, seemed to confuse the besiegers.

Ferd Smith still lay in irons on the floor. His eyes had panic. "Gimme a gun," he pleaded, "and I'll help you stand 'em off."

"We can't trust you," Johnny said.

"Sure you can," the man begged. "It's me they're after, not you."

Johnny laughed coldly. "They're after anybody who knows the truth about 'em. Which included all of us. Was Orme at the Circle D last night?"

"Not when I got there. They had to send to Chico for him."

Johnny looked at Chuck Wiggins. "Not hard to figure out what happened, Chuck. Orme brought the money and they paid it to Smith. Smith took it and rode here to keep his part of the bargain. His own neck was at stake, too, if I was left alive. But they followed him close enough to keep in sight."

"Why?" Chuck wondered.

"Two good reasons. To make sure he put a slug through me, and if he didn't, to do it themselves. Then they would shoot a few holes through Ferd Smith and take back the money they'd paid him."

Johnny looked at Flo, saw the pale horror on her face. She was still crouched under the creekside window. He said gently, "I wish you'd go huddle in a corner, Flo."

Volleys crashed from three directions. Rifle shots. They smashed the panes of three windows and riddled the door. Others drove with dull thuds into the log walls. One bullet pinged through the water bucket. Ferd Smith rolled out of line with the door and got to his feet. He stumbled toward a safe corner. The irons on his ankles tripped him and he sprawled prone there. "Take these dang things off o' me," he screamed, "and gimme a gun."

"I'll give you a tap on the head," Wiggins promised, "if you don't shut up."

"Which way's the wind?" Johnny asked.

"It's blowin' downcrik, what there is of it," Chuck said.

Johnny grimaced. With an upcreek wind, there

might be a faint chance of rifle fire being heard at the Rivera ranchhouse, six miles up the valley. He peered that way from the west window. He saw that two men had found cover behind a low sand dune in that direction. They lay prone and were firing over it.

A shot from the creekward window made Johnny turn. He saw Flo there. She'd raised her head above the sill to take a shot at some target. "I saw him," she said. "That awful fat man from Chico."

"Get down," Johnny said desperately. He dragged her below the sill level just as bullets streamed through.

"Buckshot!" Wiggins muttered. "It's Orme with his shotgun, all right."

Again came Sansone's voice from the cottonwoods. This time in a coaxing tone. "Come outa there, McBride. And bring that woman of yours. We won't bother you any. All we want's Ferd Smith. We're after him for gunnin' Johnny Diamond."

Ferd Smith himself yelled back: "You're a liar by the clock. You paid me to gun Johnny Diamond."

A puzzlement grew on Flo's face. "Why would they think Slim McBride's in here?"

"It's *his* cabin," Johnny reasoned. "He'd be riding a Lazy M horse like they found out there. And they saw your hair above the sill. Slim wasn't plannin' to get married till after roundup time, but they figure he moved it up. They figure if a woman's in here, she must be Mrs. Slim McBride."

Wiggins fired two quick shots from the east window. A yell in that direction meant a hit. Then a puzzled voice from the trees—Slim McBride ain't got red hair, has he, Alf? Must be someone else."

"Come out," Sansone shouted, "or we'll smoke you out!"

The threat, to Johnny, seemed purely rhetorical. Then a second thought brought a crease of worry to his brow. Smoke? He looked with a sense of helplessness at the windowless north wall of the cabin. The besiegers could approach unseen from that side. Nothing to keep them from setting fire to the cabin.

Two of the logs there didn't fit snugly at one end. A crack between them had been chinked solidly with adobe plaster. Johnny found a butcher knife on a shelf. "I can't trust you with a gun," he said to Ferd Smith, "but you can have this." He tossed the knife to Smith and took the handcuffs from his wrists. "Get busy. We need a loophole on that side." He pointed to the blank north wall.

Ferd Smith, his ankles still hobbled, crawled over there. He set to work gouging at the adobe chinking between two logs.

An ominous silence came from the besiegers. Johnny moved from window to window but caught no glimpse of them. The long quiet got on Chuck's nerves. "Whatsamatter?" he challenged. "You guys had enough fightin'?"

No answer. "They're up to something," Johnny said, and had a fairly good idea of what it was.

By the short shadows outside, it was now close to noon. Daylight, he thought, was on their side. But darkness wouldn't be. It would shield an attack. He looked at Flo and felt a pinch at his heart. When night came they could slip up unseen from four directions. And they'd show no more mercy to Flo than to anyone else. She, now, was an eyewitness to the guilt.

No sound at all came except the steady clicks of the knife with which Ferd Smith, professional assassin, was digging away plaster from between two logs.

"It comes out easy," he reported. "I'm almost through."

Johnny looked from the creekside window. The strawberry roan, frightened by shots, had shied away dragging the bridle reins. He was now grazing a few hundred yards up the valley.

Minutes more slipped by without any sign or sound of the enemy. "Maybe," Flo murmured, "they've gone away."

Smith's knife punched through to daylight. He scraped away chinking until he had a crack six inches wide and half as high. He was on his knees there, and Johnny saw him peer out through the hole.

"They're comin'," the man announced hoarsely. "Gimme a gun and I'll blast 'em."

Johnny pushed him aside and looked out the new loophole himself. Two cowboys were advancing stealthily toward the cabin. Each had an armful of dry sagebrush. "I'll do the blasting," Johnny said. He poked the barrel of a forty-five through the hole and fired five times.

For a moment smoke clogged the hole and kept him from seeing out. When he did, he saw that one man lay motionless on the ground. The other had dropped his armload of firewood and was legging it away. "I guess they won't try that again," Johnny said. "Not in daylight, anyway."

He turned and saw Flo looking at his bootless feet. "We should have left it on the road," she said in dismay. "I mean the one Chuck and I picked up."

Wiggins agreed wryly. "It's tied to my saddle. And Flo's dead right. If I'd had sense enough to leave it in the road, somebody else might see it and get the same steer we did."

"Where's the other one?" Johnny asked Ferd Smith.

"Left it at the Circle D," the man said. He seemed eager to co-operate now, no doubt hoping for leniency if they escaped this trap. If they didn't, he would certainly be shot down by Sansone and Sherwood and Orme.

The ruse of setting fire to the cabin having failed, again volleys came from all sides. Bullets splintered the door and the bolt fell off. "Duck," Johnny cautioned. "And get ready for a rush."

No rush came. They'd know, Johnny reasoned, that a rush would be costly. At least the first three or four men who came charging them could be picked off. He peered out and saw a man aiming over a sand dune. But the hatted head went out of sight before Johnny could fire. Something stung his cheek and he felt blood there. A bullet had creased him just under the ear.

"Please keep down," Flo begged him. She was at his side. He turned with a mirthless laugh and put an arm around her. "I wish you'd stayed in Texas, Johnny."

She'd said that, he remembered, once before. But in a different tone and the one she used now made his heart sing. It was like a caress. "If I ever go back there," he said in a choked voice, "I want to take you with me."

Wiggins was cutting loose from the opposite window. "Got one," the redhead reported. "That makes three down and maybe nine to go. How's the ammunition, pal?"

An inventory showed only about thirty more rifle rounds and even less for forty-fives. "We better save it for the showdown," Chuck said.

Ferd Smith, unarmed, was posted to watch out through the north wall porthole. Chuck and Johnny took turns at the windows. Forcibly they made Flo crouch in a corner. Twice in the next hour Alf Sansone shouted a challenge, inviting surrender.

Johnny yelled back: "Sherwood lets you do all the talking, Alf. What's the matter? Does he think Flo doesn't know he's out there?"

Silence from Sherwood. Orme too was holding his tongue. Sansone was the only spokesman. "We'll pay you a call, come nighttime," he promised.

Inch by inch the afternoon shadows lengthened. Only an occasional shot came whirring in at the shattered windows. No doubt, now, as to their strategy. They'd wait till dark and then creep up for the kill. As the afternoon hours dragged by, hope steadily faded. "We'll be two against nine," Johnny muttered.

"*Three* against nine," Flo corrected. She still had a loaded carbine.

"Four," Ferd Smith argued, "if you'll gimme a gun."

Johnny talked it over with Chuck. "What can we lose?" Chuck said. "Maybe we better heel him, Johnny."

It was hard to decide. With a gun, the man might fight for them or against them. Smith pled his own case whiningly. "If they win," he argued,

"I'm a dead pigeon. If you win, I get a fair trial in court. Slip me a gun."

"I'll think about it," Johnny brooded. "What time you got, Chuck?"

Wiggins looked at his watch. " 'Bout two hours till nightfall, Johnny."

Johnny looked wretchedly at Flo. She came to him and wiped a smear of blood from his cheek. There was nothing he could say to her. His grimness made her try to divert him with trivia. "You missed an awfully good currant pie last night, Johnny. That new maid of Felicia's, Dolores Valdez, made it just for *you.*"

Chuck Wiggins chimed in with a grin. "It sure was good, pal. I et my slice and yours too."

CHAPTER XXVI

Six miles up Grosella Creek, named for the wild currants growing profusely along its banks, a wooden bridge crossed just below the hacienda gate. Sheriff Adam Sawyer trotted his big bay over that bridge, having ridden leisurely out from town. He wasn't at all worried about his daughter. Flo, he presumed, was with her cousin Felicia.

Tall in the saddle, his long and almost frockish

black coat buttoned tightly over his chest, Sawyer rode on to the ranch gate. There he saw a rider approaching from the opposite direction. A chunky cowman heading this way along the San Ysidro road. Recognizing Buck Perry, Sawyer waited.

Perry cantered up to him. "Hi, sheriff. Ain't seen anything of a red-headed puncher of mine named Wiggins, have you?"

"I didn't meet him on the road, Buck."

"He was supposed to bust a colt for me this mornin' but he didn't show up. Came over here sparkin' last night, the boys tell me. Can't figure out why he didn't come home."

"That boy from Texas was here too, last night," Sawyer said. "Must be still here, because I couldn't locate him in town today anywhere."

"How come you're lookin' for him, Ad? Anything new?"

The sheriff nodded somberly. "Two things," he admitted. "I thought he ought to know about 'em. In fact he predicted both of them and I want to see if he's got any more smart ideas."

"What two things?"

"They found Val Cranston in a ditch up near Huerfano. Shot full of rifle slugs. Other matter concerns Winnie Quinn. She wouldn't leave her jail cell when I offered to set her free. Not till an agent sold her beer joint and brought her the cash. Then she demanded a police escort to the depot. This morning she boarded a train for California. Which scores two good guesses for Johnny Diamond."

Perry gaped. "Whadda yuh know?"

"Felicia and Flo ought to know where those boys are," Sawyer said. "Let's go in and see 'em."

They rode through the gate and up the ranch street to the main house. Felicia admitted them there. "Hello, Uncle Adam," she greeted. "How are you, Mr. Perry?" To her uncle she added, "Flo told you, I suppose."

"Told me about what?"

"About Johnny Diamond not arriving for dinner last night. Flo was so worried she got up at daylight and rode to town."

Alarm tightened Sawyer's face. "Flo rode to town? Then why didn't she go home? Or to my office? I didn't see her anywhere. I thought she was still here."

"Nothing could have happened to her," Felicia said quickly. "She was with Chuck Wiggins. They rode in together."

The sheriff stared. "But I didn't see Chuck either."

A Mexican maid entered with a tray. On it were three cups of chokecherry wine. Dolores Valdez, in her brief stay here, had already been trained in the amenities of a hacienda. When fatigued guests arrived after a long ride, especially at an evening hour, they must be served at once with a cup of wine.

But alarm had caught both mistress and guests now, and they paid no attention to Dolores. She stood timidly by, holding the tray.

"Hell!" exclaimed Buck Perry. "Looks like they rid into trouble somewhere. That Texas boy not showin' up last night! Then Flo an' Chuck headin' out to look fer him and . . ."

Sawyer's sharp-angled face turned suddenly gray. He remembered things. Not long ago Johnny Diamond had been sniped at on that same road. The same sniper might have tried again. If Flo and Chuck had found Johnny's body by the road, what would they have done?

His eyes put the question to Perry and the rancher had a prompt answer. "Chuck'd try trackin' the killer, Ad. And Flo might tag along. You an' me better hit the saddle."

"Send Miguel in here, Felicia," Sawyer said. When the old *mayordomo* appeared he snapped brisk orders. "Rout out every vaquero on the place, Miguel. Rifles and six-guns."

Miguel left excitedly for the bunkhouse.

"I'm with you, Ad," Buck Perry said grimly. "But where do we ride and who the hell do we look for?"

"We'll comb every cave in the rimrocks," Sawyer said. "We'll ride the mesas from end to end looking for Ferd Smith. He tried it before. If anyone drygulched Johnny, it was Ferd Smith."

"All I know about that guy," Perry put in, "is he's a no-good gunnie forkin' a strawberry roan."

Dolores Valdez, standing unobtrusively by with her tray of wine cups, caught the last words. Strawberry roan!

"I have seen a horse of such color, señor." She offered the information shyly, speaking Spanish. Her knowledge of English was scant, but she understood that it concerned her benefactor, the *jóven simpático* who'd found her in the alleys of Las Vegas.

Sawyer whirled toward her. "You saw a strawberry roan? Where?"

"It is yesterday morning, señor. I know that Don Juan comes for *comida* and so . . ."

"She means Johnny Diamond," Felicia cut in. "Go on, Dolores."

"So I must make for him a pie of the wild currants. Many are growing along the *río*. So I ride a burro far down the pasture. To pick the *grosellas*, señor. It is there that I see this strawberry roan. He has a saddle on. He is tied by a cabin of logs."

They stared at her. "But how could that be?" exclaimed Felicia. "The only cabin down the creek belongs to Slim McBride. And he . . ."

"And Slim," Perry broke in, slapping his thigh, "is in Denver for a week. Ferd Smith could know it and feel safe to hole up there."

Adam Sawyer unbuttoned his long black coat, exposing a gunbelt and a forty-five. Miguel appeared to announce, "The vaqueros are ready, señor."

Sawyer and Perry strode out to their horses. Dusk had settled over the ranchyard and in the gloom they could see ten Mexican stock hands, all mounted, each with a carbine in his scabbard. "You come along too, Miguel," the sheriff said. "And bring a lantern. It'll be pitch dark, time we get there." He swung to his saddle and shouted at the vaqueros, "Follow me." Stirrup to stirrup with Buck Perry, he galloped out through the gate.

With cheers the vaqueros streamed after them. They were a kindly folk, not given to gunfighting. But word had been whispered that a *prima* of their mistress might need to be rescued. Which was enough. And if there should be a fight, how could they lose under the leadership of those two stalwart gringos riding ahead? "*Adelante, compañeros!*"

In a cloud of dust they dashed on, a bell-hatted cavalcade of armed peons behind Buck Perry and Adam Sawyer.

From the ranchhouse gate Felicia and Dolores watched them dissolve into the dusk downcreek. "Don Juan, is he in danger, señorita?" Dolores whispered.

"I have fear that he is, Dolores. But it may be that you have saved his life."

"It is he," the woman said softly, "who saved mine. May God be good to him, señorita!"

Light had faded outside the cabin. A candle was on the table but Johnny wouldn't use it. It would only make them targets. When the rush came, they'd stand in the dark and fight.

He crouched where he could cover the door and the creekward window. Chuck and Flo, each with a carbine, faced the side windows. Ferd Smith had a knife and the use of his hands. His ankles were still linked together. All the while he kept begging for a gun. "They'll kill me," he whined, "like a rat in a trap."

"Which is what you are," Johnny said.

A cloudy sky meant there'd be no moon. Pitch blackness was closing in. "Their best chance," Johnny said, "is to sneak up from the north side. Put your ear to that chink you gouged out, Smith. If you hear anything, sing out."

Ferd Smith groped to the crack in the north wall. Another ten minutes slipped by. It was completely dark now.

"I hear 'em coming," Smith warned. "Gimme somethin' to blast 'em with."

Johnny went to the crack. Through it he could see nothing but black night. He heard the sound of a crawling man, barely ten yards away, and fired his six-gun through the hole.

Answering shots came from every direction.

By now the panels of the door had been entirely shot away. Flo's carbine popped at the west window. "I shot at a flash," she said. "It was close to the cabin. He was almost to the window."

"Let's get out of here," Johnny said. "If we can't see them in the dark, they can't see us either."

The prospect terrified Flo. The idea didn't appeal to Wiggins either. But to Johnny it seemed the only chance. "Look. They'll swarm us under, if we stay here. We'll slip out one at a time. I'll go first. Wait one minute, Flo, then you come after me. Chuck, you come one minute after Flo. She'll be between us. In the dark they won't see us. Crawl to the brush, Flo. Then get up and run."

Before they could protest Johnny opened what was left of the door. It showed only a black rectangle of night. He stepped quickly out and to one side. Then he dropped flat and wriggled toward the creek trees.

A flash to his left showed a man snaking his way through grass to the cabin. He hadn't seen Johnny and was shooting at the cabin window. Johnny fired his forty-five and made a hit. He heard a yelp from the man. Others must have seen the flash of Johnny's shot, but since it came from outside they'd think it was one of their own men.

Johnny crawled on to the edge of the trees. A voice near by whispered, "Where's Alf?" It sounded like Sydney Orme. Johnny groped toward the voice, his carbine punched out before him. When the barrel collided with flesh he pulled the trigger.

A mountain of man fell against him. Johnny's fingers, groping in the dark, felt the baldness of a head. Sydney Orme went down without even a groan.

A step behind him made Johnny turn, swinging up the rifle. A flash of gunfire near by saved him from shooting. It was Flo and she came sobbing into his arms. Her nerves, like his own, were brittle and drawn fine. "Run," Johnny whispered. "Keep in the brush and run like hell." Whatever she answered was smothered in a burst of yells and shots. The raiders were charging the cabin.

Had Chuck left it yet?

"Listen," Flo whispered. "They're running away. Don't you hear them?"

Johnny became aware, then, of hoofbeats. A thunder of them. Not *away* from the cabin, but *toward* it. The sound confused Johnny. Surely the Circle Ds wouldn't charge that cabin on horseback.

"Flo! Johnny! Are you in there?" The voice rang in a roar from the night and it wasn't Alf Sansone's. Nor Rick Sherwood's.

"It's dad!" Flo cried. "Here I am, dad."

"*Adelante, compañeros!*" This in a chorus from charging vaqueros.

Johnny felt his knees go weak. Relief sapped

him. Gunshots cracked on his right and his left, from the ground, from saddles, from the cabin. "Here I am!" Flo cried again.

"You all right, Chuck?" This time the voice was Buck Perry's. There came a chatter in Spanish from Bar L vaqueros. One saddle had a lantern. The shapes of horsemen loomed in the dark.

Chuck Wiggins appeared at the cabin door with a lighted candle. He'd stayed there to draw fire and cover Flo's retreat. "How many got away, boss?"

"Not many," Perry told him. "We rid up just as they was smashin' in on yuh."

The candlelight exposed figures sprawled grotesquely near the cabin door. Most of them had stopped moving. One of them was Rick Sherwood. Another was Alf Sansone. Ferd Smith came out of the cabin, still hobbled but otherwise unscathed. Adam Sawyer put him in custody and turned gratefully to Johnny Diamond.

"Looks like the roundup's over, young man."

"All but roundin' up my boots," Johnny said. He stood there in his sock feet, fight-weary, with an arm around Flo.

"I'll round up the boots," Sawyer promised. "You take Flo to the ranchhouse. Might be some of that currant pie left up there."

When the real roundup was over, late in October, and the calves branded, and the Lazy M beef sorted from the Bar L, and the Circle D stuff driven away to the auction of a felon's estate, a great feast was celebrated at the hacienda of Don Ronaldo Rivera.

The ranchyard was full. Peons from all over the county were there and the chokecherry wine flowed freely. Gay serapes made a myriad flashing rainbows in the noontime sun. Gringos were there too, ranchers and cowboys from the San Ysidro and the Dry Cimarron, even from Stonewall on the far headwaters of the Picketwire. Merchants from Las Perdidas were there with their wives and children. A hundred saddle horses crowded the corrals, munching hay at the feed racks. Servants scurried about the big house, from patio to salas, and mozos flitted from bodega to barn.

Beyond the patio the noon sunlight shimmered on a lake, circled by gracious cottonwoods. And beyond the little lake stood the real focus of attention. It was there that most of the crowd gathered, although the small adobe church would hold only a few. From it came a chime of bells. Candles mellowed the arches of its windows.

There was no room inside for Dolores Valdez. Being only a housemaid, she stood with the overflow outside. She could hear the organ. Standing on tiptoes, she could even look over the heads of the *niños* in front and see through the open doors. To the altar, to a priest waiting there.

311

The benches crammed with guests, all the best *gente* of the Picketwire valley.

She could see her Don Juan standing near the priest, his strong young face flushed and expectant. She could even see the polished boots he wore, the ones he was so proud of, with the brand of his father on them. She could see, too, the young gringo with red hair, *el colorado*, she called him, who stood at the groom's elbow.

The organ broke into the march, then, and Dolores saw the bride herself. She moved glowingly down the aisle on the arm of Señor the Sheriff. A feeling of pride came to Dolores. Had not she herself helped in the making of that long satin gown, with its train and veil?

She watched Felicia Rivera, maid of honor, follow down the aisle. She saw the young Don Juan from Texas receive the bride and the young *colorado* take his place beside Felicia. She saw the last two smile shyly at each other. It would be their turn next, thought Dolores.

She saw Señor the Sheriff withdraw to take his seat by the distinguished host of the fiesta, uncle of the bride, the gentleman from Las Perdidas, Don Ronaldo Rivera. Came murmured intonations from the priest . . .

Then, with a sigh, Dolores had to leave for urgent duties of her own. There was a buckboard to be packed with a hundred gifts, together with all the bride's baggage. Miguel, the *mayordomo*, was attending to it but he would need her help.

They were busy at it when a great burst of bells from the chapel told them the ceremony was over.

Soon the crowd came surging out. Again it overflowed the ranchyard and again the widow of Frankie Valdez felt herself brushed aside. Not that she minded. She was grateful to be even on the fringe of an event like this. While they waited for the bride to change her dress, there were songs and toasts to her health and happiness. At last, over the heads of the people, Dolores saw Johnny Diamond lift his wife to the buckboard seat.

A big dun horse was tied to its endgate. A saddled horse wearing no bitted bridle, only a hackamore.

The hackamored horse followed as Johnny Diamond drove away. Dolores, and a hundred others, waved them goodbye.

Two gentlemen stood near her and she heard bits of their talk. "That was a mighty generous wedding gift you gave Flo, Ronaldo. The Circle D ranch."

"*De nada!*" deprecated the senator. "At the auction sale it went for a mere pittance."

"But aren't you afraid," fretted Adam Sawyer, "that it will depress them? After it's been a nest of thieves all these years?"

Again the senator shrugged his thin patrician shoulders. "They are young and brave; they will find happiness there." He sucked with mellow contentment at his cigarito. "It is the way we have built this land, *cuñado mío*. Always the good must follow evil, to replace it with peace and love."

The buckboard faded, melting into the grama distance, down the San Ysidro road.

Allan Vaughan Elston was a prolific author of traditional Western novels and many more short stories and novelettes, memorable for the complexity of their plots and the flamboyance of the villains who are often more interesting than either the heroes or heroines. He was born in Kansas City and spent his summers on a Colorado cattle ranch owned by his father. He was educated as a civil engineer at the University of Missouri and worked in various engineering companies in South America as well as his own in the United States before, in 1920, turning to ranching. Times were hard financially at the ranch so in late 1924 Elston tried writing his first fiction. His first story was "The Eyes of Teconce" in *The Frontier* (2/25), an adventure tale set in the rugged Andes, but his second was "Peepsight Shoots High" in *The Frontier* (6/25), marking his debut as an author of Western fiction, in which henceforth he specialized. His second Western story was "Triggers in Leash" in *The Frontier* (2/25), subsequently adapted for the third episode of "Alfred Hitchcock Presents" in 1955. His first Western novel was *Come Out and Fight!* (1941) followed by *Guns On The Cimarron* (1943) prior to his re-entering the U.S. Army during the Second World War. Following the war, he found his stride with *Hit The Saddle* (1947) and *The Sheriff Of San Miguel* (1949). In the 1950s he would average two books a year, an impressive accomplishment for any writer and Elston was already into his sixties. His novels tend to be precisely situated as to year and place and often contain an intriguing mystery. *The Landseekers* (1964) was Elston's final novel to appear in a hardcover edition. Henceforth, he confined himself to writing paperback originals. At his best, Elston was a fine craftsman who could unite novelty of setting and events with a plot-driven complexity to produce a generally entertaining narrative.